LIGHTNING IN THE NIGHT

LIGHTNING IN THE NIGHT

FRED ALLHOFF

PRENTICE-HALL, INC., ENGLEWOOD CLIFFS, N.J.

Printed in the United States of America
Prentice-Hall International, Inc., London / Prentice-Hall of Australia, Pty. Ltd., Sydney / Prentice-Hall of Canada, Ltd., Toronto / Prentice-Hall of India Private Ltd., New Delhi / Prentice-Hall of Japan, Inc., Tokyo / Prentice-Hall of Southeast Asia Pte. Ltd., Singapore / Whitehall Books Limited, Wellington, New Zealand
10 9 8 7 6 5 4 3 2 1

Library of Congress Cataloging in Publication Data
Allhoff, Fred.
    Lightning in the night.

    Previously published in Liberty magazine in installments between Aug. 24–Nov. 16, 1940.
    I. Title
PZ3.A4363Li 1979   [PS3501.L55895]   813'.5'4   78-23538
ISBN 0-13-536557-0

CONTENTS

LIGHTNING IN THE NIGHT

". . . I WOULD SPRING LIKE LIGHTNING IN THE NIGHT AND HURL MYSELF ON THE ENEMY."

Adolf Hitler, in a speech before the German Girls' League

INTRODUCTION: A BASIS IN FACT

by TERRY MILLER

On September 24, 1940, the World's Fair Time Capsule was buried in Flushing Meadow. Having been viewed by over four million visitors, it contained forty everyday items including a fountain pen, a can opener, a tobacco pouch (*with* a zipper), cosmetics, and a camera. It also included a microfilmed essay of the times, reflecting all of our hopes but few of our fears. This record of civilization was buried and scheduled to be exhumed in A.D. 6939.

On that same date, *Liberty* magazine published the fifth install-ment of *Lightning in the Night,* which told of an imagined invasion of the United States by Nazi forces. Americans reluctant to fight Hitler in Europe were startled by the vivid portrayal of that same struggle on American soil five years in their future. And with this first publication of *Lightning in the Night* in book form, the reader is treated to a "time capsule" of an equally fascinating kind. The story offers a unique opportunity to compare the actual course of World War II with an imagined forecast created in 1940. One finds oneself forgetting that the surprise attack on Pearl Harbor was a year distant, and that atomic chain reaction was still a wild, untested theory.

Today, the events of the late 1930s seem so clear an indication of Hitler's intent that it is hard to imagine that at the time, the vast majority of Americans had little or no interest in the European turmoil. But before Pearl Harbor, while Hitler was seizing most of Europe, the United States was consumed in a war of words.

Adolf Hitler had come to power in 1933. In 1935, he denounced the Treaty of Versailles and one year later seized the Rhineland. Mussolini invaded and annexed Ethiopia to Italy's African empire, opposed by nothing more than League of Nations sanctions. As 1936 continued, Civil War broke out in Spain, and Hitler and Mussolini established the Berlin-Rome Axis. By January of the following year, Japan had invaded China.

But despite these hostilities, the United States was gripped by a mood of pacifism unsurpassed since the time of Thomas Jefferson. A majority of Americans looked back on our entry into World War I as a mistake. Europe was simply given to war. It was considered a decadent amalgam of nations and duchies, whose squabbles were as unimportant then as a moonquake might seem to us today. After all, Europe was physically remote, five days' sailing distance away. Live radio broadcasts from Europe were still in the future. The first regularly scheduled Pan Am clipper flight to London (via Newfoundland) did not take place until March of 1939, and even then it took 27½ hours. Through most of the 1930s, many Americans took the attitude that the more we kept to ourselves, the better off we'd be. After all, we had our own problems to worry about.

Franklin Delano Roosevelt had also come to power in 1933, and while the rest of the world was sinking into political chaos, America struggled toward domestic economic recovery. FDR's domestic policies instilled hatred in most business and professional circles. His National Recovery Act of 1933 had declared employees entitled to unrestrained collective bargaining. To combat this radical notion, businesses resorted to injunctions, "company" unions, and strikebreakers. The year 1934 was marked by an automobile strike, a national textile strike, and a violent general strike in San Francisco involving both the militia and self-appointed vigilantes. Although dependent upon businessmen to restore prosperity, FDR infuriated them again in 1938, when his Fair Labor Standards Act limited workers to 40 hours per week and guaranteed them 40 cents an hour pay. FDR was variously labeled a savior and a Fascist.

A conservative Congress, acting on the will of the people, had passed the Neutrality Act of 1935, on the assumption that the way to avoid war was to avoid taking sides. This unfortunate theory, and the resulting embargo, played into Hitler's hands. Only Hitler knew that war was coming, so only Germany was arming. When Hitler chose to strike, his victims would be unable to buy arms from America.

At this early time, FDR made no attempt to "sell" a new foreign policy to an isolationist nation the way he had campaigned on behalf of his New Deal policies. Before FDR's second term of office had ended, he had established the President as the sole leader of foreign affairs, a function which continues to this day. But initially, the New Deal had established the Federal Government, and specifically the President, as ultimately responsible for domestic welfare, employment, and security only. Foreign policy was still exclusively the province of Congress.

For all the outrageous aggression overseas, FDR could do little within the existing laws, and the Germans knew it. In his December 20, 1937, report to the head of the Political Section of the German Foreign Office, German ambassador Hans Dieckerhoff reported "the United States' position in regard to foreign affairs is determined by American popular opinion, on which the President and Congress are dependent." It was clear that as long as American public opinion was split, the Germans would have a free hand.

Actually, before 1937, it was difficult to judge what American public opinion was at any specific time. The Gallup Poll was inaugurated in 1935, and from its simple beginnings FDR followed it closely. Yet well into 1939, the government had virtually no established channels for collecting and analyzing public opinion beyond the ballot box. Even more important, there were no government agencies for mobilizing public support for governmental policies. FDR's celebrated "fireside chats" were an ingenious necessity rather than a self-serving extravagance.

But the average American continued to ignore the war threats. In 1936, *Fortune* magazine asked, "If a European War could be averted by the League of Nations, should the United States join the League?" Of the respondents, 30 percent said Yes, but 57 percent said No. In April 1936, the American Institute for Public Opinion (AIPO) learned that 56 percent of the American people believed that if a European war began, the United States would not be drawn into it. And while the U.S. had cultural and ethnic ties with Europe, it was far easier to ignore the continuing war in the Far East. Our humanitarian efforts on the Chinese mainland, seen by Japan as interference, were almost an absentminded gesture on our part. Americans willingly accepted Japan's apology for "accidentally" sinking the U.S.S. *Panay* in December 1937, despite the loss of two lives. In January 1938, the Gallup Poll showed that 70 percent of those Americans with an opinion favored the discontinuance of American support of China. After all, if 450 million Chinese couldn't defend themselves against 73 million Japanese, why should we help?

Hitler confided his plan for European conquest to his closest advisors in November 1937. Those who objected were quietly dismissed. The rest of the world first sensed what was happening when Germany invaded Austria in March 1938. Two months later, Hitler "liberated" Czechoslovakia under the ruse of returning the Sudenten Germans to the Fatherland.

And still American isolationism persisted. Early in 1938, Representative Louis Ludlow of Indiana proposed legislation requiring a majority endorsement by the people of any congressional declaration of war. This would have made the government unable to conduct foreign policy at all, yet it was only narrowly defeated.

Hitler's invasion of Czechoslovakia was a gamble, but he won. British Prime Minister Chamberlain returned to England on September 30, 1938, to announce that through appeasement, he had obtained "peace in our time." Czechoslovakia was to be partitioned, with Hitler absorbing the Sudentenland and guaranteeing the sovereignty of what was left. In nine months Hitler had subjugated 6.7 million Austrians and 3.5 million Czechs.

The shift in American attitudes began in 1938. A new factor in public opinion was the inauguration of radio coverage of events as they occurred. A poll in *Fortune* showed that more people had faith in radio news than in newspapers. Coast-to-coast broadcasts began in the spring of 1938. By the summer of 1938, American radio listeners knew more about the crisis in Europe than did most Europeans. By September, CBS premiered a one-half-hour broadcast covering the European scene, coordinated through William L. Shirer in London, while Edward R. Murrow broadcast from occupied Vienna.

CBS also broadcast Hitler's two-hour address to the annual Nuremberg Rally on September 12, 1938. For the first time, Hitler's fury and hatred were apparent to millions of Americans. To an audience accustomed to short news bulletins and program interruption, the full speech, with simultaneous translation by H. V. Kaltenborn, was startling. And Hitler's calls for peace were at obvious odds with his military tactics. In July 1938, an AIPO (The American Institute for Public Opinion) poll had shown that 46 percent of those polled believed the United States would be drawn into a European war. On September 23, 1938, at the height of the Czech crisis, the figure had risen to 68 percent.

The winter of 1938–39 was relatively free of hostilities. There was more interest in the construction of the World's Fair grounds in Flushing Meadow than in Hitler. For those with money, Germany and Italy were still popular vacation spots. Hitler had cleaned up Germany, and the trains in Italy now ran on time. Yet FDR now sensed that Europe was irrevocably headed toward war, with American involvement inevitable. The English edition of *Mein Kampf* was published, and offered little hope that Hitler was now appeased.

Roosevelt's address to Congress on January 4, 1939, reflected this public uncertainty. Knowing that isolationism was being reinforced by our military weakness, FDR submitted a record $9 billion budget that included over $1 billion for defense. Assistant Secretary of War Louis Johnson publicly stated that the Army was "unprepared in everything," from machinery and materiel to the men to use them. Our Navy ranked only third behind Britain and Japan, but it was a single Pacific fleet of obsolete vessels, only 15 percent of them manned. (Although Japan continued to press for domination of the Pacific, Roosevelt ordered the American Pacific Fleet into the Atlantic in February 1939, in a salute to the New York World's Fair.) And as for planes, we had no modern Air Force whatsoever. There were fewer than 2,500 licensed military or commercial pilots in the United States. Yet the Chicago *Tribune*'s answer to FDR was that "the greatest danger to the American people is not over the water, but rather the fiscal, economic and political theories of its own government."

Roosevelt's budget did not include funds for atomic research, and no one would have suggested it. Although Enrico Fermi succeeded in measuring uranium atoms at Columbia University on January 25, 1939, this was considered "pure" research of no practical value.

Scientists knew that 95 percent of uranium was too stable to be split. A new technique for refining pure, unstable uranium was needed. And a chain reaction of atoms splitting atoms, resulting in an explosion, was still theoretical.

The pollsters themselves reflected a change in attitude, even if the people did not. While still asking if Americans expected to be drawn into a European war, AIPO framed a new, more straightforward question: "Should the United States send forces to Europe against Germany?" As of March 12, 1939, 83 percent said No.

Three days after that poll, Hitler struck again. Czech President Emil Hacha was summoned to Der Führer and given an ultimatum. Czechoslovakia was either to be absorbed by the Third Reich or annihilated. Before the world knew what was happening, Hitler's troops rolled into Prague in the early morning of March 16, in clear violation of his promise to Chamberlain. That evening, Hitler crowed into microphones, "Czechoslovakia has ceased to exist!"

Chamberlain's "appeasement" had become a dirty word, but no one was prepared to act in the face of Hitler's duplicity. The map of Europe changed weekly. On March 21, the Polish Ambassador to Germany was told that the port city of Danzig was rightfully German and was to be returned to the Reich at once. The following day, Hitler seized the Baltic port of Memel from Lithuania. No one wanted to play intercessor, which left the citizens little to do but cheer their new leader.

Poland was clearly Hitler's next quarry. Britain and France, now convinced that Hitler's future aggressions had to be contained in advance, hastily concluded a mutual protection pact with Poland and Romania. Had they also signed with powerful Russia, the agreement might have had some muscle, but as it turned out, the March 31 pact forestalled the Nazi invasion of Poland by a mere five months.

Our national uproar intensified. In a letter to Nevada Senator Pittman, Envoy to Belgium Joseph Davies warned that Chamberlain's pact with Poland meant that war in Europe was certain. On the other hand, isolationist Senator Borah of Idaho proclaimed that Hitler's seizure of Czechoslovakia was Chamberlain's doing, and that Hitler could want no better friend. On April 9, an AIPO poll showed that if England and France declared war on Germany, 95 percent of Americans wanted the U.S. to abstain from joining them. FDR could do little more than appeal to Hitler for peace. Hitler's reply on April 28 was clear enough: "Roosevelt's role as the guardian angel of Europe is finished!"

Clearly the only stopgap for averting war was a peace treaty between England and Russia. In a letter to Secretary of State Cordell Hull, Envoy Davies wrote: "There has been nothing short of a revolution in war thinking here in the last three months. The picture has changed violently. The only hope now is that the British-Soviet military pact will be shortly concluded. It has been obvious for the past two and one-half years that Germany will only be deterred by the fear of having to fight on two fronts."

Hopes for such a treaty dimmed on May 3, 1939, when Stalin removed Foreign Commissar Litvinoff. His successor, Viacheslav Molotov, was known to be less interested in peace than in political expediency. Later that same week, Mussolini—fresh from his conquest of Albania—signed a full military treaty with Hitler. Italian mistrust of Hitler was officially submerged, and *Il Duce* mouthed Hitler's anti-Semitic slogans, which had never been popular in Italy. In the Axis camp, all was harmony.

With the belligerent nations rapidly choosing sides, an isolationist Congress passed a new Neutrality Bill that embargoed commerce and travel to both friend and foe. Once again it seemed even-handed, but its only effect was to hamstring our friends. Hitler was now free to do as he pleased.

The Gallup Poll revealed that the Congress no longer reflected the will of the people. With 57 percent wanting the Neutrality Laws changed, 65 percent favoring a boycott of German goods, and 80 percent sympathetic to the Allies, public opinion was clearly against Hitler. But Congress moved toward its annual summer adjournment. By now everyone was expecting a war in Europe, but according to Gallup, only half of the American public thought it might start by year's end.

The first indication that war was imminent came during the first week in August. All German military leaves were being canceled. The German army was to be fully mobilized by August 10.

Then on August 24, all hope for a second front against Germany vanished when Hitler signed a nonaggression pact with Stalin. An inevitable but seemingly distant war was now just around the corner. Americans expected their Labor Day weekend to be the last peacetime holiday for several years.

After a series of loudly protested "border incidents," that no one believed, Hitler invaded Poland on September 1. On Sunday, September 3, 1939, Britain and France—the only nations openly committed to defend Poland—declared war on Germany. But there was little the Allies could do. Danzig fell within a week. The Luftwaffe bombed Warsaw indiscriminately. On September 17, Stalin sent Russian forces into Poland from the east. By the end of the month, Poland was split between the two invaders.

With the war a reality, newspaper circulation soared. Most of the nation's 30 million radios were left on all day. Street-corner orators were everywhere. Congressional mail topped half a million items per day. There was even a fistfight on the floor of the House. On September 3 the AIPO reported that 76 percent of the American public felt we would be drawn into the war, willingly or unwillingly.

Yet AIPO data through 1939 clearly show that as the war in Europe became more likely, American desire to enter such a conflict *decreased*. In March 1939, in response to the question "Should the U.S. send forces to Europe against Germany?" we answered No by 83 percent. After the Axis seizure of Czechoslovakia, Memel, and Albania, American opposition to the sending of troops rose slightly, to 84 percent. In the week between the signing of the German-Russian pact and the invasion of Poland, it jumped to 90 percent, and during the first week of the war, to 94 percent.

Virtually no one in America wanted any part of a European war. But as early as mid-summer 1939, the Gallup Poll found that over 90 percent of the country would fight willingly if America were *directly* attacked.

Obviously, a victory by the Allies in Europe would prevent such an invasion. Conversely, a defeat of the Allies in Europe would make the unthinkable quite thinkable indeed. The question was how well the Allies could stand up to Hitler without our aid.

Roosevelt began a campaign to lift the arms embargo. On September 8, he declared a Limited National Emergency. Army and Navy recruitment was stepped up, reserves were called to active duty, and government investigative agencies were strengthened. FDR also created the Office of Government Reports, OGR, which transmitted public opinion to the President and government positions to the public.

Members of Congress atacked OGR as a propaganda machine,

which in part it was. An editorial in the the Chicago *Tribune* screeched, "The Allies' problems are their own, and if they make a mistake in solving them, they will have to pay the bill!" At the same time, the American Ambassador to France wrote Cordell Hull, "If France and England should be unable to defeat Hitler in Europe, American forces will have to fight his forces in the Americas."

Deprived of American weapons, the Allies did little to engage Hitler. As Poland was overrun, Senator Borah said, "The way the French and British are pulling their punches on the Western Front, there is something phony about this war." But Hitler was in no hurry to open a western front. The French were secure if unprepared behind their "impregnable" Maginot Line extending to the Belgian border. The English were equally secure (and nearly equally unprepared) across the Channel—a moat which the Royal Navy could surely guard—and German air bases were too distant to launch an air raid. Everyone was marking time.

On October 2, 1939, Congress began debate to repeal the arms embargo, and once again, the country was at war with itself. The gallery of the Senate was packed with hand-clapping partisans, cheering first one side, then the other. Senator Borah gave the performance of his life. But the bias toward the Allies had turned the tide. AIPO revealed that if repeal helped the Germans, only 4 percent were in favor. If repeal helped the Allies (as everyone knew it would), 58 percent were in favor. Congress got the message. Exactly one month after the debate began, the arms embargo was lifted.

Warring parties might now buy arms and ammunition from the United States on a "cash-and-carry" basis. This legislation, technically as unbiased as the Neutrality Laws had been, clearly favored the Allies, as Hitler was quick to see. His only comfort was that France and England would need months or years to match the strength of his own war machine. Time was on Germany's side. So while the Allies armed and Hitler regrouped, the "phony" war continued.

Before the year's end, France had placed orders for $18 million worth of American aircraft and aircraft parts. Since the "cash-and-carry" laws prohibited American companies from shipping the goods, steamships and tankers owned by American companies reregistered their ships in Panama, which enabled them to ship war cargoes legally. Atlantic ports were taxed to capacity. The stock market rose and unemployment fell.

But then the harsh European winter brought a lull. Except for the Russian invasion of Finland, there were no military engagements. Each week that passed without the United States being dragged into the conflict persuaded Americans that we might not get involved after all. By March 1940, a peace treaty was signed between Russia and Finland. Perhaps the war was over?

Senator Borah died suddenly in January 1940, and three months later, Hitler invaded Norway and Denmark without warning. On April 9, Denmark was vanquished and Norway survived a mere three weeks. British efforts to save Norway failed, although the Royal Navy sank 10 destroyers of Germany's Baltic Fleet.

Americans now accepted the war as real and Hitler as a threat. But the April losses were a mere curtain raiser; Hitler stormed into the Netherlands and Belgium on May 10. Belgian King Leopold III had been so intent on neutrality that his nation was virtually defenseless. Conquest of Belgium allowed the Nazis to slip behind the Maginot Line and down into France. By May 15, with Rotterdam in ruins from air strikes, the Netherlands surrendered. On May 21, the German Army gazed out across the English Channel. And on May 27, Belgium surrendered.

On that date, as the evacuation of British and Belgium forces from Dunkirk began, FDR stated what had long been obvious: the United States was no longer neutral, but merely not warring. According to Gallup, 36 percent of Americans were now ready to help England, even at the risk of war. Americans had a national topic of conversation: "What if Hitler wins?"

As the German army thundered through northern France, the world was shocked and infuriated when Italian forces invaded France on June 10. Four days later, the Nazis stormed Paris, and France fell. By the end of June, Winston Churchill, now British Prime Minister, pronounced the Battle of France over: "I expect the Battle of Britain is about to begin."

Americans realized that the defeat of England—a real possibility—would put Hitler within striking distance of the United States. When the war had begun nine months earlier, the U.S. had ranked nineteenth as a world military power. America could not risk military unpreparedness any longer.

Roosevelt proposed the first peacetime conscription in U.S. history, which a Gallup Poll showed the public equally favoring and opposing. Chief of Naval Operations Admiral Stark urgently requested $4 billion to build a "two-ocean Navy." (The enormity of this request is clear when compared with Roosevelt's $9 billion budget for the entire government only a year earlier.) But Americans objected to war, not to defense. Although the request was granted, Roosevelt was told that the United States would remain vulnerable to a sea attack for two years. As Admiral Stark put it, "Dollars can't buy yesterday!"

On June 15 the public learned that a National Defense Research Committee had been formed under Vannevar Bush. This group of civilian scientists initiated most of the scientific research used by the army. (What the public did not learn was that FDR had secretly given specific orders the previous October for research into the possible development of an atomic bomb.)

Hitler's first bomb fell on England on July 10. Throughout the summer, hundreds of bombers rained death and destruction on England. Hitler planned a full-scale invasion of England for September, but the bombings, supposed to soften up the English, had exactly the opposite effect. Britons steeled themselves to resist Nazi efforts to destroy their morale. The valiant RAF flyers were coordinated with a massive radar network which stretched across the south and east of England. Ten months passed before the nightly raids subsided, leaving over 60,000 civilians dead.

On August 24, 1940, as Edward R. Murrow's "London After Dark" broadcast brought the Battle of Britain into American homes and newspapers filled American breakfast tables with photos of London in ruins, *Liberty* offered the first segment of *Lightning in the Night*. The title was taken from Der Führer's own words: "Unlike Mussolini, I would spring like lightning in the night and hurl myself on the enemy." It had been written by Fred Allhoff with the advice and counsel of Lieutenant General Robert Lee Bullard, Rear Admiral Yates Sterling, and George E. Sokolsky. Bernarr MacFadden's popular *Liberty* magazine published the novel in thirteen installments between August 24 and November 16, 1940.

The impact of the serial was overwhelming. A fictional blitz of New York seemed more real in light of the bombing of London. After our Navy's imagined fate was published, its vulnerability to attack became clear. Allhoff's use of Hitler as a character was both innovative and startling. *Liberty* sales reached an all-time high. Whether in praise or opposition, everyone had his own, strongly held opinion of the book.

Even the Nazi propaganda machine broadcast a five-minute harangue, branding the novel "outlandish exaggeration," and ignoring the Nazi bombing of England, then at its height. But by mid-September, when the Burke-Wadsworth Act passed, public acceptance of a peacetime draft had risen to 71 percent. And by December 16, 1940—exactly one month after the climactic final chapter had been published—Gallup found that willingness to help England despite the risk of involvement had risen to over 60 percent. That *Lightning in the Night* played a role in emotionally preparing Americans to confront a Nazi threat cannot be denied.

On June 10, 1939, *Liberty*'s own publisher, Bernarr Mac-Fadden, had stated in an editorial that there would be "no war for a year, maybe five years" with Germany. Thus, Allhoff's own World War II does not begin until 1945, based on three quite logical premises: first, that Hitler would never gamble on a two-front war and thus would honor his nonaggression pact with Stalin. Second, that both Germany and Japan would settle down to assimilating their conquered territories, preferring to extend their power by diplomatic coups and international blackmail. And third, that with the European war at a standstill, America would slow her own rearmament efforts and retreat to an isolationist position.

To bridge the gap in time, *Liberty*'s serial began with a prologue by Edward Hope, in which "future" newspaper clippings and broadcasts record the march of world events. . . .

Extra! Extra! Extra!

BRITISH SIGN NAZI PEACE, YIELD NAVY, POSSESSIONS TO SAVE UNBLASTED CITIES

Empire Broken, as Canada, Australia, South Africa Refuse Terms, Secede

Canada a Republic, U. S. Ally

MEDITERRANEAN FLEET SCUTTLED, HOME FLEET GIVES
UP UNDER THREAT OF CIVILIAN EXTERMINATION

BERLIN, Sept. 17—While hysterical street crowds
thundered adulation of the man who has made Germany unquestioned master of half the world, dis-
armed officers and men of the defeated British Army,
Navy, and Air Force paraded the streets of their con-
querors' capital, to be spat upon by holiday-making
spectators. The British Plenipotentiary Mission, under
the leadership of Sir Samuel Hoare, today signed the
most abject peace terms of modern history. . . .

**Reich Claims All Former British, French,
Dutch, Danish Colonies in Western Hemisphere**

WON THEM, SAYS BERLIN

Monroe Doctrine Not Applicable in Transfer Between European Powers, Nazis Hold

WASHINGTON, Sept. 19—In a strongly worded note handed to the United States government yesterday, Greater Germany contends the historical aim of the Monroe Doctrine is to prevent the acquisition of new territory in the Western Hemisphere by European Powers, and not to interfere with the agreed transfer of colonies in the Americas from one Old World government to another. Thus, the Nazi Foreign Office holds, this country should agree without question to Germany's occupation of the former British possessions in the New World, as well as of the insular and continental holdings of France, the Netherlands, and Denmark, which have been provisionally held by the United States since shortly after the capitulation of France.

It was learned here this morning that an emergency meeting of State, Navy, and War Department heads, which lasted most of the night, adjourned without any decision being taken. At the Navy Department, it was stated on good authority that in the event of a threat of force, the United States fleet, even with the addition of naval units from the Republic of Canada, is not strong enough to hold European possessions in the Western Hemisphere.

These territories extend from Greenland to the South Shetland Islands just north of the Antarctic Circle, and from Bermuda in the Atlantic to French Marquesas in the Pacific.

Senator Chad Fillgus of the Foreign Relations Committee gave out a statement to correspondents in which he said that the logic of the German position was unassailable. In the interests of peace, Senator Fillgus told the . . .

"And now back to the news . . . Berlin: In making the announcement of Herr Himmler's departure for the British subject area, Propaganda

Minister Goebbels said, and I quote, 'It is not the Führer's intention to impair the essentials of life in Britain, which had many admirable features before it fell into decay. However, there are elements of the population which continue recklessly to attempt to sabotage the Peace of Berlin. If these groups have missed the significance of the punitive bombing of Westminster Abbey and the razing of Oxford, we will find means to bring the facts home to them,' end quote. DNB, the official German news agency, announces from London that the bodies of the seventeen schoolboys found guilty of subversive activities by the People's Court at Leeds and subsequently executed before a Gestapo firing squad were buried at once within the prison walls to avoid further unhappy incidents. . . . And here are the baseball scores: The Yankees continued their winning streak . . ."

NEW GERMAN EMPIRE: A map of the world shows the changes in status of the former British, French, Dutch, and Belgian colonies under the Treaty of Berlin, since the German-American Colonial Commission decided in favor of the Nazi contention that the Monroe Doctrine does not prevent the transfer to the Reich of European colonies in the Americas. Alsace-Lorraine and Normandy, Belgium, Holland, Denmark, and the Scandinavian peninsula have become integral parts of Greater Germany. Britain, Ireland, France and Switzerland are designated for the present simply as "subject areas," each with its *Gauleiter*. The administration of the new so-called Führer Colonies is under the direct control of Chancellor Hitler.

The only Führer Colonies in the continental Americas are the Guianas and what was formerly British Honduras. Nearest to the United States are Greenland, Clipperton Island, and the former British, French, and Dutch West Indies. Negotiations have been started, however, between Greater Germany and the Republic of Canada over the ownership of Newfoundland and Labrador, which the victorious Nazis claim as former British crown colonies.

South Africa, after a brief resistance in an attempt to gain its independence, has become a German colony. India, which seceded from the British Empire just before the Treaty of Berlin was signed, has disintegrated into the hundreds of small states of which it formerly consisted. The status of the new Australian-New Zealand Republic is in doubt under the increasing pressure of the Japanese from the (once Dutch) East Indies and of the enormously strengthened German navy. The U.S. State Department is debating a proposal to grant the Philippines immediate independence and to call an international conference to settle the future of other United States possessions in the Pacific which have become a dangerous burden to our Navy.

TILL HELL FREEZES OVER—Seven U.S. senators of the World Peace Bloc are now in the third day of their filibuster against the McRoy-Polter Bill, which would provide one billion dollars in new appropriations to build gigantic modern naval and air bases on the Florida east coast and the island of Puerto Rico to neutralize Greater Germany's alleged fortification of Jamaica and Trinidad, which German officials have often denied.

"The war is over," Senator Grooven told reporters yesterday, "and we don't want another. Give the warmongers these bases, and they'll be right back for 50,000 more planes and a couple of hundred new warships to defend them. Why, there isn't any reason to believe that German fortifications are being built! We are going to kill this dangerous legislation if we have to talk till hell freezes over. Germany won the war fair and square, and the sooner we realize that and start to treat her like the good customer she would like to be, the sooner business in this country will get back on its feet."

"And now for our news commentary . . . Greater Germany wants peace and good business, and she is ready to co-operate with other nations with similar aims. Three separate items received here in our newsroom tonight all tell the same story.

"From Mexico City first—An agreement has been reached to establish two Mexican bases for the new high-speed German ocean-transport planes. The terminal for the Atlantic service will be at Tampico, and the one for the Pacific at Ensenada, Lower California. Building of these two completely equipped modern airports in Mexico will start at once from plans that are already drawn up in Germany. That's one item, folks.

"The next is from Buenos Aires, where the Argentine government has signed a trade treaty with Greater Germany. The Reich will buy seventy-two percent of Argentina's annual beef output and pay for it in industrial machines and war materiel. German experts in animal husbandry and veterinary medicine will sail from Bremen next week to direct the Argentine cattle-raising and meat-packing industries.

"And here's item number three. It comes from Washington, D.C. The German ambassador announced tonight that his government has canceled all outstanding German orders for American wheat, corn, scrap steel, raw cotton, and cotton textiles. Do you want to know why? Here's what the ambassador says in his announcement, quote: 'There is a systematic persecution of Germans in the United States. The refusal of the American government to permit employment of skilled German-born workmen in munitions and airplane factories, the repeated violence of local and federal policy in breaking up meetings and parades of peaceful German organizations in this country, and the unceasing anti-German press campaign—vile, scurrilous, and wholly unjustifiable in time of peace—these and many other signs of systematic persecution make it impossible for us to carry on friendly commercial relations with the United States. Greater Germany does not force her business on anyone.'

"Well, that's what he says, folks, and in my opinion there are a lot of politicians in Washington who ought to paste it in their hats. . . ."

To the Editor:

Sir: I am amused to read that our State Department has seen fit to protest the creation of German naval and air bases at

Jamaica, Trinidad, and other islands in the West Indies. When these islands belonged to Britain, the Royal Navy used them freely as bases, and the United States never uttered a syllable of objection. How, then, can it be a cause of alarm or annoyance if the present owners of the islands use them in the same way?

Many of the warships to whose presence in the West Indies we are so strongly opposed are the identical vessels that used to do as they chose in the Caribbean without so much as a tut from our State Department. The more modern units of the British Navy, handed over to Germany in part payment of war reparations, have been renamed and incorporated into the German fleet.

Sauce for the goose, you know.

F. W. Liss

Brazilian plantation and mine executives, superintendents, even foremen were dismayed one morning last week as Bureaucrats of the totalitarian-minded Brazilian government watched the first step toward Nazefficiency under the trade agreement between Brazil and Greater Germany. New executives, superintendents, and foremen were imported from Germany the week before in the luxury liner *Edda Goering* (ex-*Queen Mary*) to take over.

With precision that was suggestively military, they stepped into their new . . .

According to U.S. tourist David Pardin, his smuggled candid-camera shots show the heavily fortified new naval and air base on the island of Jamaica, only ninety miles from Cuba and not much farther from the U.S. Navy base at Guantanamo Bay. Although construction of these fortifications has been repeatedly denied in Berlin, the tremendous work now seems virtually complete, with heavy (probably 16-

inch) guns. In Washington yesterday, German Ambassador Otto Schimpfholz branded Pardin's pictures as "phony" . . .

BERLIN, May 19—In a strong protest to the Mexican government over the killing of two German nationals during the riots in Mexico City yesterday, Nazi Foreign Minister Joachim von Ribbentrop warned today that the patience of the Reich is close to its limit. "Greater Germany," he said, "will not stand idly by while her subjects are maltreated." Herr von Ribbentrop dismissed as absurd Mexican charges that the riots were fomented and led by Germans.

"The Germans in Mexico," he said, "want only their just rights, and we are here to see to it that they get them. We hope a peaceful solution can be reached." He declined to elaborate his statement.

The presence of the German Caribbean fleet off the coast of Mexico, according to naval officials in Berlin, is quite normal for "spring maneuvers." . . .

It's Not Too Late by Martin L. Tresholm, New York: Greenway Press. $3.50. Reviewed by James Jackson Hobbs, former attaché, United States State Department.

Mr. Tresholm has written a brief and poignant history of the past ten years. No one can deny his skill in presenting his facts. It is his reasoning that spoils what might otherwise have been a valuable book.

Dismissing repeated German guaranties of American neutrality, disregarding the virtual impossibility of an invasion of the United States by a European power, sneering at our standing army of 400,000 men, he holds that the United States must soon fight Germany for domination of the Americas; and that unless we arm ourselves to the teeth and give all our

energies to preparation, such a war will end dis-
astrously for us. Mr. Tresholm swallows his inter-
nationalists' mythology hook, line, and sinker. . . .

MEXICO CITY, June 18: Events in Mexico have
moved so swiftly during the past few days that it is still
difficult for the intelligent reader to be sure just what
it all means.

Last Tuesday, Mexico received a sharp note from
Berlin over the killing of five more Germans in street
clashes with the police of the Cuevas regime. Wednesday morning, the Governor of German Honduras
reported that Mexican soldiers crossed the border
and fired on German guards, who returned the fire
and drove them off. That afternoon three German
cruisers steamed into the harbor of Vera Cruz on
what they called "a goodwill visit."

President Cuevas consulted the United States Ambassador, and they talked to Washington by telephone. When news of this consultation was told to
German Ambassador Schmick Thursday afternoon,
he made a statement to correspondents that any
alliance, or even any unofficial collaboration, between
Mexico and the United States could be taken by
Greater Germany only as being anti-German in
intention. The consequences of anti-German action,
he said, might be extremely grave.

On Friday morning, however, the whole situation
was changed. During the night, the Blue Shirts of
General Arranza loosed their well-organized revolution in a score of cities at the same time. When foreign
correspondents came down to breakfast, they learned
that the government had changed hands and that
General Arranza was now dictator of Mexico.

With Arranza's well-known admiration for and
friendship with the Nazi regime . . .

". . . Bureau predicts a hot sunny day with occasional thundershowers tomorrow for Fourth of July vacationists . . . Berlin: The German Foreign Office refused to take official notice of the Canadian protest over recent alleged incidents in Labrador. Canadian sources have reported that several times during the past week, German fighting planes from the new Greenland bases have appeared over Labrador and machine-gunned villages and fishing boats. Nine Canadian citizens have been reported wounded, but none killed. Unofficial German spokesmen say that German patrol planes have strict orders to remain over Greenland territorial waters, and that any Canadian fishing boats fired upon must have been violating Greenland fishing reserves. Such violations, they said, must cease . . ."

CONFIDENTIAL   CONFIDENTIAL

Memorandum to Newspaper Editors and Publishers

In the present unsettled condition of international affairs, the United States Department of State, with the approval of the President, feels it necessary to point out that articles and reports unfriendly to the German Empire have a profoundly disturbing effect on our relations with a great Power with whom we are at peace. Recently commercial negotiations with Greater Germany, which had been making favorable progress, were broken off because of publication in the American press of unfavorable comments on the pogroms in Britain, France, and Belgium. Several months ago, harbor facilities in the German West Indies were denied to American ships when United States newspapers were publishing reports of the deaths in the Hebrides concentration camp of Messrs. Churchill, Eden, and Duff Cooper.

Without wishing in any way to impair the freedom of the American press, the Department of State cannot too strongly urge coolness and great moderation in the handling of foreign news, particularly when it concerns the German Empire.

James Biddle Carleton,
Undersecretary of State

STUDENTS BURN U. S. EMBASSY, BEAT ATTACHÉ IN MEXICO CITY
Troops Mass Along Rio Grande

GERMAN, JAP NAVIES NEAR

Arranza Expresses Regret but Calls Rioters "Morally Justified"; Proposes Arbitration Talks

MEXICO, D.F., Sept. 9—While fresh divisions of the powerful Mexican mechanized army poured hourly into the stupendous new fortifications along the American border, students in the capital rioted last night without interference from the police. By the time Dictator Miguel Arranza's Blue Guards appeared on the scene, the U. S. Embassy was a heap of smoking ruins and Arthur Y. Gorrick, Second Secretary, had been severely beaten for disrespect to a policeman.

Pedro Joquera, Foreign Minister, made public early this morning his messages of thanks to Vice-Admiral Yoshimimo Oti, in command of the Japanese fleet in the Pacific off Lower California, and to Admiral Hans von Rauschpinck, whose German Caribbean fleet is maneuvering off Panama . . .

"Ladies and gentlemen, the Associated Broadcasting stations bring you, direct from Hitlerhafen, the speech of Wilhelm Holtrich, Military Governor of Greenland, being translated into English and directed to the people of Canada. . . .

". . . Germany is strong. Germany is determined. Germany is not lightly to be insulted. Der Führer-Kanzler has said: 'I will defend every German in the world, in the German Empire or out of it. Whoever lays a finger on one of my people will have to reckon with the power of two hundred million Germans. Cities will burn. Men will wallow in blood!'

"Yesterday five Germans were set upon and beaten by a mob in St. John's, Newfoundland. Two of them died. This morning three Canadian bombers flew over Davis Strait and attempted to take pictures of military objectives. They were driven off by our fighters.

"Such aggressions are not to be tolerated. German patience is exhausted. For the last time, we offer to negotiate the Labrador problem. This offer is final. If the reckless leaders of the Republic of Canada want to put the issue to the test of force, we are ready. *Heil Hitler!*"

To the Editor:

All right-thinking Americans and Canadians will sleep more soundly now that the International Arbitration Commission has reached an amicable settlement of the Labrador-Newfoundland question. All of us, except certain warmongers who masquerade as patriots, will see the common sense of the agreement that gives Greenland a year-round outlet for her merchant shipping and deprives Canada of practically nothing. As has been pointed out, Labrador and Newfoundland belong geologically and geographically to Greenland, and the Canadian Republic's decision to cede them is a triumph of reason.

The new arrangement will be vastly more satisfactory to all concerned. During the past few weeks we have all been needlessly worried by the danger that our Canadian ally might prove stubborn and drag us into hostilities with the German Empire. I am in hearty agreement with Senator Tolley's statement that nobody in this country wants to be drawn into a war over a lot of Eskimos.

John P. Fripton

EL PASO CLASH GRAVE

Mexico Admits
Guards Crossed Border

TANKS, PLANES MASS

Arranza Says U. S. Soldiers Kidnaped Two Juarez Customs Guards

DEMANDS INDEMNITY

Mexican Planes Over Houston, Dallas, San Antonio, as U. S. Protests

EL PASO, Feb. 12—State Department officials who arrived here this afternoon are still trying to get at the truth of the border clashes between Mexican and United States troops, which reached a sudden climax this morning with the appearance of swarms of Dictator Arranza's bombers over all the principal cities of southern Texas. There is still no definite news of the casualties inflicted when one Mexican flyer, apparently by mistake, dropped a high-explosive bomb on Sam Houston High School . . .

CHAPTER 1

THE PRISONER OF CORVO

It was on such days as this, when an angry sea whipped the sheer volcanic sides of the little island and the rain lashed dismally from brooding skies, that the old wounds bothered him most.

He could no longer remember the day on which he had received those wounds; that winter day on the Alpine front in 1917 when the trench mortar he was firing had exploded, killing five of his comrades and spraying forty-two splinters of jagged steel into his own back.

There were so many things he could no longer remember clearly.

Son of a blacksmith, he shrugged broad, strong shoulders against the dull aches in calves and thighs and back. He hitched forward in his chair and cupped his huge, fine head in his hands. His dark eyes stared dully, vacantly, into the fireplace.

At a table near the door sat the young guard. He was tall and strong and hard of face. He had unbuttoned the collar of his field-gray uniform.

As he cleaned his pistol he hummed the Horst Wessel song. But his heart was not in it. Back home was a girl. A tall, blonde, healthy girl with a big fine bosom. And for three months more, until they sent fresh guards, he must rot on this Godforsaken island in the Atlantic where now, since the war, no ships called. It was enough to drive a man mad.

He held his pistol up and looked through its gleaming barrel. The older man took his head out of his hands and said: "What day is it?"

The question brought surliness to the face of the young guard. "Must you keep asking that?" he said. "It makes no difference to you."

"What day is it?"

"Thursday."

"The year? What year is it?"

"Nineteen forty-five. Third year of the Greater United German Reich. Heil Hitler!"

At the name, a sudden gleam lighted the older man's eyes. It flickered out, and again he stared into the fireplace. The young guard went on cleaning his already clean gun.

Late that afternoon the rain stopped and the skies cleared. The guard went to the window. He grinned and consulted his watch.

"It is time," he said.

"Time?"

"The people wait."

The older man's eyes grew bright and his shoulders straightened. As he got to his feet, listlessness dropped from him. He put on a tunic over his black shirt. He fastened his belt. He hurried up the staircase to a second-floor room. At the door to its tiny outside balcony, he halted, gave his tunic a final pat, pushed out his chest.

The tall young guard swung open the door, clicked his heels, offered a sharp, mocking military salute. It was nonsense, this daily horseplay, but it relieved the hideous monotony.

The black-shirted man strode out on the balcony. He looked down gravely at his "audience."

On all the island of Corvo there were not more than nine hundred persons. A dozen of them were gathered now to hear this man—this stranger they called "Papa Napoleon." Some had brought with them their diminutive, waist-high native cows. All of them were barefooted.

For one terrifying second, bewilderment clutched at the man on the balcony. Then out of the deep well of memory flowed brave words and phrases. He rested his hands on the balcony railing and began to speak:

"Soldiers of the land, sea, and air! We are entering the battlefield against the plutocratic, reactionary democracies of the West."

He leaned forward, his right hand gesticulating, pointing.

"This gigantic conflict is only a phase of our revolution. It is the conflict of poor, numerous peoples who labor against starvers who ferociously cling to a monopoly of all riches and all gold on earth."

His voice rang. His imperious postures and gestures awed his peasant hearers. On and on he went: "Everything within the state. Nothing without the state. Everything for the state."

An old man below whispered to another, "Who is he?"

The other shrugged.

"What does he say?"

"I do not know that, either. But he is a brave speaker. His words blow like bugles."

The man on the balcony thundered:

"Fascism is a religion! Liberty is a putrid corpse! Now the die is cast, and our will has burned our ships behind us. According to the rules of Fascist morale, when one has a friend, one marches with him to the end. We salute the Führer . . ."

For the first time his voice trembled uncertainly. Then a rush of new words came:

"Italian people, rush to arms and show your tenacity, your courage, your valor!"

He was silent. Below, the handful of Portuguese peasants were silent too. But only for a moment. Though they understood not one word of what he had said, his oratory had kindled in them a fierce excitement. They shouted and clapped their hands wildly.

And, on the balcony, Benito Mussolini imperiously turned his back upon them and disappeared into the gray lava-stone house.

From *National Weekly,* issue of February 17, 1945:

Prime puzzle of World War II has been the fate of Adolf Hitler's onetime pal and axis partner, Il Duce del Fascismo Benito Mussolini.

Until last week, since Hitler's incredibly executed Double

Trojan Horse coup in Naples and Rome on Black Friday, May 2, 1941
(*National Weekly,* May 10, 1941), no word had come from Europe concerning Mussolini, who, according to the German government radio,
had been taken prisoner.

Of rumors there had been plenty. Sample rumors:

Mussolini had been shot to death in his great office in the
Palazzo Venezia.

He had been sent to the political prison camp in the Lipari
Islands.

He had been taken to the German concentration camp at
Buchenwald, where he had died of castor-oil "treatments"—a technique devised by the late Italo Balbo.

Last week Mussolini's fate was no longer a mystery. Since the
summer of 1941 he has been Adolf Hitler's prisoner, exiled to Corvo—
northernmost, westernmost, and tiniest of the nine islands of the
formerly Portuguese Azores.

Many American travelers, flying the Atlantic, have seen Corvo
from the air while approaching Horta. Until last week, there was no
reason to believe that any had set foot upon it. Until a radio station was
built, the sole means of communication with Flores, the neighboring
Azorean island, was by signal fires.

In a house on Corvo today lives the exiled Mussolini in the
glory of a dead past. Each day, from a balcony, under the watchful eye
of a Nazi guard, he speaks to such peasants as gather to listen admir-
ingly, if uncomprehendingly. His "speeches" seem to consist of
strangely jumbled excerpts from speeches he made years ago when he
was Europe's Number 2 Dictator.

Such was the story brought back to America last week by
Miguel Graciosa, a cranberry grower in Massachusetts' Cape Cod
region. Born in Corvo, now a United States citizen, Mr. Graciosa long
had been worried concerning the fate of a brother and sister from
whom he had not heard since leaving Corvo, as a youth, for the United
States. When Nazi Germany took over Portugal and its Azores, he
worried even more.

Having saved up his money, one day last month he boarded a
Clipper bound for Horta. There, Nazi customs officials told him that
he was free to visit any of the Azorean islands—except Corvo. No
reason was given for the exception.

He went to Flores, bided his time, and one dark night hired a fisherman to take him to nearby Corvo. He found his relatives. They told him of the island's mysterious prisoner. Barefooted and in peasant clothes, he went with his brother to hear the stranger speak. He recognized at once the sixty-two-year-old Mussolini. He said nothing of his discovery, but returned the next day to shoot several candid-camera pictures of *Il Duce* (as Mussolini used to be called) on the balcony.

That night, undetected by the German guards, he returned to Horta, emplaned for the United States. Arriving at LaGuardia Field, he told his story and produced his films in proof of it.

Solved is the mystery of Europe's missing man, Benito Musso-lini. He is not dead. But when reporters had pieced together Mr. Graciosa's story, there was ample evidence that under the strain of exile one of the shrewdest minds of pre-Nazi Europe has cracked; that tranquil Corvo has bestowed upon Mussolini the anesthesia of madness.

BULLETIN: Grenoble, Feb. 12—*Le Petit Dauphinois,* Nazi mouth-piece of the French Fascist State, today branded the Graciosa story 'a sheer fabrication.' That Benito Mussolini is, as reported, an exile on the island of Corvo, the Azores, was described as a 'typical American fairy tale in the stupid tradition of democratic wishful thinking.'

BULLETIN: Berlin, Feb. 19—Adolf Hitler's *Volkischer Beobachter* today confirmed the Graciosa story, admitting that Il Duce has been in exile on Corvo. His exile was termed 'a matter of natural and entirely under-standable political expendiency.' No comment was offered concerning his mental state.

May 10, 1945—

Despite snow-white hair, the little slender man did not look his fifty-six years. His womanish hands clasped before him at his waist, he stood alone at one end of the Great Hall, facing its vast window.

A bitter mystic, a brooding neurotic, he seemed somehow a pathetic and slightly ridiculous figure as he stood, silhouetted against the window, watching a late sun empurple the snow-capped crags of the Bavarian Alps. But the little man at the immense window of the Berghof outside Berchtesgaden was far from ridiculous. He was Adolf Hitler.

To the German people he was Triumphator, Lord of Battle, Rouser Out of Stupor, Leader from Darkness into Light. To the rest of the world he was the most dangerous and the most despised man in Europe. Both to those who worshiped and those who despised him he was the acknowledged master of all Europe. In exactly twenty cataclysmic months, he had pulled into his sphere of domination virtually all of Europe's five hundred million persons.

In those twenty months, as many nations had been smashed, divided, or had jumped eagerly under German control. France had collapsed. Great Britain, her lifelines severed, had been forced to sue for peace. Italy, onetime ally of the Reich, had been seized in a strategic coup.

The rest had been mop-up work, which was still going on. He had sent his trained "Little Führers" to administer the former French, British, and Portuguese colonies in Africa.

Long before, on Africa's north coast, he had seized the French naval bases, the Italian naval and plane bases, and the strategic British naval bases at Port Said and Suez, controlling the doorway to the Red Sea. Greece had ceded him her naval base at Salamis. He had had a bad moment when Russia had threatened to contest his seizure of Izmit, Turkey, at the entrance to the Black Sea. But he had bluffed—and won.

Adolf Hitler turned from the window of the Great Hall. To his right, on the wall, was a vast map of the world. He was fond of studying it. What his eyes now fell first upon pleased him. The coastal line of the Greater United German Reich ran from North Cape to Gibraltar, east to the Suez Canal. The Mediterranean was virtually a lake within the Greater United German Reich.

Its eastern boundary was less pleasing. Along that jagged line, Stalin, cruel and cunning, had tried to match Adolf Hitler's territorial grabs by seizures of his own—bites into Poland and Finland and Romania, the Sovietizing of little Latvia, Estonia, and Lithuania.

After annexing Bessarabia and northern Bukovina, Stalin had tried desperately to plunge deeper toward the Dardanelles, control of which would have made him impregnable to sea attack. He chose for this attempt the moment that found Hitler busy subduing Great Britain. Hitler's answer was a sharp "Hands off!" and a threat of total war. And Stalin, faced with the prospect of a poor crop and a food shortage, hedged on his bet and settled back in the hope of a war of attrition between Germany and desperate England.

Events disappointed him. England made peace. Hitler tore up
the Russo-German nonaggression pact. The Burma Road, supply
artery for China, was closed. Stalin, who wished to hold Japan away
from his throat by keeping China alive and fighting, could pour only a
trickle of supplies along the long rough road from Russia to China. It
was a hopeless task. China, whose brave long fight had aroused the
admiration of the world, fell into the hands of Japan—an arrogant,
apishly Fascist Japan. India was divided by a Berlin-Tokyo axis.

Europe, broken under a Hitler-dictated peace, had become a
single gigantic union of nations in bondage. And Europe and Asia had
become a gigantic powder keg in which three—and only three—great
Powers awaited the day of explosion: Japan, the Greater United
German Reich, and the Union of Soviet Socialist Republics.

In the United States, the impact of the Second World War had
had a devastating effect. With Canada as its sole ally, the world's last
great democracy had plunged into an inescapable economic war of
attrition.

Germany had taken over three-fourths of Britain's shipping
and one-fourth of her navy. Now Germany set out to take over the role
of mistress of the seas. In the resulting naval armament race, which
promised to bankrupt the United States, the Greater United Reich had
a tremendous edge. Available to it were the shipbuilding facilities of
most of the countries it had seized, as well as the ships that they had
been building.

By early 1945, the United States found itself still two years
away from having the two-ocean navy it had begun to build in 1940—
this even though Canada had turned over to it the shipbuilding facilities
at Vancouver, Quebec, and Victoria.

And, for the United States, this crippling naval rearmament
race was but a part of a black picture. In July of 1940, the State
Department of the Roosevelt administration, believing that a Hitler-
dominated Europe able to conscript cheap labor would deal the
United States an economic body blow, attempted to soften that blow by
calling an Inter-American Conference at Havana in an effort to work
out with the other republics of the Western Hemisphere a trade-cartel
plan whereby the resources of the Americas would be pooled.

The conference proved costly and something less than completely successful. Some of the South American republics accepted
American cash in the form of loans, then later declared the plan

unworkable and turned to the German Reich as their best market for products which the United States also hoped to sell abroad.

There had been other severe financial drains. When, in the winter of 1940, famine had trailed after the armies of Hitler across most of Europe, the Reich had asked America for help in the gigantic task of relief, repatriation, and reconstruction.

Pictures of children near starvation crowded United States newspapers. They were Belgian and English and French and Romanian children, and against the mute misery in their eyes, it was not possible to say no. Money was loaned and the American Food Relief Committee, headed by former President Herbert Hoover, sailed for the Greater United German Reich, from whence Hoover issued reports of conditions so horrible that a greathearted nation raised millions of dollars by subscription for the conquered starving peoples.

By 1943 war-ravaged Europe had regained its feet. The Greater United German Reich had become the best customer both of South America and of the United States. Outwardly, at least, Hitler manifested friendliness. While foreign trade had sunk to a mere dribble of its former flow, optimistic economists predicted that the United States would eventually emerge from the doldrums.

But for every dollar of foreign trade regained, ten were poured into the hungry maw of national defense. Hitler's lightninglike subjection of Europe had caught the United States wholly unprepared. By the time France had fallen in 1940, the United States had not even drafted a careful and thorough and clear defense program. Still unprepared when, in 1941, Hitler subjugated all Europe, America would have been an easy prize for his armies. But the years passed— and Hitler did not attack.

The year 1945 was a year in which anything might happen. Despite his manpower, his ever-growing army and navy, crafty Stalin lived in sickening dread of the fanatical little Adolf Hitler. Meanwhile Japan, gorged with new conquests and still building a "mystery" navy, no longer bowed from the waist to anyone. On the surface, her relations with the Greater Reich seemed good.

It was on just this strained situation that Americans pinned their hopes. It seemed certain that a European-Asiatic explosion was imminent. Such an explosion, it was believed, would—for a time, at least—keep war from American shores.

Hitler still despised Russia. With Japan as his ally, he might decide that his destiny (as he had predicted long years before in *Mein*

Kampf) lay to the east. He might march into the Ukraine—and on beyond.

But the United States dared not rely upon probabilities. It strove to match the Greater Reich and any possible ally, ship for ship, gun for gun, and plane for plane. And, in doing so, it teetered on the verge of complete national bankruptcy.

Given two more years, the United States might be unassailable. Meanwhile, it must cling to what seemed a reasonable hope— that the boundaries in Europe and Asia had now so arranged themselves that any possible assailant would fear to leave his homeland lest one or both of the other Old World powers march in.

This was the world in the month of May 1945.

What terrifying things the future held in store, only one man knew. That man was Adolf Hitler, who stood in his Great Hall at Berchtesgaden studying the map. To the east lay Russia; to the west, the Western Hemisphere with its rich prizes—South America and the United States.

East? West? In one of those directions lay his destiny. And as he turned away from the map, his mind was made up. He knew in which direction he would strike.

He left the Great Hall, ascending the eight steps to his own private study. He stopped for a moment to bend over and smell some white flowers in a vase on a table. Then he sat down at his desk, on which was a neat stack of sheets of manuscript. He glanced at one of them, and then, selecting a fresh sheet, began to write.

He was writing a sequel to *Mein Kampf.*

As he sat there, no man could have looked less the part of a conqueror. Yet his driving desires had made a seemingly mad dream come true.

Frail Adolf Hitler, with his burning eyes and sensitive face, had been welded in the two frames of love and hate. Above his desk was a portrait of his father, Alois Hitler—an Austrian customs official who had died in a drunken stupor in a dingy cafe.

Adolf Hitler had learned hate as a child. He had hated his father. He had hated his studies, preferring to become an artist. Failing at that, he had hated the social system that forced him to work at uncongenial tasks, reduced him to the status of a beggar. Those had been hard days—but they had made him hard.

He had loved few things: the mother who had died, his fanatical dream of a Greater Germany—and himself. The First World

War had put more steel into his frail body and had intensified the fires of soul that burned within him. He had been wounded and gassed. But he had fought well and bravely—though that bravery at times had been melodramatic and hysterical.

And now he wrote the story of the dream come true. But not all of it could be written now. There was yet a glorious chapter—a daring and dangerous chapter—to be enacted. But that would come, as everything else had.

As he wrote, the highlights of his conquest of Europe flashed before his mind.

The day Gibraltar fell—after prolonged and (as he acknowledged) heroic die-hard resistance to bombing by his air force, bombardments by the lightly armored and cautious Italian fleet, and finally, assault by Generalissimo Francisco Franco's troops, who crossed the neutral strip between Spain and the Rock and attacked under cover of bombing, machine-gunning Stukas.

The gateway to the Mediterranean fell under German-Spanish-Italian control, and Britain's Mediterranean fleet, driven toward the captured Rock to be hammered by land batteries, was scuttled, almost to the last ship, by its officers.

Later, when Adolf Hitler had recovered the African colonies Germany had lost following the First World War, he brought ivory from Cameroon and had a statue carved. The statue was 150 feet high—twenty feet higher than the famed Christ the Redeemer on the mountain peak overlooking Rio de Janeiro. It stood on a fifty-foot pedestal trimmed with gold leaf, and showed Civilization, in the form of a buxom German mother, cradling Adolf Hitler, "Liberator of Europe," in her arms. The statue looked out to sea from Breakneck Stairs, south of Mount Misery, highest spot on the Rock of Gibraltar.

Of these glorious exploits Adolf Hitler now wrote in detail as he sat there in his study.

It was immeasurably satisfying to write the full account of his most spectacular victory, the Double Trojan Horse coup that in one afternoon had reduced Italy from the position of an axis partner to a vassal state within the Reich. The conception had been all his own. Not until the last possible minute had he called in the members of the German High Command, told them his plan in detail—and forbidden, under severest penalty, any leak.

Following the conquest of Europe, Italy had been a disappointing ally. Despite their Duce's exhortations, her people did not have their heart in the business of conquest. They lacked what Hitler had and what his soldiers had—that driving, single-minded passion that he himself termed "grim fanaticism."

They had complained that they had been "caged" in the Mediterranean; yet when, with joint German and Spanish aid, they had been released, they swelled with pride and took all the credit to themselves. They now decided that the sphere of influence lay east and north, beyond the Mediterranean, and they clamored for a greater slice of the European spoils.

The tension grew. The people had never shared Mussolini's regard for Hitler—had, in fact, sardonically referred to him as the Voice that Mussolini abjectly obeyed. And Italy's King Victor Emmanuel III had been known to speak of Hitler as "that insufferable man."

With the conquest of all Europe—excepting Italy—an accomplished fact; with the Russo-German nonaggression treaty discarded, Adolf Hitler conceived this most daring of his plans for a Greater Germany.

No longer relying upon Stalin, he began anew to taunt him, reverting to an appraisal of the crafty Georgian that he had made before joining hands with him. At that time he had referred to Stalin as "the bloodstained scum of humanity."

Stalin, for his part, proclaimed through his controlled press that the Italian-German axis was collapsing.

In the spring of 1941, Hitler called Italy's "Little Casino," Foreign Minister Count Galeazzo Ciano, to Berlin for a conference. He bestowed extravagant compliments upon young Ciano and explained that he had a plan. This stupid nonsense about an impending break between Italy and Germany must be squelched. Now, as at no time in the history of the two nations, must they put up a united front against this filthy Russian propaganda intended to drive a wedge into their relations.

The plan Hitler outlined was simple. In May of 1938 he had visited Rome where, with Mussolini, he had watched a mass demonstration by Italy's young fighting troops. On the following day they had gone to Naples to review a great naval display. All this had been costly, but it had succeeded in its purpose—to demonstrate to the world the formidable might of two united Fascist nations.

It was time, Hitler said, for that show of unity and strength to be repeated. On May 1, 1941, Stalin would parade his great army in Red Square. On May 2, let the fighting forces of Italy and Germany again show their teeth. Italy would gather her officers, her finest troops, in the square outside the Palazzo Venezia, and would line the Cento-celle military airport at Rome with her fighting planes, to be sent up in great formations as a welcome to Germany's air fighters. Simultan-eously, the finest units of both the Italian and German fleets would lie at anchor in the Bay of Naples.

It would be more than a show of unity: it would be a day of honor, of recognition for Italy. Hitler had already struck off com-memorative decorations that officers of his High Command would pin on the tunics of those Italian soldiers who had helped Germany master Europe. Upon the King and Queen, Il Duce, and the cream of Italy's naval and army commands, Hitler himself would bestow special gold medals of appreciation aboard Germany's great new 35,000-ton battle-ship *Tirpitz*.

Germany would make all arrangements for a motion-picture record of the entire demonstration—pictorial proof of the close part-nership of the German and Italian peoples. And for Count Ciano himself, Hitler hinted, there would be "special recognition."

On "Black Friday," May 2, 1941, the Rome-Naples ceremony took place. The public was excluded. German cameramen had hauled huge boxes of photographic equipment to every vantage point.

Gathered in the square in Rome were almost all of Italy's naval officers, who had left their ships in the Bay of Naples. Here, too, were most of Mussolini's army command and the pick of his crack troops. On the roofs of the buildings surrounding the square, crews of German cameramen trained their cameras down to catch the scene from every angle. From the balcony of the Palazzo Venezia, a loudspeaker roared down instructions for the grouping. Finally both troops and officers were massed in long, compact lines.

At exactly three o'clock, a new voice roared through the loudspeaker:

"Soldiers of Italy, listen well and do not touch your guns. Under no circumstances are you to move or make a demonstration.

"At this moment, aboard the German battleship *Tirpitz,* in the Bay of Naples, are your King and Queen, Il Duce Benito Mussolini, Marshal Pietro Badoglio, Admiral Cavagnari, and General Francesco Pricolo, your chiefs of staff for Army, Navy, and Air. Aboard the *Tirpitz,* too, are Count Ciano and Crown Prince Umberto.

"They are all prisoners of Adolf Hitler!"

The officers and soldiers stirred.

"Do not move!" the loudspeaker bellowed. "Rash actions will only bring disaster. Each of you is covered by a gun. If you value the lives of your King, your Queen, of Il Duce and the officers you love, you will wisely stand silent until the order to throw down your guns. Look on the roofs above you!"

They looked aloft. Beside each camera was the outline of a German trooper pointing a machine gun.

"If one German is harmed, ten men will die. Resistance will be stupid and can bring nothing but destruction to you and those you revere. Germany's planes, loaded with bombs, fly at this moment above your massed air force on the Centocelle Airport. If one of your planes attempts to leave the ground, every one of them will be destroyed before it can move.

"To you officers of the Italian navy, be assured that boarding parties, disguised as German tourists, have taken over your ships and submarines while your crews gathered ashore. Your government buildings are at this moment occupied by German soldiers.

"You shall receive today something more than a medal. You shall receive the glorious opportunity to be absorbed within the Greater United German Reich. No longer are you merely a separate state. Today you become a part of the Reich.

"Once more I suggest that you avoid rash stupidity. For a long time this plan has been conceived. Every move has been studied, every chance weighed, by the Führer.

"Soldiers of Italy, throw down your arms!"

Utterly fantastic. This bloodless conquest—later to be known as the Double Trojan Horse coup—succeeded.

Only one man dared offer opposition. Aboard the *Tirpitz* in the Bay of Naples, as Hitler's ultimatum was delivered to the white-faced little King Emmanuel, sixty-nine-year-old Marshal Pietro Badoglio rushed angrily at Benito Mussolini. Years before, when Mussolini's men had marched on Rome, Badoglio had pleaded with his King: "One battalion of royal troops, sire—one battalion—and I'll sweep away those Black Shirt upstarts."

But the King had refused. And now, as the old soldier charged angrily at Mussolini—who, he wrongly suspected, had a hand in this carefully planned treachery—a Hitler guard raised a gun and shot him down.

Sitting at his desk, Adolf Hitler described the bloodless conquest. "The world," he wrote, "pretended to be aghast at this strategy. It was described, with stupid emotionalism, as despicable treachery. The peoples of New World nations professed to be unable to believe that the close ties of the German-Italian axis could be so abruptly transformed. They were unable to find a single reason for my action. They were—or so they said—shocked, dumbfounded. They should not have been. Long years before I had predicted exactly what happened in *Mein Kampf.* At that time I had written:

'The political testament of the German nation . . . should and must always read substantially: "Never tolerate the establishment of two continental powers in Europe. See an attack on Germany in any such attempt to organize a military power on the frontiers of Germany . . . and regard it not only a right, but a duty, . . . in the event that such a one be already founded, to repress it." ' "

It was long past midnight. Hitler stopped writing and put the manuscript away. He pushed back his chair and, getting up, paced the floor. Tireless, he enjoyed work. Now that comparative peace had come to Europe, he was restless.

He thought, in a coldly detached way, of Benito Mussolini. He had felt a certain admiration for the man he had exiled to the Azores. Il Duce had been a clever man—too clever to be left at large for long. A prudent man, too. In the march of the Black Shirts on Rome in 1922, Benito Mussolini had remained behind. Hitler, who had patterned the abortive Munich Putsch on that bold move, had been more intense, less cautious. And to Mussolini Hitler owed much for the idea of the Fascistic corporative state.

He shrugged. It was ever so. The peoples of other nations invented political systems, and tanks, submarines, and airplanes. And the superior Germans improved upon those inventions and found new and devastating uses for them.

He thought of the night when—three months after his seizure of Italy, and with Europe quieter than before and his work lighter than it had ever been—he had gone to bed to toss restlessly before falling into a deep sleep.

What happened after that had been like a scene relived from his childhood. He had awakened to find himself sitting up in bed, screaming hysterically, shouting: "No! No! Never!"

He could not remember the dream. He did not know why he

had shouted those words. In the morning, when he looked in the mirror, he was shocked to find that his hair had begun to turn white.

Now he pushed these thoughts away from him and returned to his desk, where he picked up a telephone that was a direct wire to Berlin. Tersely he issued orders for a conference in the Great Hall the following morning.

Then he sought the only relaxation he really loved. He began to sketch—an architectural drawing, a design for a new public building in Berlin.

Until the early hours of the morning he worked. The work rested him. Then he looked at his watch and frowned. It was time to go to bed. Yet he did not want to. He strode back into the Great Hall and stood quietly before the great map. Then he clambered up on a sofa against the wall, to examine the map more closely.

Gently he placed the tip of one finger on Berchtesgaden. To the right of it—to the east, beyond the boundaries of the Greater United German Reich—lay vast Russia, his most detested enemy. There, conveniently close, was the fertile Ukraine. Under Nazi efficiency, it would become the great breadbasket of all Europe. It was a rich prize.

Years before, in *Mein Kampf*, he had said that Germany's destiny lay to the east. That was still true. Despite Stalin's Red Army, the Ukraine would be his—and soon!

He looked to the left of his finger—to the west. His eyes spanned the Atlantic, rested upon the Americas. South America— Nazi-infiltrated, economically dependent upon his United Reich, and ever ripe for revolution—was closer ideologically and, in place, geographically, to Europe than to the United States.

And America! He frowned. The last remaining democracy in the world—a heterogeneous, politically squabbling, internally shaky mass—America was now staggering under the heaviest economic blows in its history. Many times in the months now past, it had seemed on the point of falling apart, on the verge of revolution or complete collapse.

Somehow—he could not understand it—it had held together. A rich country, a fat country, a wasteful country. Its people fought among themselves and called their own leaders names and criticized everything and anything they did not like. The right to do these things they called liberty!

And that word rankled. In the Greater United German Reich, he had given his victorious people four years of peace. He had put butter into their mouths and brought coffee (America had none) to their tables once more. He had given them great museums and public buildings. The young, the soldiers, liked it. But Himmler's agents, eavesdropping on some of the older citizens, would overhear, even now, whispered conversations of men and women who wished they might live in America—might worship and read and speak as they pleased.

Such things were bad for the Greater United German Reich.

He wondered, contemptuously, how what he had called the "blatant and superficial" patriotism of America would stand up against that "grim fanaticism" that he and the young soldiers of the United Reich shared.

It was one thing to talk wistfully of liberty. It was another to do as his soldiers had done—to rush, eyes blazing with white-hot zeal, into the fire of machine guns until those guns were silent and other young Germans, plodding over the bodies of their dead and wounded comrades, surged on and beyond to conquer more land for beloved Germany.

He wondered how the avowed patriotism of the United States would fare against the fanaticism of his young soldiers who, sprawled bleeding and dying, legs blown off, bodies mutilated, nevertheless managed to push themselves up and smile and whisper: "Heil Hiter!"

Could this annoying concept of liberty, of freedom, meet such a challenge?

The poised finger of Adolf Hitler's left hand began to move on the wall map. It moved slowly in the direction of his destiny.

From Berchtesgaden it traversed Oberammergau, crossed the Rhine into the Fascist State of France to Brest, moved south and ever west at a gentle ten-degree angle across the Atlantic, and came to rest, at last, on the eastern coast of America, at Baltimore, Maryland.

Adolf Hitler's destiny lay to the east. But he intended to approach that destiny through the west. His plans were careful and complete, his timetable ready.

His outstretched arm had bared the watch upon his wrist. The morning of May 11 was already five hours old.

In three months—in August 1945—America would be invaded.

CHAPTER 2

THE ENEMY STRIKES

He sat on Waikiki's sands, off Diamond Head, and watched a girl. Out in a pounding surf whipped up by the islands' trade winds, the girl clambered to a precarious footing on the wet surfboard as it slid down the advancing slope of a huge wave.

Poised easily erect, her arms slightly bent and held forward against a possible spill, she came hurtling toward him like some green-and-white goddess out of the sea. She reached shallow water near the spot on the beach where he was sitting, and a beachboy took the surfboard while she stooped to slap clinging water from young, rounded thighs.

Crossing the beach, she pulled off the white rubber bathing cap she wore and let wind and an early-morning sun play with hair that was the color of fire. As she came closer, he observed with approval that her eyes were green-flecked.

He thought of one of the United States Navy's demands of the agents who constitute its Naval Intelligence; they must be thoroughly unsusceptible to women. The brass hats who thought up *that* qualification, he decided, had never seen this girl. A man could be just so unsusceptible; no more.

She was panting a little, the surf-green bathing suit forming taut intriguing curves as she breathed. As her path brought her near him, he rose and nodded toward the surf.

"You're quite good at that."

She halted, appraised him with cool eyes before granting a friendly smile that revealed even white teeth.

"Lucky," she corrected. "I've been at it for years. Usually I pile up. Your first visit to Honolulu?"

He nodded.

"You'll love it here. It's very beautiful—and very peaceful."

The shy, friendly smile broke out again before she turned away.

Peaceful! Lieutenant Douglas Norton's lips curled wryly, and his steel-gray eyes were hard and bitter. He wondered if ever again in his lifetime the world would know true, full peace. You couldn't be in Naval Intelligence and not realize that the blow-off was near. This pretty girl talked the way Americans had still been talking back in 1940, five years ago. People kept saying smugly, "You can't stop progress"—by which they meant civilization. They never seemed to realize that you couldn't stop a war machine, either. You built one, as America even now was building, to hold what you had; or you built it as Germany and Japan and Russia had built theirs—to grab. You started it rolling and—. He checked himself.

"Norton!" he growled. "A philosopher at thirty! Cut it out!"

The sun beat down on his lean, hard body. The waves rolled in to calm him. Diamond Head in complacent majesty peered out over the water as she had in centuries past when puny men had hurled themselves at each other and died swallowing their own blood. . . . It was peaceful here. The girl was right. It would be nice to lie beside such a girl on the sand, to talk, to swim—to forget.

After a last plunge, he dressed and returned to his Bishop Street hotel for breakfast. Later, in his third-floor room, he took from the inside pocket of his coat a dog-eared letter dated May 25, 1945. He knew that last letter from his brother Jimmy by heart, but he read it again:

Dear Doug:

Van Holtz is here in Shanghai. Remember him? Tall, hard-faced gent. Sixty, but looks fifty. Well dressed. Wears a Homburg and a monocle. He was one of the payoff boys for German agents in America in 1918. A smooth customer—and dangerous. Professes to be anti-Nazi, but he was kicked out of one of the little South American countries last year. He's one of the best spies Germany ever had. Still is.

He's stopping at my hotel here. Has three adjoining rooms. Uses only the middle one. I figured that where there was von Holtz, there was a hell of a good story. I greased the right palms and strung a dictograph wire from the closet in his room to my room. I've been glued to it ever since. And, Doug, I'm getting my story. It's hotter than a two-dollar pistol, but it belongs to the United States government, not to any news service.

Last night von Holtz had a visitor—little Tojo Koichi of the Japanese Foreign Office. Von Holtz nearly scared little Koichi out of his pants. He showed him credentials that must have been signed by Hitler himself. And he told him that by the end of this month, Germany and Japan would break off relations— violently.

Doug, it's a plant—a fake. I couldn't get all of their conversation (it was in German, thank God), but here's the setup: Within one week an "unpleasant incident" involving Japanese-German relations will occur. I think the fall guy will be Heinrich Dietrichsohn of the Nazi Foreign Office. He's in the bad graces of the Ribbentrop clique in Berlin. They'll "promote" him to a post in Japan—where something unpleasant will happen to him. I don't know what they have planned for him. A beating by Jap soldiers, maybe. Berlin will howl and denounce the Japs and withdraw her ambassador and demand indemnities. Japan will snap back at Germany. And Russia will woo Japan as an ally.

Japan will ally herself with Russia. Tojo Koichi is close to Stalin. Actually, things will be the same except that Japan, working with Russia, will report directly to Berlin.

What the purpose of this maneuvering is, I don't know. To trick Russia, certainly. To lull America? Perhaps. Maybe it's the opener for that invasion of the States that we've worried about so long. I hope not. But watch Heinrich Dietrichsohn.

A friend leaving here on the Clipper tomorrow will bring this
letter. Von Holtz and Koichi are having another get-together
tonight. I'll have more letters for you—if I can get them out.
Good-bye now.

Jimmy

Norton had received no more letters from his young brother. Instead, two days later, a cable from Shanghai had informed him that Jimmy Norton had "accidentally" fallen to his death from the window of his Shanghai hotel room.

Within a week, Heinrich Dietrichsohn of the German Foreign Office had been shot to death by Japanese "students" in Tokyo and the Tokyo-Berlin axis seemed smashed. Japan and Russia had smoothed out old differences and become allies.

Baron von Holtz had vanished. Until last week, nothing had been heard of him. Then Lieutenant Douglas Norton had been called to Washington, where a superior told him, "Von Holtz is in Honolulu. He's vacationed there before. Hangs around with the money crowd. Whether he's up to anything or not, I don't know. We could kick him out, but I'd rather let him move around freely—under observation. You think he's responsible for your brother's death, don't you?"

"Yes, sir."

"If you were assigned to watch him, would that fact affect your work?"

"No, sir."

"Take a plane to the Coast. Pick up a reservation there on the Clipper. He's been in Honolulu a week. See what he's up to. I don't want him arrested—unless it's necessary. We'll save that pleasure until wartime. It's less complicated shooting a spy then. Here's a copy of our dossier on him. Study it, then destroy it. You'll find he's a frequent guest at the home of Wilma Joyce. Sugar heiress—long on looks and money, short on brains. She and her kid sister think 'adventurers' are smart. Good luck, Lieutenant."

And so Lieutenant Douglas Norton had come to Honolulu the day before—to trail Baron von Holtz, the man responsible for his brother's death.

Discreet questions had obtained for him the location of Wilma Joyce's showplace home. That much of his quest had been simple enough. But this slender girl with flaming red hair whom he had spoken to on Waikiki Beach this morning—the thought of her was both puzzling and disturbing to him. He had seen newspaper photographs of the "Sugar Queen," as the tabloids called Wilma Joyce. This girl looked a great deal like Wilma Joyce, only better. She couldn't be Wilma. Then who was she?

It came to him—with a pang—that Wilma Joyce had a kid sister. That was it! You just don't go around falling for heiresses—or their sisters. Not on Navy pay.

That evening, on his way to the hotel dining room, he cut through the bar. A voice that had lilt and warmth said, "Hello, there!"

It was the red-haired girl. She was as beautiful in an evening gown as she had seemed on the beach. Before he could speak to her, a suave—too suave—voice said:

"May I buy your friend a drink?"

Reluctantly he took his eyes off the girl to find himself staring at a face that looked at him with indifferent appraisal over a highball glass. A lean, shrewd, sardonic face. Close-cropped gray hair. The inevitable monocle—Baron von Holtz!

It took tremendous effort to keep his own expression from revealing the hatred that welled up within him. There were confused introductions (he had told them his name was Arthur Weller) and as his long lean fingers clasped those of the older man, Lieutenant Douglas Norton wished fervently that they might have been clamped around von Holtz's neck instead.

In that moment he hated both of them: von Holtz for what he knew him to be; the girl for being with von Holtz. Her name, he learned, was Peggy O'Liam. It matched her hair and voice, but otherwise it meant nothing to him—beyond the fact that she was *not* Wilma Joyce's kid sister . . .

"A drink, Mr. Weller?" asked von Holtz.

"No thank you."

The baron's eyebrows lifted. "It is true, Mr. Weller, that in the United States Navy, members of the Naval Intelligence must be teetotalers?"

It *was* true. This one-eyed devil was cunning. Well, if he wanted to play . . .

"I wouldn't know about that," Norton said. "My line's insurance. Ask me anything about insurance, and I can tell you. We've got a policy you should look into sometime. Double indemnity—in case of accidental or violent death."

The baron frowned. "How depressing!"

The girl seemed amused. To von Holtz's annoyance, they all dined together.

As the coffee was served, Peggy gave a long look at the silver coffee pot.

"Remarkable," she breathed. "Miss Joyce has one just like it."

"You know Wilma Joyce?" Norton asked.

"I live with her."

Norton disregarded the baron's disapproving glare. "But your last name is O'Liam. You're not—"

"I'm Wilma Joyce's secretary."

Later, in his room, Norton added up the day. It was both good—and bad. Bad because he had "burned himself up." Someone else would have to trail von Holtz; you can't shadow a man who has met you. On the other hand, he could regard Peggy coldly now, not as a desirable woman but as a possible source of information about von Holtz. . . .

Trying to sleep that night, he found it a little difficult not to think about Peggy O'Liam as a desirable woman.

Next day he tried to reach her by telephone at the Joyce home. He failed, but learned incidentally that she was to attend a dance at his hotel that evening. When evening came, he stood in the ballroom doorway until he had caught sight of her. She was with a crowd of young people, some of them men in Navy uniforms. Von Holtz wasn't there, apparently. He went down into the lobby to wait.

He remembered, later, that the last time he had looked at his watch, it had been 11:40.

Perhaps a minute later, Peggy O'Liam stepped out of the elevator, and he rose to cross the lobby and meet her. She smiled in recognition.

"Leaving early?" he asked.

"Sneaking out for a breath of air."

"Mind if I go along?"

"I'd like that," she said.

They were thirty feet from the street door when he stopped suddenly, his body tense, his face alert and grim.

"What is it?" she asked.

"Listen!"

The increasing roar sounded like the surging swell of voices from a distant stadium.

"Planes," she said. "Our shore patrol . . ."

He shook his head. "Too many."

In the distance there were sharp explosions—like vicious cracks of thunder that rolled and blasted and echoed. Something whistled and thudded outside in Bishop Street. A blinding, jagged sheet of yellow flame rose and spread. A portion of the street shivered and buckled, and chunks of paving rattled against the hotel. Where the street had been was a great deep crater. A ten-pound piece of concrete hurtled through the glass of the lobby door and bounced to a stop near their feet.

He had just time enough to notice three things: the location of the stairway off the lobby; the white bloodless face of the girl beside him; and—most horrible of all—the knee-high billow of low-crawling vaporous stuff with the smell of horseradish that, sucked into the lobby from the street, was rolling toward them.

Then every light in the hotel went out. There were more blasts outside—farther away. After that confusion—hoarse voices and aimlessly running figures. And outside, a sudden hush between explosions . . .

Lieutenant Norton grabbed for the girl's wrist and found it. His eyes fought the darkness as he pulled her, stumbling, in the direction of the stairway. They collided with a whimpering woman and a fat panting man who pushed them to one side. "Let us out of here!" the man growled. Peggy fell to her knees. Norton bent down and got her in his arms and went lunging up the stairs. He was on the second-floor landing when another high-explosive bomb went off outside. He wondered what had happened to the woman and the fat man.

Peggy O'Liam's bare arms were about his neck and her hair brushed his cheek. She was light in weight, yet by the time he reached the third floor his arms ached and his heart pumped a violent protest.

"Can you walk?"

She nodded. He put her down, and she followed him down the corridor and into his room. As he went over to close the windows, he saw a black shape hurtling down, and sprang back. The whole building shook, and glass shattered and flew into the room. His head ached violently. The girl clapped her hands to her ears and screamed.

"That won't help," he snapped.

"I'm sorry. It hurt my ears." She paused, added truthfully, "And I'm scared."

"We're both scared. But we're as safe here as anywhere. We're high enough above the gas, though. If they manage a direct hit we could use some floors above us."

Across the street, an incendiary drop bomb plunged through the roof of a building and exploded. The inside of the building began to burn, casting yellow flickering light into his room. He went into the bathroom and turned on the tub faucet. There was still water at least. In the distance he could hear the chatter of three-inch guns and the less rapid crackling of the 105-millimeter anti-aircraft batteries.

Norton came back into the garishly lighted room.

"Go into the bathroom," he told the girl. "Take off all your clothes. Everything. Get into the tub and let it fill. Don't empty it when you're through. There may not be any more water. I'll be back."

"But . . ."

"Do as I say!" he snapped.

He took a hand flashlight and his gun from a dresser drawer and went out into the corridor. He found the supply closet and tried its door. Locked! He fired four shots into the lock, got it open, and found what he was looking for—bars of strong yellow laundry soap. He returned to his room, got a fresh pair of his pajamas, and walked into the bathroom.

The girl gasped and slid down under the water.

"Will you get out of here?" she shouted.

Norton said nothing, paid no attention to her. He found her clothes on the floor. He gathered them up—all of them—opened the window, and threw them out.

"Have you gone mad?"

Norton's nerves were ready to snap. In the distance, guns and bombs still clattered. He thought of von Holtz—von Holtz, who had found it convenient to run out on this little raid. Turning back, he let the whole blast of his anger, worry, and hatred loose on the girl.

"I'm not interested in you or your German playmate, but if you have room for anything in that conceited head of yours, listen: That stuff in the lobby tonight was gas. Mustard—or worse. It goes through fabric and gets into clothes and contaminates them. It goes through skin—and you don't feel anything because it doesn't attack the sensory nerves. It gets in your eyes, and you don't notice it, but seven hours later you're blind. It blisters and destroys and sometimes kills.

"Maybe we got some of it, maybe we didn't. If you want

advice, here it is: Use that bar of laundry soap—not the scented hotel stuff. Use plenty of it. Then get into those fresh pajamas."

He went out, rummaged for another pair of pajamas, and walked along the corridor until he came to a room whose door was open. Its occupants had fled. He managed to fill the tub half full before the faucet sputtered and the water gave out. He undressed and threw his clothes away, lathered himself carefully with the coarse yellow soap, then got into the pajamas and felt better. He went back to his own room. Except for loud groans from the street, it was quiet outside.

Peggy O'Liam stood in the middle of the room. The pajamas were too large for her and she had rolled up their trouser cuffs. A pair of his house slippers flopped on her feet as she moved toward him. She had his trench coat over one arm.

"It seems to be over. If I can borrow your coat, I'll not bother you any further."

"You can't go," he said quietly. "The lobby's full of gas."

"I'll find another room."

"As you wish."

Flame flickered in the building across the way. She had her lower lip between her teeth. But the tears and hysteria came anyway.

"I want you to know," she said in a choked little voice, "that I'm grateful for what you've done for me. But"—she began to stutter— "d-d-did you have to be so d-d-damned nasty about it?"

He didn't answer. He opened his arms and she came into them, sobbing, and clutched him blindly as a child clutches. Lifting her, he crossed the room and sank into an armchair with her in his arms. He felt rotten and ashamed. He stroked her wet red hair, and after a while exhaustion won. She became limp and quiet and slept cradled in his arms. His own nerves were played out, and he wished bitterly that the man who was dying out in the street would go about it more quietly. And after a while it was quiet and he, too, slept.

Early the next morning, the Chemical Warfare Service boys came around, spreading dry chloride of lime to decontaminate gas-drenched streets and buildings. Then soldiers to remove the bodies. Labor gangs began filling in the shell holes.

Lieutenant Norton dressed and went down and arranged for food to be sent up to his room. He returned and had breakfast with Peggy O'Liam.

"What does it all mean?" she asked him.

"War," he said bluntly. "We're in it this time. That was just a sample last night. If they can grab our naval base here, our fleet will have to operate from the Pacific Coast. They'll push us back and at the same time increase their own radius of operations to our mainland. They'll bring the war right to our front porch. They haven't taken this place yet, of course. Landing their men won't be easy. But if they knock it out, if we can't base here—" He shrugged.

"Is there anything I can do?"

"Tell me about von Holtz."

She told him—simply and sincerely. The Joyce sisters, who found von Holtz amusing, had often had him as a guest in their home. They were in America now. Von Holtz had come out to the house, found them gone, invited Peggy to dinner. He had left Oahu the day before in a small boat he sometimes chartered, piloted himself.

"I don't know where he went. He wanted me to go with him. Was very persistent about it, in fact. It sounded like one of those 'come-and-see-my-etchings' things. I said no."

"I want to locate him," Norton told her. "The man's a spy. When you get home, make me a list of every person you've ever seen him in conversation with."

She nodded gravely.

He got up to leave. "I'll contact you later," he promised. "There'll be a marine here in an hour. He'll see that you get home. Sorry I couldn't dig up clothes for you. You can wear my coat over that rig." He paused at the door. "Until we find out how bad things are, don't drink any water—or milk—without boiling it first."

She said, "Thank you. Good-bye."

He left and hunted up Lieutenant Commander Dudley Fitzroy. With Fitzroy was Major Charles Hobart of the Hawaiian Department's Military Intelligence.

"Good to see you, Lieutenant," Fitzroy said. "Well, it's come at last."

"I'm afraid you'll have to tell me what happened, sir. I was sitting it out in a hotel room. Was it bad?"

"Very. They caught us flat-footed. Approached very high, at twenty, maybe thirty thousand feet, and came gliding in. Our sound locators picked them up in time for us to get a squadron of fighters of our 78th Pursuit off Wheeler Field. By the time the 78th could climb and contact them, they were all directly over the field. The anti-aircraft boys held up their fire for fear they'd shoot down our own planes."

Fitzroy scowled as he went on. "They might as well have. Our men came dropping down like flies. Horribly outnumbered. And then they were on us. They must have hit this island with three hundred planes—and they knew just where to strike and what to strike with.

"The first time over, they hit us with incendiaries. Must have been baby thermite bombs. They dropped them like rain. They caught the hangars at Hickam and Wheeler fields, and even went out of their way to set fire to Rogers airport buildings and the barracks. We salvaged just about a skeleton flight of ships: a couple out of the 5th Bombardment Group at Hickam and a couple of the 86th's observation buses at Wheeler. That's all we've got left—and we can't get them off the ground unless we learn to fly straight up. The enemy gave us three blasts last night. On the second and third trips around they dropped high explosives. Our flying fields look like cribbage boards gone wrong. It'll be days before we can patch them up."

Lieutenant Norton asked, "Casualties heavy, sir?"

"Heavy enough. They scored a direct hit on a building at Schofield Barracks. And we've got a flock of pretty bad burn cases from the airfields. All the hospital beds around here are filled, and we're putting tents outside Tripler General Hospital. They gave the civilian areas hell, too. Only place they used gas."

"I know," said Lieutenant Norton. "Ran into some of it. Trying to break down the civilian morale."

Fitzroy nodded. "The gas cases are starting to come in now. We'll have to find room for them. And evacuation's going to be a problem. Clipper service has been suspended, of course. The Japs are reputed to be fond of shooting down unarmed transport planes."

So it was Japan that the United States was at war with!

"And Pearl Harbor, sir?"

"A mess," said Fitzroy. "We're shutting it up with a net and boom in case they try to slip in any submarines. But we're not going to be able to repair any of our own ships there for a while. They scored direct hits on the foundries and on the pumping plant near the dry dock. They burned the air-station hangars, blew a traveling crane into the water, and damaged the supply depot. The hospital's all right, and they didn't hit any of the fuel-oil tanks, thank God. Our ships can still come back here and fuel—if they don't polish off the storage tanks in the meanwhile.

"Pearl Harbor was a cinch. It wasn't moonlight last night, but all they had to do was follow the coastline and blast away. We knocked down fifty of their planes—most of them Russian. Our anti-aircraft fire would have done better on a clear night."

Lieutenant Norton thought of that last letter from Jimmy. "So the attack was by both Japan *and* Russia?"

Fitzroy nodded. "Yes. They've ganged up on us. We shot them down fast. But they came faster."

"But how could they get several hundred planes here?"

"God knows. Japan and Russia together wouldn't have enough aircraft carriers for that, even if they could slip them up on us—which they couldn't. My guess is that they got a couple of carriers through our screen by traveling away from regular shipping lanes. That would put a hundred to a hundred and fifty little shipboard fighters in striking distance. The long-range bombers—those we shot down were all flying boats—either flew it all the way to rendezvous with the fighters, or gassed up from submarines, or came out of Wotje, Jaluit, or Kusaie in the Japanese Mandates. We had a patrol up last night, of course, but they either went around it or over it. And our patrol planes never got back."

Lieutenant Norton pondered the situation. It was desperately serious. Russia was strong in tanks, planes, submarines, and men. Japan had a formidable navy, plus a leadership tested and hardened in the war on China. That combination meant trouble.

But one thing puzzled him. "How," he asked the two officers, "did they happen to score so heavily here? I should have thought they would have picked a moonlight night."

It was Major Hobart of Military Intelligence who answered that one. "A little local conniving," he said bitterly. "They didn't even need to see Wheeler or Hickam airdromes to hit us with damned good accuracy. We found out why this morning. A little over a mile from each field, we found oil torches laid out on the ground. The torches were those bomb-shaped affairs used in street construction—and easily seen through night glasses. They were laid out to form an arrow fifty feet long, its head pointing directly at an objective.

"The raid occurred at eleven forty-two last night. Shortly before then, someone lit the torches."

Someone had to pay someone else to light them, Lieutenant
Norton thought. Aloud he muttered, "Von Holtz!"

Major Hobart grinned wryly. "It's probably the baron's fine
hand. The man's an eel. He got out before the show last night. I'd give a
lot to know where he is."

"And our Navy, sir?" Norton asked Fitzroy.

"Left here two days ago, supposedly on maneuvers. Actually,
we had word that the Japanese fleet was maneuvering close to the
'Fence' and the Commander in Chief of Naval Operations went out to
have a look. Our Naval Intelligence men in Russia told us that her navy
was massing, too.

"Since the raid last night—they played hob with our radio
stations—our communications have been pretty spotty. But we've been
able to pick up two things: The United States has formally declared war
on Russia and Japan. And the Japanese and Russian fleets have
rendezvoused, are already across the Fence, and are heading straight
for here."

Norton felt sober indeed. It added up to a pretty black picture.
He found himself counting on his fingers.

Fitzroy smiled. "If you're trying to figure the odds against our
Navy, Lieutenant, this is about the situation:

"The Japs have eighteen first-line battleships; Russia has eight.
That's twenty-six. Against those twenty-six, we have eighteen based out
here—not enough to tangle with them.

"However, it isn't as bad as it sounds. We have eight ships on
the Pacific Coast: four based off California, another four on this side of
the Panama Canal at Balboa. The latter four—the *Maine, Missouri, New
Jersey,* and *Ohio*—which were ready to shoot through the canal the
moment any trouble started in the Atlantic, will now join the four
California-based ships—the *Utah, Montana, Wyoming,* and *Iowa*—and
the squadron will come here at once to reinforce our Pacific fleet.
Should be on their way now.

"That will give us twenty-six against the Russo-Jap combine of
twenty-six. The CCNO can pick his own playground and then sit back
and slug it out. And if our gunnery isn't the finest in the world, then I
don't know the Old Man. The CCNO may even elect to pit his eighteen
ships against them before the coast squadron arrives."

Fitzroy scratched his head.

"Of course that would leave only nine of our total thirty-five
ships in the Atlantic. Nine ships against Hitler's twenty-two would be

useless. But before he could get his navy to America, we could re-shuffle our own fleet to the best advantage and get enough ships back into the Atlantic to give him a stand-up fight."

Lieutenant Norton sensed Fitzroy's feeling of almost devout gratitude for the fact that America had the Panama Canal. America's defense truly depended on the "Big Ditch." So long as we held the Panama Canal, our shores would be reasonably safe from invasion.

The bombing of the Island of Oahu had occurred at 11:42 on the night of July 31, 1945—a Tuesday. The next week was a nightmare, with disaster after disaster falling like the blows of a hammer.

At eight o'clock on the morning of August 1, the President of the United States announced by radio to the country that America was at war with Russia and Japan, whose fleets, even then, were headed eastward.

On August 2, tremendous concentrations of Russian planes from Wellington, Anadyrsk, Petropavlovsk, and from Big Diomede and Komandorski islands raided and destroyed American air and submarine bases of the United States at Sitka and in the Aleutians.

On August 3, having complete command of the Bering Straits, Russian and Japanese troops and equipment began the short trip across the water to Alaska.

On that same day the "Old Man"—Commander in Chief Burton Sterrett—contacted the Japanese and Russian navies off Hawaii and, without waiting for the help that was coming, went into action. He had the sun at his back and a tight battle line, and they didn't. He put Russia's 35,000-ton *Tretti International* and her 23,000-ton *Oktiabrskaya-Revolutia* on the floor of the sea and sent Japan's *Yamasiro* to join them before the enemy laid a destroyer smoke screen and took to their heels. He rubbed his nose with the bowl of his pipe and thought of the squadron of battleships now three days off the Pacific coast, and wondered if this whole thing had been a feint.

It had.

On the following day Lieutenant Douglas Norton walked into the office of Lieutenant Commander Dudley Fitzroy. With a hand that shook a little, Fitzroy showed him a radio flimsy he had just received. It read:

PANAMA CANAL UNDER GERMAN CONTROL

It wasn't easy to understand at first—or to believe. It didn't say the Canal had been attacked or destroyed. Simply, *Under German control.*

"That's all I've got," Fitzroy said. "I'm trying to get more information. But if it means what it says . . ."

It would mean, Norton told himself, that the United States Navy was virtually bottled up in the Pacific. To get out of that bottle, the twenty-six battleships in the Pacific and their cruisers and destroyers and train would have to round Cape Horn.

Such a trip would take from forty-eight days to two months! During which time the Atlantic would become the thoroughfare of the Greater United German Reich, despite the best efforts of the meager American fleet off the Eastern Seaboard. Months during which Adolf Hitler's troops, supplies, and guns could be moved almost without convoy, across the ocean.

In one swift blow, the first line of defense for America's East Coast had been rendered impotent. And on that East Coast, deprived of protective sea power, lay the great industrial triangle roughly formed by the cities of Boston, Wilmington, and Pittsburgh. Extend that triangle deeper—say, to Omaha—and you encompassed everything on which America depended.

The very jugular of the nation lay awaiting what must soon come—the sharp knife of Nazi invasion.

All of these things passed through Norton's mind with sickening certainty. He looked into Fitzroy's bleak eyes, and what he saw there made him wince.

"Our country has known some black days," Fitzroy said quietly. "But none so black as this one. God help us all!"

CHAPTER 3

HITLER SPEAKS—AND AMERICA ANSWERS

The seizure of the Panama Canal stunned all America. However it had been effected, there was not a schoolboy in the land who did not understand its significance. The Panama Canal was the key to the nation's defense. That key to the safety of the world's last remaining great democracy was now in totalitarian hands.

After Washington's official admission that the Canal was under German control, there were forty-eight hours of silence, broken only by a second terse announcement: The formerly British-owned island of Bermuda in the mid-Atlantic, little more than 700 miles from both New York City and Baltimore, was also in Nazi hands.

Following Hitler's conquest of England, a joint German-American Colonial Commission had agreed that little Bermuda should enjoy the status of an independent state. Hitler would not press claims to the island, provided the United States did not endeavor to occupy it. It would remain unfortified and uncontrolled. Now, without warning, the Greater United Reich had seized it.

In Honolulu, Lieutenant Douglas Norton dropped in to see

65

his friend Lieutenant Commander Dudley Fitzroy. A radio on the desk, tuned to a station on the mainland, was playing dance music. Over the sound of it, Fitzroy boomed, "Any luck? Locate von Holtz?" Norton shook his head.

Fitzroy turned down the radio.

"Hitler," he explained. "He's on at ten-thirty. Too bad about von Holtz."

"I don't see how he could have got out of the islands," Norton said. "He left here in a little motorboat the evening of the raid. Peggy—Miss O'Liam—gave me a list of persons he knew. Intelligence, here, has most of their names. Nothing likely to turn up there. Out at the Joyces' they have a plane, a little two-place cabin job that Miss O'Liam flies. It occurred to me that von Holtz might have gone to one of the little uninhabited islands of this group, and she flew me over some of them early this morning. He wasn't on any we covered."

"Too bad," said Fitzroy. "Pretty girl, Miss O'Liam. Very pretty," he added sagely. "What did you think of the Panama Canal business?"

"Haven't heard any details."

"That's right, you wouldn't have." Fitzroy nodded toward the radio. "It was all on there this morning. And where do you suppose the United States got most of its information? From Germany!" and he told Norton what had happened.

On the night of August 3, a fleet of the United States Navy's "Flying Battlewagons" had taken off from San Juan, Puerto Rico, on a routine neutrality patrol. Two hundred miles out, flying northeast, they came upon a tremendous concentration of Nazi planes flying southwest.

"Three hundred to three hundred and fifty of them," Fitzroy said. "Big six-motored flying boats. It would have been suicide for our patrol of eight planes to tangle with them. Our flight skipper radioed the base at San Juan and streaked for home."

Upon the news that the enemy seemed about to launch an all-out aerial attack on the Panama Canal or its Caribbean outposts, 200 planes took to the air from the San Juan naval air station, and 750 Army planes took off from Point Boringuen, the big Army field on Puerto Rico. Simultaneously the naval air base at Guantanamo put a group of planes in the air. All of them went aloft with a single mission: to locate the enemy out at sea and, at all costs, destroy him before he could reach the Canal. Meanwhile, word of the attack was radioed to Army and Navy air bases as far away as Florida and Virginia.

The original patrol of eight planes that had reported the enemy never returned to its base. Evidently it had been overtaken and shot down.

The defending air forces reached the point where, according to their reckoning, the enemy's planes should be contacted. They found none. They spread out and pushed on. Their leading plane was 300 miles from San Juan and approximately 1,300 from the Panama Canal when word came from the Colón radio station that the Canal was being attacked.

"What had happened," Fitzroy explained, "was this. After downing our eight-plane patrol, the enemy air fleet put about and flew northeast for several hundred miles; then turned again and headed for Bermuda. They took the island by surprise. Dropped two thousand parachute troops. While the troops were seizing the island, a hundred of their big flying boats sat down in the water and began to put equipment on the beach—machine guns, anti-aircraft guns, howitzers, even a number of five-ton tanks. Bermuda's pretty respectably fortified now."

"Then the move on the Canal was another feint," Norton said bitterly.

"Yes," said Fitzroy. "It served its purpose. Sucked our air forces from Puerto Rico and Guantanamo away out over the Atlantic. And while we were out there, they brought up a second air fleet from the south and bombed our fields at Puerto Rico and Guantanamo to bits.

"Meanwhile, naturally enough, the Canal Zone defense was getting braced for an attack from the Atlantic side. Moved its 14-inch mobile guns across the Isthmus railway to Colón. So what did they do then? They hit us with everything they had—from the Pacific side."

Norton listened gloomily as the older man went on. The attack on the Pacific side of the Canal had been staged by no fewer than 3,000 planes. After circling thirty miles out over the Pacific at 20,000 feet, awaiting zero hour, this huge aerial armada had come gliding down, motors cut, in a silent-approach attack upon Balboa. One hundred and fifty "smoker" planes had led. Hedge-hopping, they had roared over the channel, laying curtains of acid smoke that blanketed the mobile and 16-inch coastal batteries and the anti-aircraft defenses.

Before the smoke had blinded the Canal Zone, anti-aircraft gunners had shot down gun crews and three smoker planes. That loss, however, had scarcely ruffled the invaders' perfectly coordinated assault. Neither had it troubled them much when six more of the smoker planes, trying to smother the anti-aircraft battery near Gold Hill, crashed into the twisting wall of narrow Gaillard Cut.

Only a few objectives had been bombed. The invaders' purpose had been to seize control of, not to destroy, the Big Ditch. And by surprise and sheer weight of air force, they had accomplished it.

The radio stations at the Canal's Pacific entrance—at Gamboa Reach and at Colón—had, of course, been bombed into silence. The motor road across the Isthmus had been bombed and broken up; the Panama Railroad had been cut by bombs where it skirted Gold Hill near the Continental Divide. Incendiary bombs had reduced Panama City and Colón to smoking rubble. Albrook and France Fields, at the entrances to the Canal, had been demolished, and such last-stand defense planes as they had been able to get into the air had been promptly shot down. Rio Hato airfield in Panama and a number of smaller airfields deep in cleared jungle territory had been hunted out and destroyed. Against bombs and sabotage, the Panama Canal defenses had been as nearly invulnerable as human ingenuity could make them. But the enemy had chosen to attack not with bombs but with a mighty and lethal weapon previously considered the last resort of a losing nation at war—gas.

The Canal and its locks and dams had not been touched. Instead, huge bombers following the smoke-screen layers across the Isthmus had rained gas shells upon every spot within the Canal Zone that might conceivably be occupied by a human defender.

In a great American city of narrow streets and towering buildings, gas warfare would have been ineffective. In an exposed and concentrated area like the Canal Zone, it had been devastating. And because the preliminary smoke curtains had concealed and disguised the gas that was dropped, gun crews had worked feverishly at their posts until, sneezing and vomiting, they had realized—too late—what was happening.

Fitzroy shrugged his broad shoulders. "Well, that's the crop," he said. "The German Foreign Office itself informed our State Department of most of the details. So far as I know, we haven't a man left in the Canal Zone who isn't a casualty. Besides some of the old standbys, they used a devilish new gas their technicians have developed. It's deadly, but it can't be as persistent as mustard, because they dropped their chemical warfare boys down there the same night to decontaminate key spots in the Zone.

"Our Canal's gone, our Caribbean bases are gone, and we don't even know what the hell they used. Probably one of the arsenic-group substances that we've been experimenting with ourselves. Violent even in low concentrations. Goes right through clothing, filters—everything. Gets into the bloodstream, and a man either dies or goes mad. Pleasant little war, this."

"What happened to our aircraft from Puerto Rico and Cuba?" Norton asked.

"Their home bases were knocked out before they could get back. They were ordered to Miami. Most of them—but not all—made either Miami or Jacksonville. The Germans have been dropping parachute troops into the Canal Zone ever since. Specially trained men, by the way. Seems that in their files they've had accurate blueprints on every piece of equipment at the Canal, and for the past year trained troops have been operating and repairing a miniature Panama Canal—so they could take over and operate the real Canal without a day's loss of time. Now they're open for business."

"Why don't we go down there and destroy it?"

Fitzroy shook his head. "Not yet. We can't get it back now, but we won't destroy it until we have to."

He sighed, then scowled at the radio, which was still playing dance music.

"Well, they've walloped us blue and bloody before we could even get our fists up, but we're not licked yet. Now that the Germans have come in, we're up against a clever mob, though. Every day last week there was a rumor floating around that an attack, using gas, was planned. The rumor probably came from Germany.

"So every day down in the Zone, everybody got dressed in his rubber and oilcloth protective gear. Devilish hot outfit to wear in that climate. Men at gunnery drill keeled over after half an hour in it. Everybody got good and sick of it—and no signs of a raid. So they relaxed and they got careless. And then, when the raid did come—" Fitzroy threw up his hands.

"I still don't see," Norton said, "how they got three thousand planes to the Panama Canal. I know we've got ships with a four-thousand mile range today, but when you get into combat, you burn up gas fast. and you've always got to get back home. If they had any bases close to the Canal—any in Venezuela or even the Guianas—our neutrality patrol would have spotted them, wouldn't it?"

"They had that all worked out, too," Fitzroy said. "Remember back in 1934, when Germany started flying Heinkels from Berlin to Bathurst on the African coast, and then shuttling Dorniers across the South Atlantic to Natal, Brazil?"

Norton nodded.

"Well, in 1942, when the Vargas government was overthrown and Brazil became Nazified, Pan American Airways was tossed out of the country. And Germany flew planes in from Africa."

"But they couldn't have flown from Natal to the Canal."

"Didn't have to. They flew them into the interior—based them along what had been Brazil's domestic air route. Now and then we got a rumor about planes in Brazil that might be bombers but had windows painted on their sides to make them look like commercial transports. But nothing we could tie down. We couldn't very well patrol the interior of Brazil without making an issue of it and going to war. So we watched the coastal routes that the German airlines were flying. When we found no suspicious concentrations of planes, we figured we were safe.

"From Brazil's domestic route in the interior to the canal was more than fifteen hundred miles. Well, they made it!"

"Narrow margin, with a return trip to face, wasn't it?" Norton said.

"Not so narrow." Fitzroy grimaced. "They didn't go back to Brazil. The new Colombian government, which had been steamed up by Nazi agents since the conquest of England, threw Colombia's expanded airports open to them.

"Much the same thing happened in Venezuela. She's clung to strict neutrality—but the day before the Canal raid, a Nazi-led Brazilian army massed on her southern border. Either she'd open her airports, as needed, to the German raiders, or else! She agreed—and we can't blame her much.

"That means more headaches for us, of course. The Nazis not only have the Canal; they now have air bases all along the northern coast of South America extending from Barranquilla, Colombia, to Natal, Brazil. So they command the Caribbean and can play the devil with our oil shipments out of the Gulf States. They—"

The radio had stopped playing dance music. Fitzroy swung around in his chair and turned up the volume. He consulted his watch.

"His Nibs," he told Norton.

An announcer's voice said: "We bring you now, via shortwave from Berlin, the voice of Chancellor Adolf Hitler in a message to the people of the United States. The next voice you hear will be that of Chancellor Hitler."

A voice began to speak in a stream of carefully enunciated German. After half a minute an interpreter's voice cut in:

Hitler asserted that for many years his country had sought the friendship of America without success. That, even after the establishment of the Greater United German Reich, America had sought to wreck Germany's efforts to establish world peace by "futile rearmament" and "economic interference" in South America.

That today, virtually friendless, on the verge of bankruptcy, attacked from the northwest by Russia and Japan, deprived of her Panama Canal, and thereby of her Navy, the United States faced total and foreordained doom.

It was not, Hitler hinted, too late to negotiate an honorable peace. Even Russo-Japanese claims might well be resolved—if America truly wanted peace. There were conditions: immediate and complete disarmament; entire agreement with Germany's world economic plans; recognition of the status of Germans as "world citizens."

To the people of America, he said, he offered more than he had once offered Great Britain. He offered the hand of friendship, the hand of an ally seeking true peace.

If this offer were refused—

"Men will die by the thousands," said Hitler, "and beside them in streets running red with blood will lie the torn bodies of their wives and children—needless victims of a crass, unyielding stupidity. It is in the name of these unfortunates that I bid you think well. The choice is yours. Peace—or annihilation! It is in your fields and streets that this war shall be fought. Your houses shall crumble and in them your people—innocent civilians—shall be crushed.

"If you choose war, then this last struggle of the Greater United German Reich shall be a war without rules, without quarter—a war of total destruction. There shall be no open cities, no sanctuary for any man or woman. One of your generals has said that the serious mistake made by the Allies in 1918 was that, following the war, they did not so completely crush Germany that she would never rise again.

Germany, having risen, will not now make a similar mistake. America must choose peace now—or be forever destroyed.

"Your country has neither experienced nor appreciated the utter ruthlessness of modern warfare. In exactly four hours, from the State of Venezuela, New Germany of the Greater United Reich, one of your own countrymen will describe these terrors to you. He is the only American soldier who witnessed our conquest of the Canal Zone and who emerged alive and not subject to a chronic mental disorder. I ask that you listen well to his words before foolishly embarking upon a course of self-destruction. What happened in the Canal Zone can and will happen on the American continent if this—Germany's final friendly offer of peace—is rejected."

Lieutenant Commander Dudley Fitzroy snapped off the radio.

"Phew!" he said. "A fine choice we're offered! We can have Germany as an ally and get Japan and Russia off our backs—provided we let Hitler become master of America. The cure's worse than the disease!"

"I'd like to hear that speech four hours from now," Norton said quietly. "If you're planning to listen in, sir, and I may come back—"

"You're welcome to come back. Bring Miss O'Liam, if you care to."

Norton set out for the Joyce home. The fleet was back in Pearl Harbor for fuel and stores—probably, he thought, for the long trip around the Horn to rejoin the naval units in the Atlantic. He wondered if they could possibly make it in time.

At the Joyce home, a plain-faced, severely dressed servant woman of middle age admitted him. Peggy O'Liam, her eyes sparkling, came to greet him. She hooked an arm in his.

"I'm so glad you could come for lunch. You're just in time to meet an old crony of mine."

As they walked into the living room, Lieutenant Douglas Norton, U. S. N., stiffened automatically, professionally, at the sight of a familiar figure.

He was a blue-eyed, pleasant-featured, erect man of sixty. Admiral Burton Lee Sterrett—commander in chief of the United States fleet—took a pipe from his mouth and greeted Norton with a warm handshake.

"Did you listen to Hitler's peace offer, Lieutenant?" he asked.

"Yes, sir. Did you?"

"I did. Very much so."

"What did you think of it?" Norton ventured to inquire.

The Admiral made a wry face. "Just what you did, I imagine. What else could a man think? The Canal in his clutches—war on, in full blast—and there he was, ranting about—"

Peggy seized his arm. "Now, Burt!" she cried. "You promised!" Admiral Burton Lee Sterrett smilingly nodded and subsided and relaxed.

"We swore off just now, Uncle Burt and I," she explained. "We declared a lunchtime moratorium on war talk. Night and day, besides fighting one battle at sea, he's been thinking and talking war and nothing else. So have you and I—and Hitler too, I guess, for that matter! Anyway, we thought it was time to give the topic an hour's rest. Don't you agree? But you're in for some family palaver instead, I'm afraid.

"You see," she went on, "I haven't been in America myself since 1940. Uncle Burt saw my folks two months ago in Baltimore. He isn't really my uncle, he's my godfather. His parents and my father's were next-door neighbors out in Illinois, went to school together. Uncle Burt always seemed to get home in time for my birthdays. The O'Liams and the Sterretts have sort of adopted each other."

Admiral Sterrett nodded a tolerant gray head. "That's true. I used to bounce Peggy on my knee when—"

"When I was a skinny-legged, freckled little squirt," Peggy interrupted. "He always begins by telling strangers about my childhood deformities. I've still got freckles. My legs have done a little better since then." She folded them under her. "How," she asked the admiral, "were Mary and Dave when you saw them?" She turned to Norton. "Mary Greenwood's my married sister. She lives in Baltimore. Dave is her little boy."

"They were fine," the admiral said. "Davy's as fat and husky as any kid of three is entitled to be."

They talked on, and an overpowering sense of nostalgia crept over Norton. In this room, he thought, America was talking. The real America. The plain everyday sort of America that you meant instinctively when you said of someone: "He's my kind of folk." It did not seem strange or strained that this girl and this man should be talking this way—the girl a pretty red-haired secretary, the man the ranking admiral of the United States fleet. They were old friends, neighbors. And that, too, was America—though generations to come might never know it. . . .

A moment later, in spite of Peggy, the war intruded.

"You'll be sailing soon?" she asked her godfather.

"Very soon. As soon as—"

The plain-faced servant dressed in black came quietly into the room to announce luncheon, then went out.

"Damn it all, Peggy, I don't like that woman," Admiral Sterrett said.

Peggy laughed. "Greta? She's a bit on the sullen side, but she's all right."

"She doesn't make enough noise when she walks," he said. "We're sailing as soon as we can."

She clutched his sleeve impulsively.

"You will be careful, Burt?"

It should have sounded naïve, ludicrous. Somehow, because of the warm intensity she put into it, it didn't.

At two-thirty that afternoon, Admiral Sterrett, Peggy O'Liam, Major Hobart, and Lieutenant Norton sat in Lieutenant Commander Fitzroy's office to listen to the German-sponsored broadcast that was later to become known as the "Lone Survivor Appeal."

In America, millions of listeners turned on their radios. From far-off Nazified Venezuela a voice—the voice of a young and shocked and badly frightened American—came over to them:

"My name is Richard Harwood Wills. I am twenty-three years old. I am a private in the Fourth Coast Artillery, Balboa, in the Canal Zone. I am now a German prisoner of war in Venezuela. I am the only man in the Fourth now left alive. I am the only American soldier in the Canal Zone who is not a hospital case or who was not killed on the night of August 3rd when we were attacked. I saw the whole attack. I have been asked to tell what I saw in my own words."

The voice halted a moment, went on:

"Before the raid, we had received word that there might be an attack from the Atlantic side. Our gun crew had been ordered to their stations. We waited and nothing happened. After a while, Lieutenant Coleman told me, 'I don't think there's going to be an attack. Shinny up a tree and see if you can see anything.'

"I climbed a tree and didn't see anything, and was going to tell him so when I heard a noise up above. They came at us so fast I didn't have time to come down. They were roaring and laying smoke and dropping gas shells, and their machine guns were spitting. I never seen so many planes. The sky was black with them. I could see Panama City blazing in the distance.

"The smoke on the ground thinned a little, and I could see Lieutenant Coleman grabbing at his throat and coughing and swearing. Some of the boys began to tear their clothes off. It was the acid in the smoke, I guess.

"After a gas shell burst, I could hear my brother, Private John Wills, screaming down there. I wanted to go down and find him, but I was afraid of the gas. Some of the boys were vomiting, and a couple of them that had been hit by machine-gun bullets just lay there moaning.

"It all happened faster than I can tell it, except the planes kept coming over. They came over in waves of fifty. I never seen so many. There wasn't nothing could have stopped them, and anything that got in their way was destroyed. It was awful.

"I don't know how long I was up there in that tree. I know I prayed for a while. And I kept calling down to the fellows on the ground. And after a while none of them answered. The whole Canal got it just the way we did. The Germans came back and dropped parachute troops in oilcloth suits, and they started throwing chemicals on the ground. They saw me in the tree and made me come down. They called a German officer. He asked me questions in English. He said, 'I can't understand it. You're the first one we've found that isn't crazy or dead.'

"I didn't know what he meant. A little later we saw a naked man come out of some underbrush. He saw us and stood there grinning at us. Another man came out after him. His face was raw, and part of his uniform was eaten away. I knew him. He was Captain Roberts. He went to the naked American and stuck a gun in his face and shot him. Then the German officer shot Captain Roberts. And then the officer turned to me and shrugged and said, 'Another corpse. There must be thirty thousand of them to clean up.'

"We came to a plotting room. That's a bombproof room, underground, where the plotting crews figure firing ranges and phone them to the gunnery crews. They can keep gas out, but it gets hot down there, and the air gets stale.

"This German officer stuck his head in one of the ventilators and yelled, 'Anyone down there?' The voice that answered was Corporal John Smith's—a friend of mine. He yelled back. 'Three of us left.'

"The German officer yelled, 'Come out with your hands up. Quick!'

"Corporal Smith yelled, 'Come down and get us, you so-and so! Go to hell!'

"The Germans tossed grenades down the ventilators. I guess they killed all of them down there."

There was a long uncomfortable silence broken only by the sound of the speaker in Venezuela sobbing.

Norton stole a glance at Peggy. The girl's face was pale.

The voice on the radio suddenly blurted: "For God's sake, you people at home in America, don't let them do to you what they did to us in the Canal Zone! Don't let them bring this thing to America! Make peace with them now, somehow—anyhow! If I thought we could win . . ." Strangling sobs. And then a whimpering last plea: "Please!"

In the quiet room in Honolulu, Major Hobart muttered, "The yellow pup. He needs court-martialing."

Admiral Sterrett said quietly, "*Schrecklichkeit!*"

Norton thought bitterly: A superb job of propaganda.

Peggy O'Liam said nothing.

Fitzroy said, "Poor young devil! I think he meant it. I think he believes that the German war machine is unbeatable, that our country is doomed. The Germans believe so, too. Well, we'll see."

An announcer said over the radio: "And now, the President of the United States."

The President's voice was tense.

"Fellow Americans: Today, as you know, the Chancellor of the Greater United German Reich offered the people of the United States peace. A peace based upon his terms. A peace offered at the point of a loaded gun.

"Tonight, quite graphically, he has shown us what may happen if our answer is no. Perhaps it will happen. Are liberty and freedom worth the cost of bloodshed and death? Our ancestors thought they were. Corporal John Smith, doomed in an underground plotting room in the Canal Zone, thought they were.

"Chancellor Hitler has asked for an answer to his offer of peace. The answer that I believe the people of the United States wish me to give him is the one that has already been given Germany by an

American about to die. I cannot do better than repeat Corporal John Smith's answer. That answer was: 'Go to hell!' "

Two nights later, air-raid sirens wailed in Baltimore, Wilmington, and Norfolk. Bermuda-based Nazi bombers were repulsed by American planes, after inflicting meager property damage and slight loss of life.

In Honolulu, Lieutenant Commander Fitzroy told Norton: "The Japs'll give this place hell, once the fleet and its aircraft carriers have pulled out."

"I hope not, sir," siad Norton.

"A Clipper, escorted by a couple of Navy bombers, is bringing us quinine and serums. You're to return on it to Washington at once." He grinned. "Admiral Sterrett has arranged for Miss O'Liam to fly back to the States. The Lord only knows if she'll be safer there, but the Old Man says he could never look Mike O'Liam in the face again if anything happened to his red-headed daughter. So you'll have company. Good luck to you, both of you."

But the Clipper plane was never to arrive. It was shot down, with its escort, somewhere at sea by Japanese and Russian planes.

Admiral Sterrett sailed quietly one night out of Honolulu. A few hours later, Jap and Russian planes raided the island of Oahu again, strafing gun crews and blasting airports.

When the raid was over, Norton phoned the Joyce home. The telephone at the other end rang, but no one answered. At one-thirty in the morning his own telephone rang. He lifted the receiver in the darkness and said, "Yes?"

The voice of Peggy O'Liam was taut as a stretched steel wire.

"Doug! Can you come at once—please!"

Sleepiness fell from him. "Peggy," he shouted into the telephone. "What is it? What's wrong?"

"I've just shot a woman," she said.

CHAPTER 4

THE GIRL WHO SAVED THE FLEET

The trip to the Joyce home was a nightmare.

Norton had asked Peggy O'Liam no questions, but said quietly, with a calmness he did not feel, "I'll be right out." Slipping on some clothes, he hurried down into the street.

A cabdriver with a New York accent said, "Where to, buddy?"

"The Joyce estate. It's usually a twenty-five-minute trip. For every minute under twenty-five that you can make it in, there's an extra dollar in it for you."

The driver, already moving, said, "O. K. Hang on!"

Norton finished dressing in the cab. In the distance, searchlights were poking into the skies, and he wondered whether a second raid was anticipated. The cabdriver twisted down a street cluttered with debris from bombed buildings and, on the outskirts of town, turned off his headlights and drove by moonlight.

They screeched around a turn in the country road and the driver slapped down hard on his brakes. Norton grabbed for a hand strap. He missed, slid the width of the slippery back seat, and landed on the floor.

"That was close!" yelled the driver. "Big shell hole in the road, ditch on the side. You all right? Want me to go slower?"

"No," Norton said, "keep going."

They passed what had been a cluster of native houses, now a smoldering mass of blasted stone and wood. But as they neared the Joyce place, there were no signs of the raid. They wheeled into the driveway and saw that the estate's broad, gently sloping lawn and the rambling house itself were undamaged.

"Wouldn't you know it?" the driver said. "The rich always get off easy."

Norton was not concerned with that angle. He did think it strange that the place, an excellent target, was untouched.

Peggy O'Liam let him into the house. Her eyes red from crying, she put a trembling hand on his arm. "Oh, Doug," she said, "I didn't mean to! I tried to get Dr. Horner, but I don't think—"

She began to cry. He led her to a chair. "Easy," he said. "Where?"

She nodded toward the living room.

"Stay here. I'll be right back."

He went into the living room. There on the floor lay the middle-aged servant woman. Her plain face was still—expressionless. There was a stain, wet and spreading, on her dress over her chest. A pistol of German make lay on the carpet near her.

He got her limp wrist between thumb and fingers. There was no pulse. He lifted her and put her on a davenport. She wouldn't need a doctor. He went back and said gently, "Peggy, tell me what happened."

Peggy seemed to find relief in talking.

"Greta—her name's Greta Müller—and I were here alone. It was late, and I asked her to bring me some tea. I had the radio on when she came back. A news broadcast from the States. I made some remarks about Hitler.

"Doug, she began to act like a person gone mad. I thought she was going to hit me. She said she wouldn't listen to insults about the Führer. She said Americans were a soft, wasteful lot and deserved what was going to happen to them. She said what had happened here and at the Panama Canal was only a taste of what would happen from one coast of the United States to the other unless we submitted. She said America was doomed.

"Japan and Russia—though Russia didn't realize it yet, she said—were assisting Germany in her attack upon our country. All the plans had been made by the German High Command and Hitler himself. They would be carried out with split-second accuracy. She looked at her watch and said. 'If you do not believe me, listen: In exactly three minutes there will be a raid on this island.' And Doug, in three minutes we heard bombs in the distance.

"I told her, 'You know what happens to people like you in wartime.' She said, 'I do not care. My work is through, and I would gladly lay down my life for the Führer.'

"I got up and started for the telephone. She took a pistol from her dress and made me sit down. When the raid was over, the phone rang. She wouldn't let me answer it."

That had been his call, Norton realized. Many things were now clear. It had been no accident that the Joyce estate had twice escaped bombing. This servant who had managed to attach herself to the staff of the Joyce household was a German agent! Silently, bitterly, he damned the giddy and fabulously rich Joyce sisters. They reveled in inviting to their home prominent persons, including such men high in the United States Army and Navy as would accept their invitations. Their home had been a fertile field for just this sort of thing.

The dead woman had probably been the local contact agent. She would have paid for the placing of the gasoline flares that had directed bombers during the first raid on the island. Paid with money received from . . .

"Did she mention von Holtz?" he asked.

Peggy O'Liam shook her head.

"No. I remember now that I saw him talking to her once, months ago. But, Doug, I haven't told you the worst thing. I said to her that when our fleet reached the Atlantic Coast, the Germans wouldn't find it so easy. She just laughed at me. She said that they had plans for our fleet, too—by the time the sun rose, the United States would have few if any battleships left. I asked her what she meant, and she said something that sounded like 'boot' and said, 'You'll know soon enough.' "

"Was it *Unterseeboote*?"

"Yes."

So that was it. Submarines! It was probably a submarine in which von Holtz had left the islands, too.

"I didn't know what she meant," Peggy continued, "except that Uncle Burt was in danger. It made me angry. I jumped up, and that surprised her, I guess. She almost dropped the gun, and I managed to get my hands around her wrist and bend it back. The gun went off and . . ." She shuddered.

He told her very quietly:

"You'll have to make yourself forget that now."

He began to try to piece the meager facts together. After bottling the United States fleet in the Pacific as far as the Canal was concerned, it would be quite logical for the enemy to try to destroy it long before it could reach the Atlantic around Cape Horn.

If they planned a hit-and-run attack by submarines, they could not do better than to make the attempt at dark, when the fleet was only a few hours out. Given time, Admiral Sterrett could get out into the ocean and have a better chance to maneuver and avoid a massed attack. But if the enemy were quietly lying in wait off Hawaii or Maui, their surprise attack might riddle the fleet.

True, they'd lose a lot of subs. But the subs would be those of Japan and Russia. And Russia, particularly, had enough to lose. As long ago as 1940, when it was still possible to form an idea of a nation's naval might, she had had 150, more than any other nation. Fast-diving subs, many of them, with a remarkable surface speed. And Japan had her share, including some long-range ones that could cross the Pacific and return without refueling.

Altogether, it was a foregone conclusion that at this moment, out in the path of Admiral Sterrett's fleet, a terrific concentration of enemy submarines was lying in wait.

Norton explained some of this to Peggy.

"Can't we do something?" she demanded.

"Where's a phone?"

She led him to one, and he put through a call to Fitzroy. When he hung up, his face was grave.

"Our communications are all shot," he told her. "The island's cut off—everything gone but the local telephone system. Cable's gone. Radio stations got it tonight in the raid. Admiral Sterrett left a station ship behind in Pearl Harbor to reach him at sea by radio. That ship was sunk. Combination of good bombing and local sabotage, I guess.

Fitzroy says we may have a radio working in anything from two to five hours, but even if we do, there'll be no assurance that the fleet gets the message. Admiral Sterrett won't radio back for fear of disclosing his position."

Very quietly she asked him, "How far out are they—Burt and the boys?"

He looked at his watch. The fleet had sailed around 7:30 P.M. It was now 2:29 A.M.

"Somewhere between a hundred and a hundred and twenty miles."

"Air miles?"

"Hundred and twenty would cover it."

And then, with a jolt, it came to him what she was thinking of—setting out in a tiny landplane over a lot of deep water to overtake and warn Admiral Sterrett!

"That's a pretty fancy brand of suicide you're playing with," he said soberly.

"Burt would do it for me," she replied stubbornly.

He began questioning her about the little two-place ship. It had a cruising speed of 120 miles an hour. Its range of 600 miles would be more than ample, but . . .

"There hasn't been any gas for civilian flying lately," she said. I've got about an hour and three-quarters in the tank."

An hour and three-quarters! Two hundred miles! That was slicing it pretty thin.

She produced a chart. "The fleet," she said, pointing, "should be somewhere off here—Alenuihaha Channel, between the islands of Hawaii and Maui—right now. They'll probably follow the regular lanes until they're out of the islands. We can be at this spot in an hour. In that hour, they can't make more than fifteen miles or so. If we're lucky— and we've got to be—we'll find them. If we're not . . ." She shrugged her shoulders. "We can head east and probably find a place to squat down on the island of Hawaii."

While she readied the little plane, Norton spent five minutes searching Greta Müller's room. It was five minutes wasted. He found nothing.

When he went outside, Peggy had the motor warmed up and ready. He climbed in and found that she had stowed life preservers in back of the seat.

There was no nervousness about the girl now. She gave her instrument panel a final check, gunned the motor, and "horsed" the plane off the smooth lawn so expertly that he wasn't aware when its wheels had left the ground. They cleared the wall, circled and, a few minutes later, were out over the Pacific, with Oahu behind them.

There were masses of broken clouds overhead. She climbed through them and on up to 8,000 feet where, picking up a slight tail wind, she leveled off. Between cloud patches he scanned the black water beneath them. They flew on, and once, when he lit a cigarette for her, he saw that under the tonic spell of flying, her face was relaxed, free of tension. Some minutes later he saw that the clouds had massed beneath them. They could no longer see the water.

She nosed the little plane down and they came out beneath the clouds at 1,500 feet. He looked at his watch. It was three-forty. In seven minutes they should overtake the fleet.

The seven minutes passed. Nothing! His eyes were drawn uneasily to the gasoline gauge. It looked perilously close to EMPTY. At most, they had a little more than one half hour of flying left in that gas tank.

"If we turn east now and head for Hawaii," Peggy said, "we should make it easily. The fleet's probably to our west. If we look for them, we may not be able to get back to land. Which shall we do?"

It was not an easy decision to make. He didn't find himself feeling heroic. The first light streaks of dawn were creeping over the horizon. If they turned west, away from Hawaii toward open sea, they might never see another sunrise. His stomach felt cold and uneasy. He did not want to die. Nor did he think it fair that this girl beside him— young, beautiful, happily eager for life—should have to share that fate.

And then he thought of the people at home in America—his people and hers—who might well die unless the United States could re-establish control over the Atlantic.

"We started this thing," he told her softly.

Fear had made her own face taut, but she smiled a little as she banked the plane and turned west. He half rose in the seat beside her. His lips found hers.

"I had hoped you might do that," she said.

They flew west for five minutes, saw nothing. It seemed hopeless. Then he heard her say, "Look, Doug."

She was already banking the plane in a turn to the south when he saw it. Down on the dark water beneath them was a series of whitish streaks, the thinning wake of many ships—the trail of the United States fleet. He felt like shouting.

She dove down to five hundred feet, lined the plane up with that wake, and followed it. A minute later they were roaring over the fleet's train—its oilers and their slender, alert, zigzagging destroyers. Huddled in the center of the tight battle formation was a line of "covered wagons"—the Navy's aircraft carriers—and just ahead of them were the mighty lines of America's sea sluggers, her great battleships.

On the outer edge of the rectangle of battleships and carriers hovered rows of destroyers. Beyond, in a far-flung circle, were more destroyers and cruisers, poking protective inquisitive snouts into the sea. There, beneath them, was the massed force of most of the United States Navy, and Lieutenant Norton felt an instinctive surge of pride.

In the semidarkness they flew quite low over the water and close enough so that he could distinguish the recognition letters painted aft on the *Saratoga*'s flight deck.

"There's the *Sara*," he said. "We'd better circle and come in beside her. We're not equipped to land on her flight deck. We'd probably barge into some of her planes. We'll have to take our chances on landing in the water beside her."

He saw Peggy nod. And then he made out the outlines of the Navy's new pride and joy, the 40,000-ton *Virginia*. The Old Man would be aboard the *Virginia*. He had chosen her as his flagship. She had a special fighting top built for his use.

"Would Admiral Sterrett know your plane?"

"I think so," Peggy said. "He's been up in it."

He told her to fly reasonably close by the *Virginia* several times. The mighty battleship was running, as was the rest of the fleet, under dim blue battle lights. Once, as they passed, he saw a head and shoulders silhouetted on the navigation bridge. He opened the cockpit window, leaned out, and made forward—then downward—motions with one arm.

"We're almost out of gas," Peggy said.

He saw the *Saratoga* pull out of formation and pointed her out.

"Come in on her port quarter," he instructed. "I think they're getting ready to pick us up." Or take a shot at us, he added to himself.

As Peggy dropped the left wing to bank into the wind, he

pulled down the life preservers and put one in her lap. Their safety belts had to be left on until they were in the water. In case their little plane began to break up in the heavy onshore swell that was running, they could flip open the buckles in a trice and dive out of the door. Peggy eased back on the throttle, and as she inched down through the dim light, Norton mentally rehearsed his escape procedure. There was, of course, no chance to make a normal night landing. At that low altitude, it was impossible to tell where sky and water met. However, Peggy did a masterful job. All the way down through the long pancake approach, she held the "ship" in a quarter-gun power stall, with the control column well back and her hand ready to cut the switch the instant the tail wheel touched the water. That instant was an interminably long time in coming. She and Norton could do nothing but sit there and wait while the airplane shuddered on down.

They hit with a resounding smack as a big wave reached up to grab at them. The little plane reared high into the air, hung there half over on its back for an instant or two, then fell off into a trough some three or four waves away. Norton's seamanship told him that there was no time to waste before the next wave crashed down upon them. His fingers frantically tore open the safety-belt buckle; then he grabbed for the cabin door with one hand, reaching for Peggy's wrist with the other. He had taken off his shoes, and as he tried to get up, his foot slipped. There was no time for life preservers now. As it was he barely had the girl halfway through the door before the big wave had opened its mouth to swallow them.

Too close for comfort, he thought, as he towed her on through the waves while the valiant little plane spiraled on down to Davy Jones's locker. However, in a few seconds more, they were swimming side by side on the surface.

The *Saratoga* had pulled about and already was launching a "Mary Ann"—a motored crash boat bringing a doctor and rescue party. The two were pulled aboard. A lieutenant grinned and said:

"It's a good thing you flew low and had the look and sound of a commercial puddle-jumper! We had half a dozen five-inch guns and a flock of anti-aircraft pom-poms drawing a bead on you when we got the order to hold fire. The Old Man wants to see you—and your story had better be good."

In Admiral Sterrett's quarters aboard his flagship, Norton was wearing borrowed clothes. Peggy O'Liam was wrapped in warm dry blankets as they told their story. The admiral had already issued orders for a change of course, and through a porthole, Norton could hear the noise of planes roaring off the flight decks of the carriers *Hornet, Yorktown, Enterprise, Wasp, Lexington, Saratoga,* and others.

"I've been at sea a long while," Admiral Sterrett said, caressing the bowl of his pipe, "But this is the first time I ever heard of a mass attack by submarines in darkness. It would be dangerous—for them. They'd be diving into each other, and they'd stand a chance of being rammed by us."

He put the pipe in his mouth, took it out again.

"Could be done, though. If each sub had followed a specified course during the attack, they probably could avoid ramming each other and might even get away after giving us a bad time of it all around. The element of surprise alone would have been in their favor. But now the shoe's on the other foot. If they're still hanging around out there, our bombing planes and destroyers will make it hot for them. Sandy bottom around here. Even in this light they'll be easy to find unless they can get down deep, and do it fast."

And they were found—nearly two hundred Japanese and Russian submarines, lying in wait along Sterrett's course. The scouting planes reached them first and went to work on those that had not begun to submerge, strafing their gun crews with machine-gun bullets, leaving them easy prey for the torpedo planes and bombers that followed. Submarines that had already begun their dives were attacked with shattering depth charges.

Meanwhile, Destroyers Squadrons One and Nine had steamed ahead on a fan-shaped course, dropping more depth bombs. The *Farragut* reported later that she had rammed and sunk a long-range Jap sub of the Kaigun type, while the *Warrington*, in the same fashion, had accounted for the *Dekamolka*, pride of the Russian undersea fleet.

An hour later, Norton and Peggy O'Liam sat in their own clothing, freshly dried and pressed, in Admiral Sterrett's quarters. He totaled up the score and found that 103 enemy submarines had been accounted for.

"And only two of our scout planes failed to return," a younger officer said. "A fine buy for us, sir."

The commander in chief nodded absently, "A fine buy, but we had men—nice young men—in those two planes."

Peggy, beginning to show strain, was sent away for a short nap.

"Lieutenant," Sterrett told Norton, "I'm going to get you and Peggy back to Honolulu on one of our catapult planes. You can land in the harbor, and our pilot can rejoin us. We'll need him before we're through."

"You face a hard trip, sir."

Admiral Sterrett shrugged. "It'll be hard on the men," he admitted. "Tough on the air pilots, too. We'll have to keep patrols in the air night and day. And we'll have to fuel somewhere along the coast of South America. That may be a problem, with the countries south of us none too friendly. And the subs will be on our tail. Hope I can keep my tankers intact. Well, we all have a job cut out for us."

He gave Norton two envelopes to deliver. One was addressed to Admiral Martin Nettleton, Chief of Naval Operations in Washington; the other to Lieutenant Commander Dudley Fitzroy in Honolulu.

"They'll get planes through to Honolulu in a day or two," he said. "Risky journey—both ways. Try to get Peggy back to the States safely. And don't let her brood over that damned woman that got shot. She's a fine, sensitive girl."

"She is that, sir," Norton agreed fervently.

The Old Man looked at him sharply. "Just the same, don't let her talk you into any penny-a-point pinochle. Best pinochle player I ever saw that wore skirts. Too bad I can't take her on this cruise. I guess I don't have to tell you," he said gruffly, "that the pair of you did a damned-fool thing today—and that it's lucky for us that you did."

Norton flushed. The admiral scratched the back of his ear and held out his hand.

"That's about all, I guess. Good luck, Lieutenant."

"The same to you, sir."

Fifteen minutes later they were catapulted off the *Virginia* in a seaplane. The pilot circled and waggled his wings as they roared past the fighting top that, high above the upper bridge, was the pride and joy of Admiral Sterrett. They could see him wave an arm in farewell. Peggy and Norton were silent for a while after that, their thoughts the same. Would the admiral get his fleet safely around the Horn? And, if he did, would it be merely to find himself up against the overwhelming combined naval forces of Russia, Germany, and Japan?

Thirty minutes later Honolulu came in sight. As they circled to come in, Norton saw three of the Navy's new substratosphere flying boats at rest near the seaplane ramp where Honolulu's naval hangars and squadrons had been demolished during the first raid.

They came down into the harbor and disembarked. The pilot taxied out again to take off at once for the return trip to the *Virginia*.

At officers' quarters at Pearl Harbor, Fitzroy read the letter from Admiral Sterrett and put it aside.

"You probably saw those three planes in the harbor," he said. "They finally got our serums to us. We'll need them, because I have an idea this island is going to be cut off from the world for some time. A lot of the gas casualties are showing signs of turning into pneumonia. And we've got a few cholera cases bobbing up. I hope that doesn't spread. Oh, well. The orders are that those planes are to fly you two back to the Mainland."

"I'd like to go home," Peggy O'Liam said. "I won't pretend that I wouldn't. But it seems somehow like running away."

Fitzroy grinned ruefully. "More like jumping from the frying pan into the fire. There aren't any ivory towers left in the world anymore. Things are about ready to explode in—or over—the States now. You'll get there just in time for the fun, I'm afraid.

"We haven't got our own radio communications working yet, and we're not even getting news from the Coast. I was listening to "Amos 'n' Andy" over a Seattle station last night. Right in the middle of the program, with Andy about to be hauled off to jail, they went off the air. Hell of a thing!"

"Air-raid alarm?" asked Norton.

"I suppose so. The Coast radio stations were off all last night. Well, your plane leaves at three. Don't miss it."

The three Navy planes, however, did not get off until 7 P.M. Fitzroy had come down to the ramp to see them off. Peggy O'Liam gravely kissed him good-bye. He shook hands with Norton.

"If the cable's working when you get back, let me know if they took Andy to jail, will you?"

"I'll do that. Best of luck, sir!"

"Thanks," Fitzroy said with a straight face. "We'll be cozy enough here."

That was a lie, and they both knew it. The island of Oahu, and everyone on it, was doomed. Facing an epidemic, cut off from supplies, lacking aircraft, the well-fortified island would put up a bitter but futile fight. The enemy could harass it at leisure. . . .

Once in the air, Norton took a last look at the island, basking in the rays of a setting sun. The planes climbed rapidly to 25,000 feet. In the heated, oxygen-pressured cabin, the altitude had no noticeable effect. Darkness came. They were flying without navigation lights over clouds that blotted out the sea beneath them.

Around midnight, the second pilot came back. "How are things in the States?" Norton asked him.

"Not so good," he answered frankly. "Not on the Pacific Coast, at least. When they grabbed our Alaskan bases, that gave them control of the North Pacific, knocking out any chance of our stinging them with a flank attack.

"The Russians have eight million troops pouring into the Alaskan Territory from Siberia. The Japs, with almost as many, are coming across by way of the Aleutians. That's why they picked this time of the year, I suppose. The Aleutians have tricky currents and dangerous reefs, but the Japs have been charting them in their so-called fishing boats. Their only handicap was fog. August is the one month in the year when it lifts."

"What are we doing about them?"

"We've sent a couple of divisions from the Ninth Corps Area up to join the Canadians, but the enemy's moving down from Alaska faster than we can get our men up there. Seems we never got around to finishing a highway gap in Canada that would have joined Alaska to our American transportation system.

"Alaska's been getting the brunt of it, of course—no coastal defenses. Juneau was wiped out in one night by incendiary bombs. If we can't reinforce the garrison at Chilkoot Barracks before they get there with tanks and troops, those men will be massacred.

"No foreign soldier in this war has set foot on the soil of any one of our forty-eight states—yet. But the stage is all set for it, and meanwhile, they're giving us a little war of nerves. All the coastal cities are getting it. Ketchikan, Prince Rupert and Victoria in British Columbia have had air raids. Night before last, they dropped a few bombs on Seattle. No casualties and not much damage. Then, just to show us what they could do, they flew down over Portland and as far south as San Francisco. Russian planes, I guess. They dropped some pamphlets inviting us all to become comrades before it was too late. Our anti-aircraft guns knocked a few of them out of the sky, so next time they'll drop bombs."

"And they come from our own Alaskan bases?"

"That's right. Dutch Harbor, Kodiak, Sitka. Sitka's less than a thousand miles from Seattle."

"Can't we take those bases back?"

"It would take more planes than we can spare right now," the pilot replied. "Besides, we'd have to train new pilots in arctic flying. There's no time for that now."

"It doesn't look very pleasant."

"It isn't. We've had to feel our way so far. We don't know how or where to place our heaviest concentrations of troops and guns and planes. While Hitler gets ready, he's giving our East Coast air raids and a war of nerves. The Russians and Japs are treating us to the same dose in the West. The Mexicans, under the new Arranza government, are combining occasional air raids in Texas with some of the old Pancho Villa guerrilla raids along the border towns. And the Germans can strike from South America as well.

"All of those things have to be taken into account. The Russians and Japs, for example, can send planes up from Dutch Harbor, Sitka, and Kodiak. The planes rendezvous somewhere at sea. They have a concentrated force—and a definite objective. Since we don't know what city they're going to try to bomb, we just have to sit tight."

"I notice we're flying without navigation lights," Norton said. "Safer that way?"

The pilot nodded. "The Japs and Russians have decided that, for the moment at least, the Pacific is their playground. They're flying all around it. I'd hoped we'd get away from Pearl Harbor earlier. We'll get to Frisco after dawn, now. We'll have some sun in our eyes, and it won't be too easy to spot any patrols they may have up. Keep your fingers crossed!"

They slept for a while after—the deep, sound sleep of exhaustion—as the three substratosphere flying boats roared onward.

The sun streaming in upon Norton's face woke him. In the seat across from his, Peggy O'Liam said, "Good morning. "We're one hundred and twenty miles from San Francisco. Half an hour more. We're almost home."

He was about to reply when the plane banked sharply to the left.

"Doug, what is it?" she cried.

"I don't know."

His eyes fought the bright sunlight outside. He saw something dark dive past them, and he saw the leading plane of their V formation trailing smoke. Then it dropped and spun crazily downward. He heard nothing except the roar of their own engines and the chatter of their machine guns, but he saw a row of tiny black holes appear in their right wing. Than a rattle like that of hailstones sounded against the cabin. More holes appeared in a row above their heads.

He could feel the air coming through, cold and crisp, and he felt strangely buoyant and good. In the distance, he saw a cluster of fighters wheeling, to climb and come down on them head on, for another try. Upon their wings they bore the insignia of the Rising Sun. He began to count them—and found that he could not concentrate.

With a dull shock, he realized that the exhilaration, the trigger alertness he had felt, was only the momentary result of high altitude and lack of oxygen in the plane's no longer airtight cabin. His fingers, fumbling at the buckle of his safety belt, seemed clumsy, inept, unresponsive.

He knew that unless he could act swiftly, could make a suddenly befogged mind and slowing reflexes obey him, both he and the girl would be unconscious. And it would be too late.

CHAPTER 5

THE SIEGE OF SEATTLE

Norton's head ached violently and, despite a blast of chill subzero air that streamed into the cabin, he felt an almost overpowering sense of drowsiness.

His hands groped for the auxiliary oxygen tank that he knew must be fastened somewhere under the seat. He found it, and turned the valve. He brought up a length of metal-bound rubber tubing and sucked in a long pull of oxygen.

After a moment of dizzying intoxication, his senses cleared. Across the aisle he saw Peggy O'Liam shaking her head against approaching unconsciousness. Just as he got to her side and adjusted the seat oxygen tank, her eyes closed and her head dropped forward. He put the oxygen tube's wooden mouthpiece between her lips and, pinching her nostrils, forced her to breathe in oxygen.

She revived to smile wan recognition. He said, "Thin air. Blacked you out. Hang on to this tube."

He got back into his own seat and fastened his safety belt as their plane nosed down in a roaring power dive. They emerged from under clouds at 8,000 feet in a pullout so sharp that his body ached from the downward pressure. His eardrums seemed to have buckled, and he blew his nose and swallowed hard to relieve them.

He could see nothing, now, of the Japanese planes. There was little use telling Peggy, if she had not already guessed. Either they were going to make their destination or—they were not.

A few minutes after that, he saw a group of Navy fighters flying protectively above them. Some time after they came in over the gleaming waters of the Golden Gate, and to his right, he saw San Francisco. He looked down, his eyes seeking the Golden Gate Bridge across the entrance to San Francisco Bay.

Then he found it—and he stared. The $35,000,000 bridge, longest span in the world, pride of Californians, had been severed almost midway between its two high towers. Its cables and six-lane roadway, a twisted mass of wreckage, had sagged into the channel waters.

They circled, gliding down over Treasure Island, onetime site of the Golden Gate International Exposition. The bridge connecting Oakland and San Francisco was undamaged. They landed lightly on the water, and turned to taxi toward the ramps of Alameda Airport and Seaport, which since 1940 had been converted into a naval air base.

As they were crossing the field he grinned at the girl beside him and said, "Welcome home."

She halted and her face was wistful. "Home!" she repeated. She dug the tiny toe of one slipper into the earth, hugged his arm and smiled up at him. "It feels good," she said.

Later an Intelligence officer at the air base told them of that Japanese attack upon their planes.

"We had a high patrol up this morning," he said. "Part of their job was to escort you in. They found you just after the Japs did. Of the fifty Jap planes, half a dozen had dropped out of formation and pounced on you, knocking down your leading ship. Then our interceptors came down on them out of the sun. Complete surprise. They lost forty-four planes. We lost five. You had a close squeak, though."

Norton was on the point of asking about the Golden Gate Bridge when a message arrived. He and Peggy O'Liam were to report at once to the office of the Commandant of the Twelfth Naval District, Rear Admiral Dugal O'Shane.

The Intelligence officer whistled softly. "Old Tight Britches," he said. "Ever met him?"

"I've heard of him."

"Well, you're about to have an experience. O'Shane's the Luke McGlook of the Navy. He was born with a tongue that could slice through armor plate. Years ago they gave up trying to find a new place to pin medals on him. Great man. Don't let him rattle you."

"Thanks," Norton said. "I'll try not to."

Admiral O'Shane lived up to his advance billing. He was red-faced, gray-haired, testy. When Norton and Peggy reported to him, he waved an impatient hand toward a chair.

"Sit down, sit down," he said. He did not look up. He spent a minute reading a report before tossing it aside. Then his piercing blue eyes appraised his visitor.

"So you're the young idiot that flew a landplane out to the *Virginia?*"

Norton smothered a grin. "One of them, sir. I was the passenger."

"Probably get medals, both of you. Hope you live to wear them. We have a dangerous job picked out for you. Tell you about it in a minute. Acquainted with the military situation as it stands this morning?"

"No, sir."

"Desperate," grunted O'Shane. He got out of his chair and crossed the room to a wall map. He pointed to the northeast coast of the Western Hemisphere.

"Hitler's been hammering away at the East Coast from Labrador to Virginia. His air base at Greenland doesn't amount to much— except for its nuisance value. And the raids, so far, haven't been intense. Just enough to keep the civilian population shaky and to make us wonder where we'd better mass our defense for the big push.

"It's a guessing game, to wear us thin. If he thinks he can smother our coastal defenses, he may order a head-on assault against Boston or New York or Baltimore. He may try our back door, down the St. Lawrence, through Canada. He may try a combination of those moves.

"All we've been able to find out is that he's ready. He can attack at any time on forty-eight hours' notice. We've sent a few bombing reconnaissance patrols out to Bermuda to find out what's up. Not one got back. But one of our boys did get a radio message through before he was shot down. Gist of it was that, seven hundred miles off our coast, Hitler has massed the greatest concentration of ships and planes that has ever been assembled. Troopships, supply ships, fighting ships. Planes of all kinds. Carriers, including some that once belonged to France and England.

"We might get together every plane we own and fly them all out there and try to wipe out his concentration. If we succeed, the war—with Germany—will be over; if we fail, we'll be through. Instead, we're gambling on the theory that if he comes to us, he'll lose three or more planes to our one. And maybe we can get our fleet back into the Atlantic. If we can control the air over it, we may cut his lines of communication. I know that if anyone can get the fleet around the Horn, it will be the Old Man."

Admiral O'Shane moved his arm across the map.

"Meanwhile, we've got a west coast to defend. And no navy to defend it with. Have to rely on secondary defenses—coastal fortifications, planes, troops. That may not be enough.

"Alaska's already gone. One of the last of the privately owned feeder stations of the Alaska Communication System got through to the control station at Seattle this morning. They passed the picture down to us.

"Those people are being annihilated up there. I don't know what else we expected to happen. We rigged them up some air bases, but we got around to it too late. When the Japs and Russians, with superior air power, pushed those over, Alaska was defenseless, cut off.

"The Reds sent a whole field army across the strait; the Japs sent one by way of the Aleutians. At least half a million men altogether. There are only eighty thousand people in all Alaska. People with guts. Pioneers. But what can they do? Regiment of the Thirty-Second Infantry at Chilkoot Barracks tried to stop the enemy yesterday. They were wiped out.

"When the Reds crossed into Alaska, first thing they did was to take some Russian renegade out of the jail at Ware and make him Commissar of the 'People's Recovery Party of Alaska.' He designates the traitors. Priests and nuns are automatically traitors. So is anyone found in possession of a weapon or a radio. They shoot them without trial, usually in the churches. Then they burn the churches. Territorial Governor of Alaska was executed yesterday at Juneau. That'll give you a rough idea of what we're in for."

"Didn't we send a couple of divisions up there, sir?" Norton asked.

"*Started* them up," O'Shane corrected. "Then their air forces got busy. Flew inland into British Columbia. Blasted the Canadian National Railway in a dozen places between Prince Rupert, on the coast south of Alaska, and Prince George, in inland British Columbia. Tore up a lot of the Cariboo Road south of Williams Lake, just to make sure we couldn't help up there. We pulled our divisions back before they could be trapped and blown to bits.

"Meanwhile our Canadian friends in British Columbia are having their hands full. The Russians have been flying inland and dropping parachute troops at all the commercial airline landing fields from Fort St. John to Williams Lake and from Prince George to Finlay Forks. That gives them all the nearby air bases they need to bomb hell out of the State of Washington. Of course we can raid them from every field we have along the Canadian boundary. But we have to keep as much air strength as we can on hand for a possible full-dress attack on our own west coast. It's anyone's guess but I think that's where we'll be attacked first.

"Germany can afford to wait. The Japs and Russians will move their fleet and air force and troop transports against us fast to consolidate their present gains. Then, when we have them on our backs, Hitler will spring."

Admiral O'Shane turned from the wall map. His eyes were bleak, his voice surprisingly gentle. "Son," he said softly, "we can't buy or talk our way out of this jam. And we can't underestimate our enemies. We call the Russians bums. They were bums in Finland five years ago. But eight million is still a lot of bums, especially when they do what they're told.

"The Japs are a bunch of heathen. Yet this is part of a holy war to them. Did you see Golden Gate Bridge when you flew in today?"

"Yes, sir."

"One Jap did that. He didn't drop a bomb. He dove his plane, its bombs, and himself right into the bridge. Think you'd like to try something like that?

"And the Germans. Ever laugh at that silly goose step of theirs? I did, once. Try it sometime. If you can march three steps in that stiff-legged, awkward fashion and forget that you're a soldier for one of those steps, then you'll have done something no other man has ever done. Discipline!

"And that's the combination we're up against. With luck you'll live to see this country stagger out from under it and start putting the pieces back together. Otherwise, you'll see what we like to call civilization vanish from this earth.

"My father came to this country when it was being scratched out of a wilderness. I don't know why he came here from Ireland, but I know he worked and sweated when he got here. We had meat once a week, and ate our potatoes skins and all. My father helped build a railroad. Got up at five, spit on his hands, and grabbed a sledgehammer. He swung it until dark.

"The other day I rode on the railroad he helped build. In the diner there was a fat old cluck, dressed mostly in jewelry, giving the poor shine hell because her steak was overdone. And I thought, Is this what my father spit on his hands for?

"If it is, God help us, because we're going to lose our jewelry. We're up against the lean, the hard—the seasoned, the ambitious. They know we're rich—or were—and they figure we're soft. I hope we still can remember to spit on our hands.

"That's where your job comes in. Washington figures we're certain to be invaded within the next week. Hitler from the east; the Red and Jap armies from the west. One or the other. Wherever it happens is where you're to go—fast. You'll be furnished an assistant and credentials. The assistant will be a skilled news photographer. We're taking pictures of this war to show posterity—in case there's any posterity left to look at them.

"Your credentials will entitle you to any means of transportation—Army or Navy—at any place, any time, so long as it doesn't seriously handicap a specific military operation. You can fly in bombers during a raid. You can ride in a tank during an attack. You're to take pictures—and you're to observe morale and listen to comments. We'll have other observers doing the same job you're doing.

"Understand, this is no shoofly job. We aren't creating a Gestapo. We don't want names. We want to know how morale, civilian and military, is standing up. If some private calls his C.O. an old stuffed shirt, that's his privilege. Probably he's right. If the complaint's about equipment, that's something else again. Get it back to us. We'll iron out the bugs or give them something better.

"The brass hats who mastermind the war from swivel chairs are going to learn some humility this time. Billy Mitchell told us years ago that the nation controlling the air in the next war would win. Hitler listened to him. We court-martialed him. We've chalked off a lot of our peacetime prophets as cranks. Now Panama and Hawaii, our Caribbean and Alaskan bases are gone—and we're going to build a separate air arm. It will take time. But you are to remain here in San Francisco awaiting further orders. Any questions?"

"No, sir. I'd like to know that Miss O'Liam will get back safely to her home in Illinois. And Lieutenant Commander Dudley Fitzroy asked that this letter be delivered to the Chief of Naval Operations."

"We'll attend to those things," O'Shane promised. "Ask Miss O'Liam to come in for a minute, please."

That evening, Norton and Peggy had dinner at a restaurant in San Francisco's Chinatown.

"You'll be going home shortly," he said. "I'm glad, in a way. I expect to miss you terribly, Peggy." His eyes became bitter. "We've been born a generation too late. Not so many years ago, we could have talked of plans for a tomorrow."

He controlled a sigh. "You'll be seeing your father soon," he said. "It'll be good to know that you're in Illinois. That should be a safety area."

She did not look at him when she answered. "I'm anxious to go home, of course. But I'm going to Baltimore first. My sister lives there."

He did not like that. The coastal cities were unsafe. He tried to dissuade her.

"Please—let's not talk about that now."

She didn't know, she said, when passage home might be arranged for her; now that war had come, the airlines and railroads were overburdened. Private reservations were being canceled to make way for passengers engaged upon official missions. Something about priority. After Admiral O'Shane's promise to get this girl home, Norton found himself a little disappointed.

They were together most of the next day as he awaited orders. Admiral O'Shane invited them to lunch, and had dinner with them at the hotel where Peggy O'Liam was stopping.

At the end of the meal, O'Shane put down his cup and made a wry face. "Looks like coffee, smells like coffee, tastes like slop. Those synthetic substitutes! I sometimes wish we had Brazil for an ally."

Peggy said nothing. Norton looked up to find her staring

beyond him, her face white, her lips trembling. A man at an adjoining table was reading a newspaper. On its front page, in huge black type, was the headline:

JAPS SMASH HAWAII
Oahu Overrun—Death Toll Mounts as
Defenders, Refusing "Honorable
Peace," Are Slaughtered

Heading the known casualty list of hundreds was the name of Lieutenant Commander Dudley Fitzroy.

Peggy got up. "Will you excuse me for a few minutes?" she asked huskily. "I'm afraid I'm going to be sick."

Norton took her to the elevator. When he returned, Admiral O'Shane was tracing patterns on the tablecloth with a knife. He did not look up. "What's wrong with that girl?" he growled angrily.

Norton felt a seething rage. "Nothing's wrong with her, sir," he snapped. "It just happens that she has friends in Hawaii, and they've been killed, and—"

"I don't mean that," O'Shane interrupted. "What I mean is, why in hell don't you marry her? I could have put her on a plane to Baltimore the first day you arrived in San Francisco. She asked me to let her stay here—with you—until you left. I promised her I wouldn't tell you that. She loves you. My God, and you're supposed to be in Naval Intelligence!" Admiral O'Shane threw down his knife, got up, and stalked away.

Feeling a surge of elation, Norton went up to Peggy's room.

"I'm all right now," she smiled at him.

He decided, as he took her into his arms, that she was something more than all right.

They were to be married at nine the following morning. At six Admiral O'Shane called Norton.

"Sorry," he said. "Hell's broken loose in Seattle. We've got a plane warmed up for you at the field. Get in a cab and get out there. I'll tell the girl good-bye for you."

The siege of Seattle began at 5:46 A.M. on August 18, 1945.

Three wings of Red and Japanese bombers, escorted by a patrol of fast little fighters, roared in from the Pacific across Olympic National Park on a straight line toward Bremerton and Seattle.

The air fleet of great bombers came over at 10,000 feet, flying in diamond formation for salvo bombing. A squadron of interceptor planes from Fort Worden Air Field at Port Townsend got into the air in time to meet them, but were promptly shot down.

Over Seattle droned the big bombers, each carrying two tons of bombs. The first salvo, directed at Boeing Field, smashed one of the bridges across Duwamish Waterway. Other hits claimed the Lake Washington pontoon bridge and demolished the Federal Building and a nearby railroad station. The great Boeing Aircraft plant, which was turning out three badly needed six-engined Flying Battlewagons a week for the United States Army, was left in ruins by fifty tons of bombs. The Naval Air Station Airport on the city limits was wrecked, and a number of its planes were caught on the ground and destroyed.

After passing over Seattle, the enemy air fleet turned north and headed for its Canadian air bases.

Norton's cameraman was a wiry, lean-faced young civilian named Jock Rodgers. The two of them approached Seattle less than two hours after the first raid. As they neared the naval airport, they saw the still smoldering hangars, the bomb-pocked field. "Whew!" said Rodgers. "We'll never land there!" They circled and flew back to Boeing Field.

Several years before, the United States War Department had organized a Civilian Airplane Warning Service, enlisting thousands of residents in outlying districts in every coastal state of the Union as "spotters" of enemy aircraft. At headquarters in Fort Worden that morning, after the first raid, the phone rang, and an excited member of the civilian Spotter Corps shouted, "Enemy airplanes overhead!"

Before the private at the switchboard could get the location code signals from him, the man had hung up.

A moment later a woman, less excitable, called: "Forty-seven. Arthur. Three. Enemy planes overhead, flying south. Several hundred of them."

An officer at Fort Worden consulted a huge wall map. The enemy planes were over Van Zandt, in Whatcom County, Washington, halfway between the coast and the Canadian border. "Coming at us from the north this time," he said.

For more than a hundred years, the Canadian and American boundaries had been unfortified. American-Canadian friendliness had been enduring. But the great stretch of border had constituted an open invitation to foreign invasion, particularly at the port of Seattle.

In August of 1940, however, during the war in Europe, a permanent Canadian-American Joint Defense Board had been set up. Fort Worden, on the tip of Admiralty Inlet at the mouth of Puget Sound, had been transformed into a coastal defense fortification bristling with armament. Batteries of mobile and fixed anti-aircraft guns had been installed. Massive 16-inch guns, capable of firing twenty miles out into the Strait of Juan de Fuca, had been mounted in concrete pits. Fort Casey, on the opposite shore of the inlet, had been similarly armed.

Now, the Spotter Corps member had warned that an enemy air fleet was approaching from the north on a line that would bring it within range of the forts' anti-aircraft defenses. Gunnery crew members of the 14th Coast Artillery hurried to their stations. However, after flying south as far as Burlington, Washington, the enemy air fleet swung sharply west and blasted the city of Victoria, British Columbia. Then, turning north on their way home, they unleashed a terrific bombardment on Vancouver, wrecking the Royal Canadian Mounted Police Barracks, the Royal Canadian Air Force seaplane base in English Bay, and the airports on Sea and Lulu Islands. One bomb landed on Vancouver General Hospital; another wrecked a building of the University of British Columbia.

Canadian air resistance was courageous but futile. One Canadian plane shot down was piloted by a member of Vancouver's Flying Seven, an organization of licensed women pilots.

All through that day, the raids continued. Great waves of Japanese and Russian planes came in relays, to lay their deadly eggs on Bellingham, Everett, Tacoma, Seattle, and on Vancouver and Victoria in British Columbia. American planes took off from dozens of army and naval air bases, only to go down before the overwhelming superiority of the enemy air fleets.

Seattle was raided for the second time at noon. The enemy planes came in from the east, warily avoiding the anti-aircraft fire awaiting them at Forts Worden and Casey. A number of office workers left their desks and went to the roofs of the buildings to watch the bombardment. Jap fighter planes spotted the civilians on the rooftops and, skimming down, raked them with machine-gun fire.

By nightfall Seattle had been raided five times. And still the waves of enemy planes soared overhead, dropping brilliant parachute flares to illuminate objectives that the bombers then demolished.

Outside Tacoma, enemy planes dropped incendiary bombs into the great wild forests of the "Lumber Capital of America," starting a most menacing forest fire.

Every railroad entering Seattle had been blasted, preventing the arrival of troop reinforcements that were being rushed toward the beleaguered City of Seven Hills.

Shortly after nightfall, Great Skagit Dam was destroyed and Seattle's power plants hit. Electrified transportation was halted, and as the city fell into darkness, doctors in the County Hospital on Eighth Avenue swore softly and called for candles and lanterns in order to continue emergency treatment of wounded civilians. Later that night, three direct hits on the hospital killed some twenty doctors and several hundred patients.

Near dawn, the whine of air-raid sirens and the constant tolling of church bells were joined by the shattering bellow of dive bombers dropping explosives upon merchant vessels moored at docks in Elliott Bay. Incendiary bombs, dropped on wooden houses, started fires that added to the terror and confusion.

Morning saw a proud city in ruins. Only one wall of Seattle's civic auditorium remained standing. Defiantly its people carried on in the face of new terrors. A Port Blakely ferryboat with hundreds of civilians on board was blown high into the air when it struck a floating mine, one of many deposited in Puget Sound the night before by low-flying Japanese planes.

A "splinter fleet" of wooden fishing boats, manned by daring fishermen, set out to clear Puget Sound of mines. The men perished when enemy planes swooped down and machine-gunned them.

Norton and Rodgers had watched the attack upon Seattle from a room high in the Benjamin Franklin Hotel. Between raids they had gone out—Rodgers to take photographs, Norton to talk with citizens.

Early the following morning, the voice of the Mayor of Seattle was broadcast over radio station KIRO, which had been powered during the night for emergency transmission. He asked the people of Seattle to evacuate the city, using United States Interstate Highway 10, which would take them inland and behind the Cascade Mountains by way of Snoqualmie Pass.

In the street that morning Norton found that, for the most part, people were stubbornly refusing to leave.

"By the Lord Harry," one old fellow said to him, "I saw the whole business district of this town wiped out by fire in '89. And we built her up again! I ain't gonna let no Japs or Reds run me out of my own town! If they're figurin' on landing troops in Seattle, they're crazy! If they drop 'em in parachutes, I guess we can knock 'em off before they can light. Six years ago, they might have brought their navy right through Admiralty Inlet. They better not try it today. We got guns at the forts that'll blow 'em right out of the water. They can't get through!"

But they did. At ten o'clock on the morning of August 19, 1945, the Japanese and Russian fleet, preceded by minesweepers and by submarine-hunting destroyers, steamed into the Strait of Juan de Fuca. Just before coming into range of the heavy coastal guns of Forts Worden and Casey, four battleships lined up at the head of the great fleet of destroyers, cruisers, transports, and train.

The two Russian battleships were the 35,000-ton *Internationale* and *Kornilov,* each mounting nine 16-inch guns; the two Japanese battleships were the 32,000-ton *Nagato* and *Muto,* each mounting eight. The four battleships waited in line, out of range of the coastal guns.

Suddenly a squadron of "smoker" planes appeared high over Dungeness Spit and, one by one, they came roaring down toward the miles of water separating the two forts from the enemy battleships. The forts' anti-aircraft guns sent up a barrage, but the speed and angle of the diving planes made a hit almost impossible. When perilously close to the water, they pulled sharply out of their dives and, leveling off, began to lay a thick curtain of black smoke between the forts and the battleships.

The planes offered better targets now; the American gun crews quickly downed two of them. But a squadron of hedge-hopping attack planes came skimming over, strafing the gun crews from the rear with machine-gun fire.

The Japanese smoker planes had laid a thick pall of smoke across the entire stretch of water from Port Williams to San Juan. Behind it the four battleships moved forward. High overhead flew a third squadron of Japanese planes. To the battleships hidden behind the smoke screen, they radioed instructions for firing upon the land forts.

The *Muto* opened fire. Her first shot went wide. She tried

again, her range corrected by the planes. This time she scored a direct hit on Fort Casey. A moment later she let go with a salvo that smashed the fort's guns and killed every man in the gun crews.

The gun crew at Fort Worden, faced with certain destruction, fired on through the curtain of smoke. A lucky shot tore off the fire control tower of the *Internationale*. A moment later, the *Nagato* and *Kornilov* battered the fort into silence.

Preceded by minesweepers and destroyers, the Japanese and Red fleets sailed through Admiralty Inlet and into Puget Sound toward Seattle. Into Elliott Bay steamed a number of warships that began pounding the city with a great fan-shaped barrage.

With the fall of the two forts, the civilians had begun to flee rather than await the transports carrying half a million troops of Stalin and Hirohito. A few grim snipers hid in buildings near the docks to fire upon the first troops to land. They were quickly found and bombed to death by the Japanese. Both Japanese and Russian troopships pulled alongside the docks of Elliott Bay and began disgorging troops.

Seattle had fallen. The invading armies of Russia and Japan had set foot on American soil.

Norton and Rodgers joined the throng of refugees on United States Interstate Highway No. 10. Fifteen miles out of the city they came upon a truckload of wounded men and boys waiting for army engineers to repair a crater blasted in the highway. Only a few complained.

Norton approached one young man whose left side had been torn by shrapnel. "Well, Seattle's gone," he said.

The eyes blazed. "Gone?" he asked. "Maybe! My grandfather was a baby when his folks came out here. Wasn't anything here then. He was one of the first settlers, and his folks didn't even own a cow. Had to feed him clam juice to keep him alive. He and his kind built that city. It can be built again.

"If those foreigners think they can get very far inland, they're crazy. Wait till they try to come through the passes in the Cascades. We'll pick 'em off like flies. If we have to win this war with Indian fighting, then we'll do it. They're not through with us yet."

It was not until he reached Snoqualmie that Norton was able to send a telegram, addressed to Admiral Dugal O'Shane, Commandant of the Twelfth Naval District, San Francisco. He merely said:

"Out this way, they still spit on their hands."

CHAPTER 6

MADNESS OVER MANHATTAN

Lieutenant Norton and Jack Rodgers had left the Seattle refugee line at North Bend, Washington, where they had managed to obtain plane passage to Olympia. Meanwhile, young Rodgers had taken many feet of film of the slow-moving procession of refugees headed inland.

Admiral O'Shane had been brief in his instructions. Norton was to observe American morale and to supervise the photographing of such phases of America's invasion as he himself might decide upon. The sweeping latitude of his roving commission, Norton realized, implied much more than those instructions conveyed. His job was to make such use of the wide authority given him as would best serve the interests of his country.

Photography had played a strategic role in the Nazi war in Europe. Back in 1939–40, the documentary pictures taken by Hitler's cameramen of the conquest of Poland had helped destroy the morale of the Low Countries, speeding their subsequent downfall. Now, both the Army and Navy commands were relying upon pictures taken by agents of their Intelligence sections, working closely together, to bring

107

to the American people a realization that their country was plunged into a last-ditch fight for existence.

Even now, the broadcasts and newspaper stories had not thoroughly accomplished that. The news that the Red troops of Stalin and the fanatical hordes of the Mikado had actually occupied an American city had, of course, shocked the entire nation. But to many inland residents in vast America, Seattle seemed as remote as had Alaska, Hawaii, and the Canal Zone. And on both coasts, where radio stations now often went off the air during hours of darkness lest they guide enemy air raiders, citizens seeking news set their dials for large interior stations. People were disturbed, but too many of them were not even yet quite aware. In a democracy that had no designs upon other peoples, had only the tenacious wish to live in peace, full realization, with awakening of the martial spirit, the will to fight, came slowly.

East Coast residents, from Boston to Miami, quietly accepted it as a foregone conclusion that Hitler would immediately launch his attack upon the United States.

Men and women who as late as 1940 had scoffed at the possibility of any such invasion now resignedly asked each other how and where it would get under way.

In New York's Times Square, huge crowds gathered to watch the electric news bulletin until, following an order by the Police Commissioner, the sign was disconnected. Officers of Boards of Disaster Control in every East Coast city interrupted local radio broadcasts to ask that citizens go quietly about their usual affairs, avoid congregating in the streets, refuse to listen to rumors, and wait quietly in their homes for real news, which would come to them in their newspapers or by radio from Washington.

Norton had concentrated on photographs of individuals in the refugee line because such lines were usually joined by fifth columnists intent on playing upon the terror of confused people fleeing from their homes.

In Olympia, Washington, Norton and Rodgers talked to an American pilot of a dive-bombing plane who had been sent up to the front from North Island. As they sat in a restaurant, the young pilot ordered food, then pushed it from him.

"Stomach's gone into a tailspin," he explained. "I was up five times yesterday. You do enough six-G pullouts, and you begin forcing the digestive juices through the stomach wall. Or you black out, or get nitrogen bubbles into your spinal fluid and begin turning slaphappy.

"So far, they've run rings around us in the air. We've got better planes and pilots. We've got inland factories that they can't reach with bombs, and we've stepped up our assembly lines. Given time, we can match them plane for plane—and that's what we're going to have to do. But not if they knock us out of the air the way they've been doing.

"We can afford to lose first-line planes, but we can't afford to lose first-line pilots. When we begin drawing on pilot reserves, our casualties will be even worse."

"Lack of training?" Norton asked.

"Partly. The rest of it's psychological. A pilot is more than a man who can fly and fight. He has to keep his head on afterwards. I've seen pilots get through the hottest dogfights possible, fly home, and then, over their own fields, go completely haywire and crash.

"But there's one big reason why our casualties have been so heavy. It's simply that we haven't got a unified command, a top man who can direct the whole shebang—air, land, and naval activities. If we're to win this war, we'll need perfect coordination of all three arms.

"Germany learned that six years ago. She licked Europe by building a huge air fleet, making it a separate force on a par with her army and navy, and placing it where it belonged—in the hands of men who were themselves flyers.

"Let the Navy have all the planes it needs. They've done good work. Lord, our own Navy invented dive-bombing! Let 'em have all the carriers and equipment they want for ocean fighting. But give us a separate air force able to coordinate with both land and sea fighters, headed by a man who won't let the enemy spread our defenses thin every time some politician lets out a yodel! Then we'll show you something."

The argument, Norton realized, had inescapable logic. When France had been crumbling five years before, troops as well as high officials had shouted pathetically, "For God's sake, send us planes!" The conquest of Europe had shown unmistakably that mastery of the air over a theater of operations was vital in the new modern warfare. Yet the United States had stubbornly rejected the idea of a separate air force.

The invasion of Seattle proved the one thing needed to pound home a public realization of this weakest link in America's defense chain. Long-standing opposition was crushed, and Congress passed a bill calling for creation of a Department of Defense, with separate Bureaus of Air, War, and Navy, headed by a Commissioner of War.

America faced on two coasts a war she did not want. Against the coming of this day she had, since 1940, been making feverish, incredibly costly preparations that had dislocated the whole economic pattern of American life. Every citizen in the country had been affected. Rearmament costs had shot the national debt up to a staggering $75,000,000,000. Taxes consumed 40 percent of the wages of each earner. Defense bonds, maturing in fifty years and paying only one percent interest, were a required purchase by anyone possessing more than $1,000 in savings.

The gold standard had disappeared and, except for use by jewelers and dentists, the yellow metal had little value. The underground gold repository at Fort Knox, Kentucky, was used for the safekeeping of more precious things such as quinine and antimony which, along with chromium, manganese, Manila fiber, nickel, and tin, constituted stockpiles of strategic materials not produced at home in the quantities that wartime demanded. Rubber and silk were being produced synthetically. Gasoline for civilian use was being rationed. The value of the dollar in America was maintained by government fiat.

In Europe, since 1941, labor had been paid for with commodity cards, and manufactured goods had been exchanged for food and raw materials under a barter system against which many American firms had found themselves unable to compete. Yet despite this quiet, exhausting, deadly economic warfare, America had not collapsed—as both Hitler and Stalin had freely predicted it would. America made its sacrifices willingly; talked of them characteristically as the price of peace.

And then, in the Pacific Northwest, came the incident that was to rouse seething rage, unify America, give it a will to fight, and wipe out the last of the habitual bickerings of a democratic people. That incident was the capture of Tacoma.

After the bombardment and shelling of Seattle, the Red and Japanese armies disembarked under command of fierce, vodka-guzzling Field Marshal Budenny. Field guns, light and heavy mobile artillery, tanks, tractors, motorized units—all the equipment of modern mechanized warfare on land—were unloaded and assembled.

Before the invading armies began their push southward,

American troops of the Fourth Army from seventeen states began to assemble to meet them. Three regiments of Ninth Corps troops, including a mechanized battalion, crept up from the south over highways and railroads blasted by the invaders' bombers. They were to try to hold or slow the enemy while the Fourth Army assembled, but they never made contact. Japanese planes came upon their column as it halted for engineers to repair a bridge, pulverizing the soldiers and their equipment.

Four hours before the invading armies started to roll south, a six-wheeled staff car, driven by a Japanese soldier whose uniform bore the three stars of a sergeant, roared from Seattle toward Tacoma. Mounted on the car was a white flag of truce. A gray-haired Japanese general bore with him orders and instructions for the immediate evacuation of Tacoma and the announcement that it would be occupied within four hours by an advance force of the Japanese and Red armies.

Ten miles out of Tacoma, the car in which he was riding struck a land mine and, with its occupants, was blown to bits. A great concentration of Japanese and Russian planes flying close to Tacoma destroyed all scouting forces sent out to reconnoiter, and word of the enemy's approach was not received until they were within half an hour's distance of the city.

At a hospital in Olympia, Father Bernard Schultz, a white-faced priest from Tacoma, told Norton and Rodgers of what had followed.

"It was ghastly," he said. "The enemy evidently believed that rather than withdraw we had chosen to fight a hopeless fight. They began to shell the city, and civilians who had not had a chance to get out were killed by hundreds in the streets.

"Our soldiers—a mere handful—fought bravely, but the odds were overwhelming. The Russian and Japanese soldiers streamed into the city, and the next hour was a bloody melee of street fighting. In the confusion, every person seen running was shot down. A number of our men, cornered on the Municipal Port Terminal piers, were machine-gunned and then pushed off into the waters of Commencement Bay.

"I don't know how long the fighting went on—for several hours at least. The hospitals were in flames, and I persuaded the Russian commander to let me bring some of the wounded civilians here to Olympia with me."

"Father," Norton said, "I want to talk to those wounded and photograph them."

The priest nodded and led the way. In a hospital ward room, accompanied by a doctor and nurse, Jock Rodgers took pictures of the victims while Father Schultz explained their cases.

There was a dying girl of twenty who had been struck during the shelling by shrapnel and building splinters. There was a man whose arms had been burned to the elbow by an incendiary bomb that had trapped him in the top-floor room of a wooden building. There was a young National Guardsman whose neck had been torn open by a bayonet.

But the picture that was to arouse the nation was one taken that day by Rodgers of little Dickie Roberts, a seven-year-old boy.

"His father and mother," Father Schultz said, "were killed by a shell that ripped the roof off their house. Miraculously, this little fellow was not seriously hurt. He stayed in the house with his dead parents all day. At night he crept out to ask for food. His mistake was to tug at the sleeve of one of the enemy sentries and speak to him in English. The sentry whirled and lashed out with his gun butt. He nearly crushed the youngster's skull."

That night Lieutenant Norton reported by telephone to Admiral O'Shane, who told him that he and Rodgers were to board a Navy plane that would leave San Francisco shortly for Olympia and would pick them up and fly them, their films, and reports, to Washington, D. C.

At the Winthrop Hotel in Olympia, young Rodgers paced the room where Norton was eating dinner. Rodgers' lean face was ashen, his hands clenching and unclenching.

"I know how you feel, Jock," Norton said. "You want to shoot a gun instead of a camera. But you'll have to try to forget it. Sit down and eat something."

"Couldn't," growled Rodgers. "I don't know why I should go soft now. Lord, I've been around! But accident or no accident, when a hungry kid gets it like that. . . . You don't drink, do you?"

Norton shook his head.

"Good," said Rodgers. "One of us has to stay sober. And, Doug, you're going to have to pour me on that plane tonight."

Late the next day, in Washington's Navy Building, the pictures taken by

Jock Rodgers were run off before an audience that included some of the crack Navy and Intelligence Officers of the United States.

As the film showing the Seattle refugees fleeing their city was shown, several voices in the audience shouted simultaneously to the projectionist: "Hold it!"

Halted, the film showed a group of men and women on a horse-driven cart. The driver of that cart, attired in overalls, had now been recognized as a German spy named Heinrich Grubel.

Norton did not know the man, but an FBI agent sitting beside him explained: "He's one of the old-timers. Worked with Baron von Holtz over here during the First World War. Was mixed up in the Black Tom explosion, although we could never nail him on it."

Intelligence officers in the Seattle territory were immediately notified. Armed with a description of their man, they quickly located Grubel and learned that he had been diligently spreading defeatism during the Seattle evacuation. Two days later, he was executed.

The pictures of the victims wounded during the capture of Seattle were promptly released to newspapers and motion-picture houses. They were frankly propaganda—but they were truthful. Throughout the length and breadth of the United States, the picture of little Dickie Roberts, his head swathed in bandages, had the same effect it had had upon young Jock Rodgers.

And suddenly the people of America woke up to the stern fact that it was not enough to love their country or to give willingly of their time and money for its defense. Physical, individual participation in defense—with all the dangers and hardships it implied—became their job.

Enlistment bureaus found themselves swamped. Grizzled applicants demanded that the age bars be let down. It took patience and time to explain to them that they could best serve away from the front in the more quiet posts to which they had been assigned. Local home-defense units had the job of guarding factories, railroad yards, and munitions plants against sabotage.

The peacetime conscription bill passed in 1940 had given military training to hundreds of thousands of American youths. As the inevitability of war had become apparent, more and more thousands of civilians had received military training. America had two million men already under arms and another trained million reservists on hand.

In the next week, the Red and Japanese armies were to suffer terrific casualties in the Northwest. In the State of Washington, farmers who had escaped in refugee lines stopped only long enough to get arms and ammunition before circling back toward the enemy columns. Their aptitude at hunting, plus the training they had received under the Burke-Wadsworth Peacetime Conscription Act, now stood them in good stead: hidden in the woods, they sniped at enemy patrols. In a nighttime raid that was to become known later as the Second White River Massacre, a group of three men carrying light machine guns almost succeeded in cutting the enemy communication lines outside Kent. Detachments of Red and Japanese troops were sent into the woods to wipe out these snipers, but they were separated by their hidden foes and then coolly picked off one by one.

In the nation's capital, Lieutenant Norton, awaiting further instructions, was handed a letter. His heart jumped at the postmark—Baltimore! He tore the letter open. It began simply: "Darling—"

Peggy O'Liam was in Baltimore at the home of her sister. She was safe and well. There had been air raids on the city by Nazi bombers, but they had been of slight consequence. Peggy was busy. As soon as she had attended to a number of things (she did not specify exactly what) she intended to go with her sister and her sister's child to their father's home in Illinois.

"Everywhere here in the East," she wrote, "people are asking two things: 'When will Hitler attack?' and 'How soon can Admiral Sterrett get the fleet back into the Atlantic?' I am afraid the answer to the first is, 'Very soon,' and to the second, 'Not for many days, if ever.' I do hope Uncle Burt will manage it."

He read the closing line of her letter many times: "I miss you terribly, my dear, and if God listens to the prayers of a red-haired and rather frightened girl, He'll watch over you for me."

Norton desperately hoped that he might be assigned to Baltimore next. But he was not. He and Jock Rodgers were sent to New York City.

"Ever been here before?" asked Rodgers, a native New Yorker, as they strolled about the city.

"Six years ago," Norton said.

Since wartime defense measures had been put into effect, the great metropolis had undergone many changes. Around its towering skyscrapers now floated a cordon of thousands of barrage balloons—

sausage-shaped gas bags on steel-wire mooring cables that curved down from them in 3,500-foot arcs.

"I never expected to see those things around the Big Town! They're a good defense, though. Better than England's balloons. We've got the only helium there is to be had, so they can't be set ablaze with tracer bullets. They're hard to knock down, and while they won't prevent bombing of New York, they will keep most of the low-flying bombers from coming down on us.

"We've developed another protection, too. It's messy but good. Before the war, a building superintendent used to consider the city inspectors an unmitigated nuisance. They only came around to tell him that his heating plant or incinerator was throwing out too much smoke. Now those same building inspectors, coached by our Chemical Warfare Service, have come around to give those same building supers chemicals and instructions for making smoke and artificial fog. When there's a raid, we can blanket most of the city with the stuff."

As they walked up Broadway, Norton noticed that all the shop windows were either boarded up or heavily taped against bomb explosions. He noticed, too, that America had called up her manpower fast. For the most part, buses and surface lines were now operated by gray-haired men or young women, easily recruited from the vast numbers who had found themselves unemployed when department stores and business firms had felt the pinch of war. This city, where hacking had been a major industry, now boasted only a dribble of its thousands of taxicabs. Gasoline rationing had forced most of them off the streets, and most of those left were driven by women.

The statue of Columbus had been dismantled and removed from Columbus Circle. Entering Central Park, Norton noticed that New Yorkers, as always, sat in the sun on benches. Most of the women were knitting—a carry-over from the war of 1914–18. And then a strange incongruity struck him. In their entire walk, he had seen not a single baby carriage. New York was a city without children!

When he spoke of it, Rodgers nodded. "Yes," he said, "the kids have all been evacuated, along with the mothers of babies a year old or less. Evacuation of the youngsters was a tremendous job. The New York Central had to make up a set of train schedules that had two hundred pages. But they got them out of the city in three days. The crippled and blind have been moved to reception areas, too—mostly to the Catskills or the Adirondacks. Wherever possible, to the homes of relatives living far inland. A few to Long Island, though that's considered only moderately safe. My parents have a place up in the Adirondacks. I got them to go up there."

New York seemed strangely calm and sobered. Men and women alike carried little boxes with shoulder straps, each containing a gas mask and canister. Many men and women carried canes. "They use them at night during the blackouts," Rodgers said. "If you tap as you walk, you're less likely to have a collision."

Central Park proved a beehive of activity. Elderly men, young boys, and even a few women were digging up flower beds and stretches of green grass to provide miles of trench shelters. The shelters—six feet wide by seven deep, with wooden floors and dirt-covered corrugated-iron roofs—were of little value against a direct bomb hit. But when fragments from nearby explosions began to fly, they might mean the difference between life and death.

Cleopatra's Needle, the Egyptian obelisk in the park behind the Metropolitan Museum of Art, had been completely covered with piles of sandbags. Most of the art treasures in the museum itself, Rodgers said, had been moved to the City Art Museum of St. Louis.

"New York has to take a lot of precautions," he said. "When London was bombed, the English usually had about ten minutes to get to their shelters. Since the planes will come in from the ocean, where it's difficult to spot sound locaters, we may not have that much time. And since this is a city of cliff dwellers—apartment dwellers—the average citizen can't buy himself a steel bombproof shelter. He hasn't a backyard to park it in.

"On the other hand, our steel-frame building construction is excellent. On a direct hit, a twelve-hundred-pound bomb might crash through five or six stories of an apartment building and might gut those top stories. But it wouldn't topple over the whole building—and it would take weeks of constant hammering to reduce our skyscrapers to rubble.

"The tenements and some of the old three- and four-story brownstone houses are in a bad way, though. Hit by incendiaries, they'd be certain firetraps. Nothing much can be done about that."

Late that afternoon the two registered at a hotel in the West Forties. On the inside of the room door was a sign:

TO OUR GUESTS:
This hotel possesses a shelter offering the utmost in
safety. Your hotel operator will notify you immediately by telephone in the event of an air-raid warning.
Trained floor attendants will direct you to the shelter.
Do not run, but follow instructions quickly and
quietly. Do not go near windows. The shelter, located
beneath the ground-level Arcadia Room, is protected
by sandbags, jacks, 10,000 feet of steel tubing, and
oak beams.

Newspapers, magazines, bridge tables, radios,
food, and liquor are available in the shelter.

Rodgers, grinning, spoke over Norton's shoulder: "Tsk, tsk! No floor
show?"

Dinner in the hotel's Arcadia Room that night was by candlelight. The dining-room windows were sealed with heavy black shutters.
Since air conditioning had become a forbidden luxury, it was stuffily hot.

New Yorkers, who in prewar days had fretted over inability to
find something to capture their fancy among twenty or more entrées,
now made a choice from among five. Only one of the five was meat.
Food rationing had begun.

"We're beginning to learn to eat fish, and like it," Rodgers
pointed out. "Feeding more than eight million people is a job, and
before this war is over, the Nazis will be blasting away at our fishing
fleets. Some general—I think it was Mannerheim—once said, 'Hit 'em
in the belly.' Here in New York we're wide open for that kind of punch.
I read somewhere that it takes eleven billion pounds of food to feed us.
Lot of it comes from as far away as California. And most of it comes in
on thirteen railroads—more of it than ever, now that Hitler's out there
off the coast and our shipping's unprotected.

"Right now, the Army has its hands full finding enough trains
to move troops and supplies around. What would happen if Hitler
bombed those thirteen railroads? Can you imagine a Park Avenue
dowager fighting her way to a garbage can to rummage for something
to eat? That isn't as goofy as it sounds.

"Then there's water and power. If a few central power plants were hit by bombs—they're pretty closely guarded these days against sabotage—the whole life of this city would be disrupted. Lights would go out, subways and elevators would stop. There'd be the darndest confusion you ever saw.

"As for water, there are only two great carriers for New York City. Not much danger of their being hit, I suppose, since they're tunnels two hundred feet underground. But if anything happened to them and if power were knocked out before we could even begin to evacuate the people, this city—the biggest thing man ever built—would be a howling bedlam cluttered with corpses.

"New York! Turned into a cross between a madhouse and a ghost town in three days! That's what authorities fear most, I believe. And it could happen."

"Has there been much bombing?" Norton asked.

Rodgers shook his head over a cup of synthetic coffee. "Not much. Mostly piers in the North River and a few tries—that missed—at the Jersey railroads yards and gas tanks. A bomb fell close to the Aquarium, and the concussion shattered a lot of the glass tanks and dumped fish all over the place.

"The piers, of course, are an easy target if there's any moonlight. All the pilots have to do is follow the reflection from the river waters. We've been able to drive most of them off. But needless to say, we're being kept guessing. One of these nights Hitler's going to hit somewhere—and hit hard— in an all-out raid."

They left the hotel for a breath of air that hot August night. By comparison with the dimly lighted dining room, the streets of New York seemed almost totally dark. Shielded dim blue lamps glowed faintly at street corners. Broadway—the Great White Way—was no longer ablaze; no longer a carnival of animated and neon signboards.

Taxis were equipped with black-light auxiliary headlamps, whose ultraviolet rays, invisible to human eyes, were absorbed and visibly radiated by fluorescent paints. As a cab came down the street, Norton saw a previously invisible center stripe in the middle of the street turn white, then disappear as the cab passed them.

Not many feet under the darkened street, he realized as he recalled Rodgers' dinner conversation, lay the complex arteries of a great city—cables, mains, wires, pipes. And, like human arteries, they lay within slashing distance beneath the city's skin.

He was bumped violently in the darkness. He backed away. "Sorry."

Jock Rodgers, exploring the darkness with a flashlight that threw its ray through a blue lens, began to laugh. Norton asked what the joke was.

"You were apologizing to a lamppost," Rodgers told him.

The dim blue street lamps had been extinguished. Suddenly, from high above them, came three banshee shrieks of a siren.

"Air raid!" said Norton.

Almost at once, air was filled with the chatter of anti-aircraft batteries. They groped their way back to the hotel, and an elevator whisked them to their room on the twentieth floor, where the telephone was ringing. They ignored it and, without turning on the lights, threw open the windows. Leaning on the sill, they looked west toward the Hudson River.

In the distance, great 60-inch searchlights of 800-million candlepower fingered the skies, poking through holes in fluffy cloud formations 8,000 feet above the city. The searchlights swayed and shifted, picked out the snub-nosed barrage balloons, moved on, seeking other prey. Downtown, the prying lights illuminated occasional puffs of smoke from anti-aircraft shells.

Suddenly, from the south, above the clouds, came the deep pulsating drone of the Nazi bombers. Wave after wave of planes added the throb of their motors to the increasing sound.

"This is it," said Norton. "Must be hundreds of them."

Dull explosions sounded from the canyon of downtown buildings. Parachute flares, dropping to earth, momentarily illuminated the towering darkened skyscrapers in the financial district. A plane fell out of the clouds and spun groundward—a twisting, fiery thing bathed in the glare of a searchlight.

"Got it!" Jock Rodgers said triumphantly, his camera pressed to his face.

A moment later, the searchlights found a swaying parachute at the end of which dangled the Nazi pilot. Somewhere overhead a terrific dogfight raged invisibly as American fighters, climbing with frantic speed, sought to drive back the invading planes.

Westward on the Jersey shore, a terrific sheet of yellow flame sprang into the air. A moment later, the two heard the shaking, rumbling, mighty boom of the explosion that had set it off.

"Gas tanks," Jock Rodgers said. Then, excitedly, he pointed toward southwest Manhattan.

"Doug!" he shouted. "Look!"

CHAPTER 7

THE BOMBING OF NEW YORK

Down out of the layer of clouds had come the first squadron of a wing of 250 huge new Wulf bombers to brave the blinding glare of search-lights and the anti-aircraft fire. Leveling off at 9,000 feet, the leading plane, its belly bomb-bay doors open, flew in a straight line toward its bomb-release point.

Norton and Rodgers could actually see the falling bombs as a swinging searchlight caught them for an instant in mid-air. They seemed tiny things, those huge fourteen-foot, two-ton missiles. A moment later they let go with a window-shattering blast that reverber-ated amid the silhouetted downtown skyscrapers and was audible far uptown.

One by one, the great bombers dropped down out of the clouds. Hugging the western rim of Manhattan Island at varying altitudes above the balloon barrage, they flattened out for the forty-five seconds of dangerous straight-line flying necessary to align their sights and drop their eggs. Each plane released its bombs, in salvo, just north of the plane that had preceded it. Then it turned, banking sharply toward the Jersey meadows, and thence toward the open sea and safety.

From the clouds above the bombers, smaller Nazi and American pursuit planes were dropping in flames out of a raging dogfight. Other American pursuit planes fought their way toward the ocean, where, without having to hurdle the fire of their own anti-aircraft batteries, they might meet and bring down incoming enemy bombers.

From the ground, the sleek Wulf bombers were absorbing terrific punishment. The first Nazi plane to be caught in a hell of anti-aircraft fire jettisoned its bombs and wheeled desperately to get away. A merciless searchlight pinned it against a backdrop of clouds. Up that shaft of light, an anti-aircraft battery sent a burst that scored a direct hit, ripping off one wing and spinning the plane crazily into the North River.* Another Nazi bomber, struck before it could release its tons of high explosive, blew to flinders in the air with a terrific spurt of flame.

Still they came on, and by now, the skies over lower Manhattan were a sullen, shivering red. Methodically, precisely, and with uncanny accuracy, the bombers were blasting and setting ablaze the wooden piers and covered pier sheds along West Street. The great Pennsylvania Railroad terminal for perishables had been struck. Washington Market and West Washington Market were in flames, their tons of foodstuffs ruined.

The eerie scream of the "whistling" bombs, the roar of their explosions, the deep drones of planes, and the clatter of anti-aircraft fire did not drown out the whine of fire trucks and the clang of ambulances.

Norton and Rodgers made for the roof. The elevators were not running, but they found the staircase door. On the roof, a gray-haired man—a civilian "spotter"—pointed southwest.

"Looks like the whole of downtown's afire," he said. "Jersey's getting it, too."

They looked across the North River in time to see a sheet of flame leap 2,000 feet into the air. The storage tanks of the Bayonne oil refineries had been struck. Other bombs were bursting in New Jersey, and Norton guessed what their objectives would be: warehouses, sheds, stockyards, and factories from the Ford plant near Edgewater (now manufacturing warplane engines) to the floating grain elevators

*As the Hudson used to be called.

beyond the Black Tom flatlands. But the Nazi bombers' prime target in New Jersey would be the twelve great trunk lines over which New York's food came in.

The bombers fought their way toward uptown Manhattan. Waterfront property was burning furiously from as far south as the United Fruit Line piers to the great piers at Fiftieth Street, where the luxury liners *Normandie* and *Queen Mary* had docked before the war in Europe.

A squadron of German fighting planes swooped down and riddled three barrage ballons. Slowly deflated, they collapsed and fell earthward. But ground crews instantly sent aloft new balloons, and an American fighting squadron fell upon the attacking planes. A Nazi bomber pilot, attempting to sneak between a pair of barrage balloons, was blinded by a searchlight. His left wing struck a balloon's mooring cable and was sheared off.

All that night the raid continued with undiminished fury. Wave after wave of Nazi bombers came over. The Fifth Coast Artillery battery at Fort Hamilton was blasted out, but not before downing an estimated fifty enemy planes.

From the hotel roof, Norton and Rodgers watched the assault upon a blacked-out city from whose chimneys rose blankets of smoke and artificial fog. Once a screaming bomb fell so close that the two instinctively dropped to the roof and curled up in the tightest possible position. The bomb missed the hotel, exploding with a roar in the street. And though that explosion was twenty-seven floors below them, they could feel the building tremble.

Uptown, beyond the piers, new fires raged as incendiary bombs plunged through the roofs of brownstone houses off Riverside Drive. Striking inland, the bombers chose as targets some of New York's greatest skyscrapers, whose upper floors towered above the smoke. The great RCA Building in Rockefeller Center suffered a direct hit that ripped out its east wall from the seventieth to the sixty-fifth stories. A bomb directed at the Chrysler Building struck, instead, the nearby Chanin Building, ripping off a corner of its fifty-second to fifty-fourth stories.

In Brooklyn the Bay Ridge Terminal, stored with food, was set afire, and the tracks of the New York Connecting Railway were twisted and uprooted by bomb hits that knocked out the New York, New Haven and Hartford service linking the city with New England. Directly across the upper bay, the Greenville railroad yards in New

Jersey—the main artery by which Manhattan received freight from the West—were demolished. Brooklyn's Army piers and the Navy Yard also suffered bomb hits.

Before dawn, roaming bombers had demolished the huge Sunnyside yard of the Pennsylvania Railroad in Queens, severed three of the five bridges across the East River, and put out of operation the Point Morris and Hell Gate electric plants.

Low-flying Nazi mine layers, operating outside Manhattan's balloon barrage, skimmed up the East and North Rivers during the night, sowing scattered fields of floating mines. On their return flight, close to the New York shore, they raked fireboats with machine-gun fire, killing crew members who were trying to save the burning piers.

It was around dawn when Nazi bombers, flying beyond range of ear or eye, had come over New York City to release tens of thousands of tiny six-inch parachutes that floated down to alight on roofs and window ledges, in streets, in buildings already bombed. Not until later were Norton and Rodgers to learn their significance.

At seven o'clock of the sultry morning of August 27, a siren sounded the "all clear" signal. New Yorkers, shaky from a sleepless night, came out into the streets to inspect the damage. It had been strategic rather than intensive. Subways had stalled, surface lines had stopped running. Thousands of persons had spent a night of terror in subway tubes, some of which ran fairly close to the surface. When the "all clear" signal had sounded, Rodgers and Norton had gone down to their room from the hotel roof. They found the telephone dead. No water came from the faucets in the bathroom.

"No shave this morning," said Rodgers.

Norton shrugged.

Secretly each man wondered whether the hotel's high-pressure pump had failed, or whether the lack of water was caused by something far more serious.

The morning found the city without power or gas, its transportation disrupted, its population virtually isolated. Faced with an immediate shortage of food, the Army had taken control of every restaurant in New York. Army jeeps with loudspeakers drove through Manhattan advising people that for the moment it had been necessary to ration food; that they should apply to the restaurants nearest their homes for individual allowances.

Other warnings were issued: Since electrical refrigeration had broken down, civilians were cautioned against tainted meat. Since water mains had been smashed, all water must be boiled before drinking; and the utmost conservation of any available water was ordered.

Rodgers and Norton walked down the many flights of stairs to the street level. There was a long line of hotel guests waiting to enter the coffee shop. They took their places in the line. Breakfast—in a dining room presided over by a watchful Army sergeant—was skimpy: one slice of toast, one egg, fruit juice, and one cup of tea or synthetic coffee.

A waiter dropped a knife upon the tiled floor. A woman at the table next to theirs half rose from her chair and screamed. Civilian nerves were on edge. But if the merciless bombardment had made New Yorkers jumpy, it had also served to bring them closer together than they had ever been in their hurried peacetime lives. Perfect strangers in the line were exchanging experiences of the night before in easy conversations. Potbellied businessmen who had been digging trench shelters were as inordinately proud of their newly calloused or blistered hands as steel-helmeted members of Home Defense units were of their armbands. Elderly men and women who came patiently to take their places at the foot of the waiting line were promptly smuggled up near its head—and no one complained.

"There's nothing like an air raid to bring people together," Jock Rodgers grinned.

And it was true. In days long past, these same people would have squabbled among themselves over defense measures and policies. Their seeming disunity had incurred the contempt of the "virile" dictatorships. But one night of bombs—of bombs that blasted rich and poor alike—had united them in the cause of democratic freedom.

They were nervous and shaken, true. Unshaven men were hollow-eyed, women pale. But there was a new dignity about them. They had not asked for this war, but now that it had come, they were bearing it uncomplainingly. Since they had never known the grim fanaticism of Hitlerian regimentation, they accepted whatever was in store for them with confidence and easy good will.

A man sitting at a nearby table told his companion: "The more damn noise they make, the better I'll like it! Then I'll know our own anti-aircraft guns are in there banging away!"

As he watched them, Norton felt a surge of pride. He and Rodgers set out for a walk about the Times Square section. Along Broadway great queues of people were lined up, awaiting their turns to enter restaurants. Before the Paramount Theater, where Jimmy Durante was making a personal appearance, high-explosive bombs had blasted a huge crater in the street. A crew of the Disaster Control Board's 100,000 emergency workers had roped off the gaping hole, from which issued a cloud of live hot steam. New Yorkers, natural-born "sidewalk superintendents," had lost none of their insatiable curiosity. They were crowded three deep about the gully while workmen struggled with shredded wires, pipes, water mains.

The two turned west on Fiftieth Street and headed toward the still smoldering docks along the North River. They were opposite a citizens' food line when sirens overhead shrilled warnings of a new raid. Part of the line broke to seek shelter; the best stubbornly remained huddled against building walls. Norton saw a man look aloft and thumb his nose.

Ten squadrons of bombers, trailed by their higher-flying fighter escort, came over in open-V formation. American fighter planes were seeking to get above them.

Rodgers halted a moment in midstreet to aim his camera above. Then, at the wail of a "scream" bomb, he ran with Norton for shelter in the doorway of Polyclinic Hospital. The bomb exploded in the street, close to the line of waiting people.

"When you get the 'all clear,' go out and get 'em, boys," a man in a surgeon's apron said to half a dozen men standing by with stretchers. To Norton he said, "Got a cigarette?"

He proved to be a military surgeon. Norton noticed that his hands trembled.

"Operating all night?"

"Yes. By candlelight."

"Casualties very heavy?"

"Heavy enough. Our people are pretty reckless. Lots of them stay outside to watch the raids and get hit by pieces of our own shells."

"How's civilian morale?" Norton inquired.

"Incredibly good. Half of those we have to operate on are proud of their wounds. Makes 'em feel they're taking part in the war. And the place is cluttered up with would-be blood donors. We've got plenty of blood banks—don't need them. But we can't very well turn them down. They're so pathetically eager to do something—especially for the other fellow who is worse off than they are. I guess that's as good a brand of democracy as we'll need to see us through this war."

The air raid had moved farther uptown. Occasionally the dull boom of a bomb burst came to them.

"You saw the parachutes come down last night?" the surgeon asked. "They're giving us a headache. Brought down delayed-action bombs—explosive, incendiary, and some gas, chiefly mustard and Lewisite. They go off unexpectedly. The firemen and mop-up squads have been getting it. That isn't our most serious problem, though."

"What is?"

"Water. Thank God, when the alarm sounded last night, we had sense enough to fill every bathtub and washbasin in the hospital. We can still sponge off the burn victims—but what are we going to do for them when the water's all gone?

"I don't know whether you know it or not, but New York City is without water. The Germans are trying to stampede seven million people into panic. Day before yesterday I'd have said it might be done. Not any more! In the next two days, people are going to be dropping like flies. But they're not going to stampede! Raids won't split us apart, they'll drive us together."

"Where did they hit the water supply?" Norton asked.

"At its source. They bombed our water systems last night, knocking out reservoirs from Kensico to the Schoharie Reservoir. They even got to our new Delaware System, just completed this year. Now they'll be after the few bridges and tunnels we have left, and then they'll have us both thirsty and isolated. How we're going to evacuate our people I don't know, but it'll have to be done—somehow."

The clang of an ambulance came near. The surgeon turned to the groups of stretcher-bearers. "Want to try it now?" he asked.

They went out into the street, and Norton and Rodgers followed. Near the great crater where the bomb had exploded there was little aid to be given. Farther up the street, where concussion and bomb fragments had worked their havoc, were men and women. Some were prone and quiet, others sitting dazedly on the curb. A few, uninjured, were trying to help those that had been hit.

The first man they came to had suffered a jagged abdominal

wound. Before he was lifted to a stretcher the surgeon, with a piece of charcoal, inscribed an H on his forehead.

"Hemorrhage," he explained tersely.

They came to a man sitting on the curb, his head between his hands. Leaning down, the surgeon asked:

"Were you hit?"

The man looked blankly ahead of him.

The surgeon straightened. "Concussion," he said. "Split his eardrums. That bomb was the last earthly thing he heard. Probably shell-shocked, too."

At the curb, near a wrecked building, they heard someone whimper. Norton looked up to see a pretty girl of twenty, her features frozen, her eyes staring out into the street. A wounded man lay at her feet. She looked down at him without expression, stepped carefully over him. In the street she stooped near a pile of debris, picked up an injured kitten. She cradled it in her arms, sat down in the street, and began to cry. Norton looked at the surgeon.

"A few of them get that way, too," he said. "Something snaps—and human life doesn't mean a thing to them. They only feel sorry for animals."

An attendant led her, weeping, into the hospital. The surgeon called after him, "Don't try to take that kitten away from her just yet."

He turned to Norton. "That's the worst they can do to us— and only a few of us. Smash our minds." He waved a hand toward the wrecked building, the street cluttered with corpses and debris. "This," he said with savage intensity, "is nothing. They can't smash our spirit. Let 'em try! They say we're soft. We've looked soft, we Americans, because we've taken our freedom for granted. We've juggled it and abused it. But no one in the history of our country has ever quite succeeded in taking it away from us. And they won't now!"

The surgeon grinned. "Give me another cigarette," he said, "and I'll shut up. But this damned dirty bloody business gets me this way, I guess. You can't hear some poor guy that's been hit by a shell say, 'Look, Doc, tend to some of the others first. I'm all right'—when actually he's dying and knows it—without realizing that this country has what it takes! Well, thanks for the smokes—and good luck, Lieutenant."

Norton returned to the hotel with Rodgers, and in the crowded lobby a soft voice behind him called:

"Doug!"

He whirled incredulously—and there was Peggy O'Liam. Oblivious to those about them, he swept her into his arms and embraced her.

Gruff Admiral O'Shane was with her. "You and Rodgers," he said, "are to leave here at once for Washington. I flew up here to bring you both back. Miss O'Liam insisted upon coming along."

"Oh, I did so want to see you, Doug!" Peggy whispered.

"I never want you out of my sight again," he told her.

They left the city between air raids. A car took them to the shore of the Hudson, where a motor launch was waiting.

They were in mid-stream when Nazi planes swooped down on the city for the fourth time that day. The planes, their formation broken up by a terrific barrage of anti-aircraft fire, dispersed and were turning back when one escort plane sighted the launch, threading its way through a field of floating mines. It came roaring down. Norton could see the machine guns protruding from its nose and wings.

This is it! he thought.

Suddenly a burst of anti-aircraft fire ripped across the sky, tearing away part of the German plane's tail assemblage. The plane rocketed upward in a crazy zoom, power-stalled, and came whirling down in a tailspin to hit the water.

"We seem to be learning how to fight their kind of war," O'Shane grunted dryly.

On the New Jersey side of the river, a car took them to Newark Airport. O'Shane tactfully took a seat beside Jock Rodgers in the transport plane they boarded. Norton and Peggy found seats together. She told him she was to leave the plane in Baltimore.

"But why?" he demanded. "It's not safe. Why don't you go home to Illinois?"

"I can't just yet," she said. "Baron von Holtz is somewhere in Baltimore, and Admiral O'Shane has asked me to help find him."

"How do they know he's in Baltimore?"

"A Naval Intelligence agent located him there."

"And was killed?" Norton said.

Peggy nodded.

"Darling, it isn't fair!" he protested. "The man's dangerous. Suppose you do find him—what will happen? I'm going to ask O'Shane to let me go to Baltimore."

She tugged at his sleeve. "No, Doug. I have my work to do. Let me do it. Then—I promise you—I'll go home."

It seemed no time at all before their plane settled down on a runway at Baltimore's Logan Field. He saw her off the plane, kissed her again. She waved to him as the plane took off for Washington—and he wondered, sitting alone, whether a day might ever come when he and she would have no need for good-byes.

During the next few days, news from New York drifted into Washington. The great city was being raided almost incessantly now. While the German aerial armadas were suffering terrific losses, they were also inflicting horrible damage.

The water shortage had created a ghastly situation. By the second day, civilians standing thirstily in line to receive their water rations refused to break up their lines when Nazi planes came over. Some who did run for shelter dropped exhausted; those who remained were often struck by bombs. Casualty figures began to skyrocket.

Between raids, efforts were made to evacuate some of New York's millions. It was difficult and dangerous work. All bridges over both rivers had now been destroyed. Civilian owners of small motorcraft—members of the United States Power Squadron—volunteered to clear the East and North Rivers of floating mines dropped there by Nazi planes. They succeeded, but only at a heavy cost due to raiding Nazi dive bombers.

Most of New York harbor's shipping had gone up in flames; but at night, between raids, tug-drawn barges and ferryboats that had not been destroyed in their slips worked with the privately owned fleet.

Staten Island's pumping stations, too, had been wrecked, and the water famine in all of Greater New York became a hideous problem. Cholera broke out on the lower West Side.

Small boats braved the bombs and machine guns to lay a water line across the North River from New Jersey—itself feeling the pinch of bombed pumping stations. But this proved to be only a slight alleviation of the suffering.

Not until after the third day of New York's siege did America gain mastery of the air over New York—by bringing nearly every plane she could spare from strategic spots elsewhere along the coast and from far inland. The incessant Nazi raids tapered off.

But they had brought death and destruction to the proudest city in America—even though they had not crumpled its morale. And they had pulled America's defenses together and left other possible objectives exposed.

Now Hitler could strike!

Since docks, railroads, and bridges had been destroyed, it seemed obvious that he contemplated no invasion of New York itself. The best guesses seemed to be that he would attempt to establish beachheads along the flat New Jersey shore, or send his fleet and troops down the St. Lawrence to invade America by her "back door." It was a time-honored, obvious invasion route. In the 1940 army maneuvers, imaginary battles against just such an invasion had been fought in the Plattsburg area. And to invade America by way of the St. Lawrence, Hitler would have to leave his left flank unprotected. His ships, in the narrowing river, would be easy targets for the shore-based artillery.

Yet these two—New Jersey and the St. Lawrence—seemed the only possible routes. And in either move, he would be unopposed by sea, for America's Atlantic Squadron, hopelessly outnumbered, could not challenge his navy and was, at the moment, keeping its distance.

But Hitler made neither of the expected attempts. On the night of August 29, 1945, he struck—boldly, surely—in a frontal assault upon Baltimore.

Such an assault had been held suicidal, for the defenses of Chesapeake Bay had been built up to a point considered impregnable. Yet by a treacherous ruse, those great coastal guns had been rendered impotent in a brief few hours.

Baltimore fell that night. And in Washington, Doug Norton thought of Peggy O'Liam and sat sleeplessly before a radio awaiting reports. They were few.

Late in the next afternoon, films of the evacuation of Baltimore were shown to Rodgers and Norton and a group of members of Naval and Military Intelligence and the FBI. All present were asked to watch the film carefully for any spies who might have joined the stream of refugees. At a sequence that showed a black-robed priest apparently comforting a tired mother who carried a wounded child in her arms, Norton was one of those to shout "Hold it!"

He had recognized the face of the "priest." Though he wore no monocle, it was von Holtz. And then suddenly Norton felt an impact of emotion like a blow in the pit of the stomach.

In his absorption, he had missed another face in the film's background, several rows deep, behind Baron von Holtz in the plodding procession of refugees. A wan and tired and very dear face.

The face of Peggy O'Liam.

CHAPTER 8

THE FALL OF BALTIMORE

As they left the Navy Building that afternoon, Jock Rodgers was tactfully silent. He knew how dangerous Peggy O'Liam's mission had been, and—with no word in Washington concerning either the girl or von Holtz—how worried Norton must be.

Before leaving, they had sought out the Intelligence agents

who had taken pictures of the evacuation of the "Monumental City" early that morning along U.S. Highway 1 between Elkridge and Savage, Maryland. Their information was not reassuring.

The scene—as their pictures had shown—had been one of indescribable confusion. Frantic women separated from their children, young mothers trudging south, carrying babies and bulging suitcases stuffed with what belongings they had been able to salvage. Men, their faces numb with shock or twisted with hatred, plodding along the congested highway. A few had been unashamedly crying— the bitter tears of impotence and rage.

At least a third of the refugees had failed to escape. Their long line had been severed outside Savage when German dive bombers, swooping low over the defenseless people, had machine-gunned a swath through their line at an intersection where a connecting road to Ellicott City crossed the main highway.

As the unarmed civilians dragged their wounded from the highway, a Nazi column of infantry in trucks, preceded by tanks—the left flank of the German Expeditionary Force—roared and clanked northwest on the connecting road in an enveloping movement about Baltimore.

"We narrowly missed being cut off from escape ourselves," one of the agents told Norton and Rodgers. "We were just south of the intersection when the line was cut."

They had been up and down that slow-moving line in their covered picture truck several times, often traveling off the road shoulder to get their pictures. Neither he nor his fellow agent could recall in what part of the line they had taken the pictures of von Holtz and the girl.

Communications between Baltimore and the Capital—only thirty-eight miles away—were disrupted. Intelligence had not yet been able to obtain for the General Staff a complete and authentic picture of how the fall of Baltimore had come about. There was nothing to do but wait.

As Norton and Rodgers walked wordlessly along Constitution Avenue, both realized that one of three things could have happened to Peggy. She could have been among those wounded or killed at the intersection by machine-gun fire from the dive bombers. The chances for that, happily, were small. She might have been trapped in now German-occupied territory when the trailing third of the refugee line had been cut off. Or . . .

Jock Rodgers stole a glance at the grim face of Norton as they turned between the Labor Department and Internal Revenue buildings and walked up Twelfth Street toward their hotel. He could hold his silence no longer.

"Chances are," he said with forced cheerfulness, "that she's perfectly all right. Remember, Doug, two-thirds of those people got through safely."

Norton shook his head. "Thanks, Jock," he said softly, "but that isn't true. She's trapped. She was behind von Holtz in the line. And he would be deliberately hanging back so that he would be among those caught in the encircled territory."

Against that frightening logic, Jock could offer no counter-argument. When they had reached their hotel, he persuaded Norton to attempt to get some rest. Exhausted by a sleepless, worried night, Norton agreed. Jock Rodgers left the hotel without him.

Washington—shrine of a mighty nation, capital of the last great democracy—was the scene of feverish, saddening activity. With almost overnight suddenness, the mighty military machine of Adolf Hitler had established a base on American soil within gunshot of the capital. Now the streets of Washington were alive with soldiers and filled with the rumble of trucks loaded with infantry, carrying troops north. Twice in three blocks Rodgers was stopped by alert sentries who passed him only after a careful examination of his identification papers.

Although the sudden and mysterious fall of Baltimore had come unexpectedly, Washington had not been caught unprepared. At almost every government building, great vans—most of them commandeered under a plan worked out long months before—were being filled with the records and equipment by which a great nation had been run. Days before, when the Panama Canal had fallen, the historic and art treasures of the nation, from the Declaration of Independence and the Constitution housed in the Library of Congress, to the corset of Queen Elizabeth in the Folger Shakespeare Library, had been crated and sent to the Midwest.

Virtually the entire contents of the Smithsonian Institution, the National Archives Building, and the Library of Congress, which alone contained ten million separate items, had been carted to unspecified warehouses in Missouri, Kansas, and Colorado.

The evacuation of Washington was being hastily but calmly carried out.

Now employees and departments, already skeletonized to the bare necessities of maintenance, were leaving the capital. Clerks, stenographers, congressmen, and senators were leaving the city by auto, train, specially chartered buses. Plane service had been reserved for the exclusive use of Army and Navy officers who alone planned to maintain headquarters for the present in Washington.

The President of the United States and members of his family, guarded by Secret Service cars, had already been driven to the station, where they had boarded the Presidential Pullman *Roald Amundsen*. The government of the United States, under the threat of invasion, was moving to Springfield, Illinois.

The reason was not—as the German press later was to thunder—cowardice on the part of the nation's officials but, instead, a deep-seated hope that a city of beautiful and majestic buildings, beloved by the citizens of a great country, might be spared the destructive ravages of modern warfare.

True, weeks before, Adolf Hitler had threatened that there would be no open cities in the war he intended to wage upon the United States. Yet it seemed unlikely that he would foolishly waste ammunition upon a capital that was fast becoming a ghost town; that— if his troops did succeed in reaching it—would offer no resistance. It was in an effort to preserve such shrines as the home of George Washington at Mount Vernon; the great domed Capitol; the Lincoln Memorial; the stately and beautiful Supreme Court Building; and the White House, partly burned by the British in 1814, when foreign troops last had invaded America, that Washington now was being evacuated.

At the Navy Building, Jock Rodgers ran into Admiral O'Shane, who told him quietly how the city of Baltimore had been so easily taken by the Germans. Rodgers listened—as millions of Americans later that evening were to listen beside their radios—in stunned incredulity.

Rodgers was still sitting with O'Shane when the noise of explosions sounded in the city. He looked up, startled.

"Demolition bombs," O'Shane said. "The Army's engineers are blowing up every bridge across the Potomac. National Guard's doing the same for a lot of railroad between here and Baltimore. We're keeping the B. & O. Main Line intact until we can get our people out of here."

When Rodgers returned to the hotel later, newsboys were shouting extras along streets that seemed almost empty. He bought a paper. Its headline read: NAZIS NEAR WASHINGTON!

At the door to his room, Rodgers hesitated. He hated to face Norton. He let himself in, and Norton sprang up out of a chair to ask, "Well?"

Jock Rodgers did not look at Norton. "I'm sorry, Doug," he mumbled. "Talked to O'Shane. There's no word—nothing—about von Holtz. Or Peggy."

"I'm going to Baltimore. I'm going to find her."

"You can't," Rodgers said softly.

"Why not?"

"O'Shane forbids it."

"To hell with O'Shane! He got her in this mess."

"Easy," said Rodgers. "O'Shane's almost as badly floored by this as you, but it's no time to go off half-cocked. We have men in Baltimore, too, you know. Sooner or later they'll get word of her to us. A few days, a few weeks, perhaps. Wait! That's bitter medicine, but I think I'd rely on O'Shane instead of spouting mutiny."

"Sorry," said Norton.

"Forget it."

They ate, in glum uneasy silence, in an almost deserted dining room.

They listened to the radio news broadcasts that night and read extras from the newspaper office adjoining their hotel. Rodgers told Norton of Admiral O'Shane's account of how Baltimore had fallen.

At noon of the day before, what seemed to be the entire German navy, followed by a tremendous train of merchant ships, had boldly steamed into sight twenty-five miles off the entrance to Chesapeake Bay.

The incessant and intolerable aerial attacks upon New York City had stripped other air bases along the Atlantic Coast of all but a handful of planes for scouting purposes.

The United States General Staff fully realized that the overwhelming attacks on Manhattan might be under way for just such a purpose. But—with seven million persons facing death by thirst or starvation—they had no choice but to meet force with force.

In 1940, when America had come to the grim realization that its coastal defenses were outmoded and pitifully weak, a part of its national defense program had been to build giant bombproof fortresses at strategic points along its coasts.

For the protection of Chesapeake Bay, three massive outer-line forts had been constructed. A deadly barrier, they stretched across the mouth of the bay: one on Cape Charles, another on Cape Henry, and a third between the two capes on Middleground Shoals.

Since the war in Europe, the United States had come to rely less upon supporting railway guns (track beds could easily be destroyed by roving enemy aircraft), and the outer-line forts of Chesapeake Bay bristled with fixed 16-inch and 14-inch guns and with 12-inch guns and mortars.

The huge 16-inchers, most powerful coast-defense guns known, were able to hurl more than a ton and a half of steel and explosive at a battleship thirty miles at sea. They were the sluggers, ready and able to engage in duels with unseen targets.

A zigzagging destroyer, the leading ship of Hitler's navy, was first sighted by a scouting plane flying a patrol out of Hampton Roads. He radioed in a warning, and then wheeled and flew toward shore. A squadron of German fighters rolled off the flight deck of the *Graf Zeppelin*, one of the German fleet's twenty aircraft carriers, and pursued the Scout plane for twenty minutes before returning to the *Graf*.

Meanwhile, the Coast Artillery guns were being readied. Members of the gun sections had gone to their stations. In hidden observation posts, where bells sounded at thirty-second intervals, Coast Artillery observers picked out the leading destroyer through powerful telescopes and, by a throat transmitter, relayed its compass bearing to the chartroom at each bell tap.

There, on a harbor map, men with earphones received the compass bearings and plotted them in straight lines. The intersection of those lines gave the position of the target.

After that, the plotting room went to work in the complicated business of firing big guns at an invisible target. Twelve soldiers made individual corrections—for wind velocity, the temperature of the powder room, even the curvature of the earth.

Yet within half a minute of receiving compass bearings from the observation posts, Captain Robert McNeil of the Cape Charles battery had reported: "Number One gun ready!"

And at a jerk of the lanyard, Number One had sent a twisting shell twenty-five miles out into the Atlantic Ocean. It fell a few scant yards to the right of the destroyer.

Passing the leading destroyer, the German battleship *Bismarck* rushed in to hurl a salvo from her 16-inch guns. Her shells fell hopelessly short, and the American gun crews began to batter away at relentless half-minute intervals.

The *Bismarck* turned and fled at thirty knots, while the rechristened 35,000-ton *Himmler* (formerly the *King George V* of the British Navy) came in for a try with her ten 14-inch guns.

The American gun crews, firing at these unseen targets, were jubilant. It was destined to be a one-sided battle, for the fort batteries could outrange the guns of the German ships and—if they dared come too close—destroy them one by one.

Cautiously changing speed and course, the German ships came ever closer. First blood was drawn when a gun at the Middleground Shoals fort blasted a hole in the bow of the 10,000-ton *Prinz Eugen*.

The battle of forts and ships raged on. One Nazi destroyer, caught by a salvo from Cape Charles, sank with most of her crew. Two other Nazi destroyers, badly crippled, limped away over the horizon. A reserve supply of shells was ordered up from the divisional munitions dump that served all three forts.

At the munitions dump occurred the event that was to alter the entire course of the battle. Nazi planes overhead had been braving anti-aircraft fire to attempt to drop bombs upon the three forts. A number of gas shells had exploded near the underground munitions dump, whose soldier attendants had donned gas masks.

A huge olive-drab limousine braked to a stop at the munitions dump, and a man in the uniform of a major general got out, followed by seven soldiers. All wore gas masks.

Two soldier guards at the munitions dump saluted sharply. A moment later they were clubbed into unconsciousness, and the "officer" in the American uniform entered the munitions dump with his escort. With timetable precision and complete surprise, they took over.

During the preparedness program of 1940–45, the United States government had hit upon the ruse of manufacturing stores of "false" shells for its big coast artillery and field artillery guns. These shells deceptively identical in outward appearance to those regularly used, actually had a deadly difference. Some were filled with thermite, a highly incendiary mixture of iron oxide and powdered aluminum. When ignited, thermite burns at a temperature of between 4,000 and 5,000 degrees Fahrenheit. Exploded in the muzzle of a gun, it destroyed that gun's rifling, rendered it useless. The second type of "false" shell contained a full explosive charge, but was constructed so that the first sudden twist given it as it engaged the rifling was enough to explode it prematurely, bursting the gun.

The false shells, carefully stored in a separate room at the munitions dump, were to be rushed up to the forts only in the event that it became necessary for the gun crews there to abandon their positions. There these shells would be left conveniently near the abandoned guns. Such ammunition, fired by the enemy, would destroy the captured armaments.

Now, unknown to the gun crews, a group of eight spies routed this ammunition up to the defending forts. The first intimation of this treacherous switch came in the heat of firing, when the lanyard of a gun commanded by Captain McNeil was jerked. Out of the long gun muzzle issued a blinding flash of white, and a shell plopped into the water a few scant hundred yards away. Almost simultaneously, a gun in the Cape Henry battery burst with a mighty roar, killing all its crew.

So furious and constant had been the firing that half a dozen of the defending guns were ruined before firing could be halted. And as firing ceased, an advance unit of the German fleet quickly closed in, got the three forts within easy firing range of their own guns, and began to hammer away. Methodically they smashed salvo after salvo of shells against the great fortresses, rocking them on their bases, throwing out of alignment the great guns that still remained uninjured.

Cut off from the munitions dump by planes from the enemy carriers, the American gun crews bravely and defiantly fought a desperate battle. They could not be sure which of the mixed shells that had been sent up to them were good, which false. But—despite the sickening realization that their guns might burst—they pleaded to be permitted to "try."

Three more Nazi destroyers were sunk, two more guns burst before the unequal contest ended.

From the decks of Nazi airplane carriers came bombers and fighter planes to blast Fortress Monroe, at Old Point Comfort, Virginia, commanding the Hampton Roads entrance to the naval base at Norfolk. The skeleton force of planes from Langley Field that had already taken to the air had been hopelessly outnumbered and shot down.

That afternoon, preceded by efficient minesweepers, the navy of the German Reich sailed into Chesapeake Bay, whose mighty fortifications had been believed invincible.

Up historic Chesapeake Bay, where the British fleet had based in 1814 off Tilghman Island, sailed Adolf Hitler's navy. Overhead droned his advance guard of planes, a watchful aerial cavalry alert to smash any shore-based opposition.

Annapolis, bombarded from the air, was wrecked. Its Naval Academy was reduced to rubble and its Statehouse, where George Washington had resigned as commander in chief of the Revolutionary armies, destroyed by a direct bomb hit.

Darkness had fallen by the time the German fleet's leading ships turned into the Patapsco River and unleashed their guns on the inner-line defenses guarding the city of Baltimore. Fort Howard was destroyed quickly by attack from sea and air.

Fort McHenry could offer no resistance—it had been converted into a national park years before. Ironically, this famous fort had stubbornly and successfully defended the city when attacked from both land and sea by the British in 1814. It had been during that bombardment that a Maryland lawyer, prisoner aboard a British vessel, had thrilled at dawn to the sight of the American flag still waving from the fort and had written an inspired poem. The lawyer had been Francis Scott Key; his poem, later set to music, became "The Star-Spangled Banner," America's national anthem.

With Baltimore's shore defenses hammered into submission, the German train of cargo ships began swinging their equipment overboard onto the concrete docks under cover of the guns of her men-of-war. Except for three transports containing a compact division of crack Nazi infantry, no troops were being transported to Baltimore by water. Instead the huge train of cargo boats carried ammunition, tanks, food and medical supplies, trucks and heavy motorized artillery.

Troop transportation was being carried out entirely by means of huge long-range land- and seaplane transports that, landing in Delaware and Chesapeake Bays and on airports from Langley Field to Dover and Baltimore, came over in regular waves of five hundred. Each fleet of five hundred planes was capable of landing a division of men, and they were promptly shuttled to Baltimore's Municipal Airport, whence they marched to the docks to assemble and man tanks, infantry trucks, and motorized guns. The initial landing force of one division had already swung into action to batter down the last resistance of the invaded city.

Twenty-five hundred American troops of the Fifth Regiment, determined to offer enough resistance to cover the flight of Baltimore's civilians, had taken posts in a building of Johns Hopkins University. There, manning half a dozen light field pieces, light and heavy machine guns, and sniping with side arms and Garand rifles, the American "Suicide Regiment" made a last-ditch stand.

The heavy guns from Nazi battleships lying in the northwest branch of the Patapsco River might have shelled them out of their nest in a long-range bombardment. Instead, a regiment of German infantry was sent out to demonstrate the incredible firepower and clocklike teamwork of the German troops. Two sections of a Nazi heavy-weapons company took up posts on either side of the building and began pouring a withering crossfire of shells into it from their light field guns. Meanwhile, to prevent the bringing up of any reinforcements from the rear, big 150-millimeter howitzers lobbed shells over the building into University Parkway.

Caught in this merciless heavy barrage, the beleaguered American defenders fought stubbornly on, were slowly being subdued as heavy shells smashed men and weapons. But they had not yet seen all of the methodical German attack. Grenade throwers, crawling on their bellies to within 150 feet of the building, poured a constant rain of grenade fire at the building from concealed vantage points, while the two flanking companies, armed with howitzers and field guns, brought up their deadly crossfire, reinforced by seventy-two infantrymen manning heavy machine guns. As they moved in, ever closer, against the diminishing resistance from within the building, light-grenade throwers added their missiles to the inexorable crossfire.

Within half an hour all resistance—except that from a few desperate American troops sniping pitifully away with rifles—had been crushed. Not a field piece or machine gun seemed left intact.

A reserve mop-up company of Nazi troops entered the building, threaded their way among the dead, one of whom—a broad-shouldered, plaster-smeared Irish sergeant—lay grotesquely, still clutching a machine gun.

The company of German troops inspecting the ground floor

of the building were about to leave when a voice calmly inquired: "Which one of you homely galoots speaks English?"

The Nazi soldiers wheeled. From around one of the few remaining pillars on that floor protruded the homely snout of "dead" Sergeant Michael Donovan and the homelier snout of his machine gun. Half a dozen Nazi troops brought up their weapons, only to find themselves caught in Sergeant Donovan's mercilessly accurate fire.

Into the air went a hundred pairs of Nazi hands. Sergeant Donovan grinned. "I asked a civil question," he said. "A question, anyway. Who speaks English?"

A German officer stepped forward. "I do."

Sergeant Donovan of the Suicide Regiment, one wary eye on the floor entrance, told the German officer to order his men to remove their tunics and helmets and substitute those taken from American dead and wounded.

"Then pick up your guns—with your backs to me—and go to the windows and start shootin'," he ordered.

There was a mutter of protest, which Sergeant Donovan quelled with a burst of fire at their feet. They went to the windows, to be greeted by a withering barrage from the confused German troops outside.

"Ha!" said Donovan as they ducked. "You don't like it. Well, tell 'em so. Fire away, you Dutch dopes!"

His machine gun put a period to the order. They fired, half-heartedly, into the air. One of them, during a lull, shouted to his comrades outside in German.

"That won't help you," shouted Donovan. "They want this building. To get it, they got to take me. To take me they got to take *you*— the whole hundred of you. A hundred to one! And there's millions more of us Americans when I'm gone. That'll give you some idea of your chances. Now shoot, and shoot straight. You're a disgrace to the upper half of your uniform."

Three Germans wheeled from their window posts and sent bullets toward him. Six of them ripped into his left leg. He shifted his weight to the right and his machine gun chattered, killing the men who had shot him.

For one hour Sergeant "Hundred-to-One" Donovan held the building with his conscript army, while confused German officers outside pondered the problem. The solution was the grim expected one. The Nazi forces outside unleashed a hell of bombardment that, at the cost of their own mop-up squad, finally crushed the enforced resistance.

An Irish ex-truck driver became the first individual hero of the invasion of America. The story of heroic Sergeant Donovan, later learned from the lips of a German prisoner, inspired Americans from one end of the country to the other. A monument in his honor was erected at Springfield, provisional capital of America. "Hundred to one!" became the slogan, the rallying cry of American troops everywhere.

It was a slogan that at first proved difficult to follow. But, though the untried soldiers of a peace-loving nation were pitting themselves against the awful odds of the greatest war machine ever created, their spirits did not buckle.

"Remember Donovan," they told each other quietly.

After the fall of Baltimore, the German High Command sent division after division of Nazi troops into the city. They were flown in from assembly points as far away as the Azores, secret landing fields in the interior of Mexico, captured Canal Zone airports, and Brazil. By noon of the day after Nazi troops first had landed, roaring Panzer divisions had encircled Baltimore and its environs. The Nazi concentration and supply zone was enclosed in an arc that swept out from Sherwood Forest to Ellicott City to Bel Air and Havre de Grace.

When invading German troops established a line from Perryville to Delaware City, virtually the entire state of Delaware and portions of Maryland and Virginia were cut off. The flat sandy beaver-shaped peninsula formed by Chesapeake Bay and the Delaware River became a Nazi-controlled zone of the interior.

Meanwhile, the American General Staff, drawing its troops from as far north as Maine and as far south as Richmond, had concentrated its First Army in the Cumberland Valley. The United States Second Army was being mobilized in the Columbus, Ohio, area. General Headquarters for the United States air fleet had been moved from Langley Field to Port Columbus. First engagement between the Nazi and American forces occurred at Dug Hill Ridge, southeast of York, Pennsylvania, near the Pennsylvania-Maryland state line.

Norton and Jock Rodgers, ordered to the front, participated in that initial engagement. The first German drive had started northwest, and on the morning of September 1, 1945, German scouting planes and dive bombers roared above a clump of woods where an American mechanized division, its tanks hidden beneath trees, awaited the attack.

A fourth tank had been added to a tank platoon so that motion pictures could be taken. Jock Rodgers, his camera ready, sat deep in the light-armored ten-ton tank to the right of the driver, while Norton rode in the turret beside the tank's sergeant-commander. They were equipped with crash helmets and goggles.

"You're going to be black-and-blue tomorrow," the sergeant said. "These hell buggies weren't built for their riding qualities. We'll try to get you your pictures, but if the going gets too hot, you'd better forget about the pictures and go to work with your machine guns."

"What happens," Rodgers inquired, "if an antitank gun puts a bullet through our armor plate?"

The sergeant grinned. "It bounces around inside here until it gets tired. So don't forget to duck."

"I'm not sure I'm going to like this," said Rodgers.

They heard the German attacking forces before they saw them. Out of the southeast came a clattering, clanking rumble that swelled to a mighty thunder. Suddenly, around a road curve skirting a forest, burst the leading tanks of a Panzer division of 450—cloaked in dense smoke, guns cracking, steel tracks clattering, motors roaring as they lunged forward in a narrow column to attempt a breakthrough of the American lines of defense.

As their own combat car platoon went into action, Jock Rodgers found himself slammed from side to side and up and down in his seat, but he kept his camera grinding away through a machine-gun slot. He attempted to shout something to the driver, found his words drowned in the roar of motor, tracks, and guns.

Out of the smoke came the huge 70-ton steel monsters leading the Panzer division. He wondered desperately how anything devised by man could stop such land battleships. As they thundered on in wave after relentless wave, he saw the American heavy tanks charge them, blasting away with 37-millimeter cannons.

He saw a massive German tank come to a grinding halt as a shell ripped loose its track. He saw an American light tank veer crazily and driverless as a penetrating bullet sent a spray of steel splinters into the bodies of driver and port sponson gunner.

The American mechanized division's oblique attack from

ambush forced the thundering column of Nazi tanks to the right through a flat field. And for a moment, victory seemed assured as land mines, carefully planted for just such a maneuver, were tripped and let go with devastating explosions as the leading Nazi tanks ran over them. But the following tanks of the Panzer division quickly swung back onto the roadway, matching their own heavy-fire power with that of the American mechanized division.

Recklessly the Nazi tanks charged on toward the American artillery lines where antitank defenses, manned by men in trenchlike foxholes, awaited their approach.

The leading tanks had spread out in "gangs" of three, and when they were within 1,000 yards of the first group of concealed antitank guns, the American crews fired. Norton saw the sergeant riding in the tank turret beside him scowl. He could not hear the words he uttered, but reading his lips, he caught the phrases:

"Damn it! Hold fire! Hold fire!"

What he saw next was another macabre nightmare of modern warfare. In firing, the defending American gun crews had revealed their positions. Nazi tanks, charging them, ripped the foxholes with bursts of fire. One American ground crew, unhit by the guns of the advancing tanks, was trapped in its foxhole and cremated by a twenty-foot stream of liquid fire. Still another gun crew, crouching helplessly in its pit, was raked with bullets fired from the Nazi tank's machine guns against a rear splash plate that deflected the stream of death into the subterranean gun trench.

And then Norton saw the tank sergeant wheel about beside him in the turret to man his .30-caliber anti-aircraft gun. Norton ducked as the roaring Nazi dive bombers came down at them. He heard the chatter of the anti-aircraft gun, saw a bomb drop ahead of them and pit the earth, felt his head smash against the steel sides of their tank as they slammed down into the shell hole and tipped up precariously to ride its far slope to level ground. And, to one side, he saw the smashed and burning plane that the tank sergeant had brought down.

Most of the dive bombers had gone on ahead to blast with bombs and rake with machine-gun fire the gun positions that until now they had been unable to spot from the air. Screaming down out of a one-sided dogfight that raged high above, they attacked tanks and anti-tank gun crews with efficient ferocity.

Under the precisely coordinated onslaught of the Nazi Panzer division, American resistance had crumbled. The German breakthrough had been accomplished. The American mechanized division was split and scattered, its artillery defenses wiped out. A flanking movement now might pocket those tanks remaining. The sergeant signaled the driver by kicking against his right shoulder. Their combat car wheeled swiftly and fled to the right.

They reached bivouac that night and talked with other tank commanders who had escaped. From their observations, Norton compiled a report. Some of the American medium tanks had blind spots that needed correction. More streamlined tanks, capable of offering minimum area of vulnerability to enemy fire, were needed. Antitank guns of greater velocity were required. But . . .

Sergeant Graves, who had commanded the tank in which Rodgers and Norton had engaged in the "Battle of Dug Hill Ridge," summed it up. "Coordination," he said quietly. "A long word for training, training, and more training. And training under fire. We're up against veterans. They have planes helping them. We haven't—yet.

"You saw our antitank defenses get it this afternoon. They fired too soon. I don't say you or I wouldn't have done the same thing. When seventy tons of steel is charging down on you, you're liable to get an itchy trigger finger. But our men have got to learn that fire has to be held until those big fellows are within a thousand feet of them. Then's the time to blast away. If they score a hit—and they should at that distance—they've got a Nazi tank. If they miss . . ." He shrugged. "Then they're dead pigeons. It's nerve-racking to wait for a sure shot when all hell is coming at you. But we're going to lose a lot of men and tanks and battles until we get the knack of those two words, 'Hold fire.'

"This is a brand-new kind of war to us. Once we get the hang of it, we can kick the hell out of those Germans. We've got the equipment. Except for a few bugs, it's all right. Now we've got to learn to use it."

The next day, Rodgers and Norton flew to Springfield, Illinois, the new seat of America's government, to deliver their report and motion picture record. Their bodies ached from bruised muscles received the day before.

A newspaper they picked up at an airport en route to Springfield carried dismal news. The German Expeditionary Force had pushed across the Susquehanna. Even as they read the accounts of the battle in which they had participated, Nazi troops were marching up Market Street in Wilmington, Delaware.

And the Second Army of the German Expeditionary Force had pushed southwest to America's deserted capital.

Up Pennsylvania Avenue, in Washington, marched three divisions of Adolf Hitler's crack and seasoned troops. And as they marched they sang triumphantly:

> *Make way, make way, here come the brown battalions!*
> *Make way, make way, the Storm Troop men are here!*
> *Upon the Swastika the millions look with longing.*
> *The day of freedom and of bread is near.*
>
> *At last, at last, we hear the bugle calling!*
> *It finds us armed and eager for the fray.*
> *Soon Hitler's flags will fly throughout the nation,*
> *Soon bitter slav'ry will have passed away.*

The words were those of the Nazi anthem—the Horst Wessel song.

" 'Freedom and bread,' " snarled Jock Rodgers. "Why, that son of a—"

"How about his flags flying throughout the nation?" Norton inquired. "Can you imagine the swastika flying from the Capitol?"

It was no longer something that required imagination; for even as Norton spoke, the German emblem floated in the breeze from a perch atop the bronze statue of Freedom on the Capitol's dome.

In the bustling, confused, and suddenly expanded city of Springfield, Illinois, Norton felt a stab of nostalgic, painful remembrance. Close by this city that had become the nation's temporary capital was the little town of Clinton, Illinois, home of Peggy O'Liam.

He and Jock Rodgers were taken to an office building. A black-and-white painted sign over its entrance proclaimed it to be the WAR AND NAVY BUILDING. In a tiny unpretentious cubicle on the third floor they found Admiral Dugal O'Shane.

"Glad to see you, men," he said. "We took a hell of a beating our first time out. We'll get better."

Rodgers left his motion-picture record; Norton submitted his report. Admiral O'Shane asked to speak to Lieutenant Norton alone.

When the door had been closed behind Rodgers, Norton began. "May I ask, sir—"

Admiral O'Shane waved him to silence. "You want to know about Miss O'Liam."

"Yes, sir. Has there been any word?"

"There has," said O'Shane gruffly. A muscle in his jaw moved. His eyes dropped under Norton's eager stare. "Sit down, boy! Sit down!

"When the Nazis cut off the peninsula—and most of Delaware with it—one of the first things they did was to establish a concentration camp. Did you know we have a concentration camp on American soil?"

The blood drained out of Norton's face. Cold fear seized him, and he wished desperately that the older man would come to the point. "No, sir," he replied politely.

"Well, we have. Concentration camp. Never thought I'd live to see one established in America. It's on Assateague Island. Know where that is?"

"No, sir."

"Well, it's down near the tail of the peninsula. Narrow, uninhabited strip of land that lies between the eastern tip of Maryland and the Atlantic Ocean. Right on the ocean.

"Now, in addition to the concentration camp, they've set up a 'People's Court.' It's at Salisbury, Maryland."

Norton could stand it no longer. "For heaven's sake, will you get on with it, sir? What's happened to Peggy?"

Admiral O'Shane drew himself erect and his eyes became hard. "Mister Norton!" he snapped.

"I'm sorry, sir. Believe me, I'm very sorry."

"You needn't be," the older man said softly. "I'm doing a hard job rather poorly. Anyway, in the Nazi-occupied peninsula, farmers who destroy crops, insult Hitler, refuse to work for the German officers, or who hoard food are brought into the People's Court. I guess I don't have to tell you what their system of 'justice' amounts to. No trial. They listen to evidence. The offender is sent to the concentration camp. Hard labor. Our agents in that territory have managed to get word out to us. Scores still awaiting trial. Miss O'Liam is one of them."

In a voice that was hoarse and without hope, Norton asked: "Is her trial scheduled?"

"Yes. The day after tomorrow."

"And the charge, sir?"

"She is charged with being a spy."

"Has she any possible chance, sir?"

Admiral O'Shane got up and walked to the window and, turning his back on Norton, blew his nose lustily.

"She has no chance whatever," O'Shane said gently. "She will be convicted of being a spy. The penalty, to be carried out after twenty-four hours, will be—death."

CHAPTER 9

A HAZARDOUS ENTERPRISE

Death! The grim finality of the word left Norton numb with despair. And yet he realized with horrible certainty that O'Shane was not painting a distorted picture. From the sentence of a Nazi "People's Court" there was no appeal—except to Hitler himself.

These secret tribunals, presided over by five judges (three of whom would be military men), promptly rewarded treason with death. And the charge of "treason" had many definitions, espionage being one of the most common.

True, if Peggy O'Liam were able, she would be permitted to plead her own case at her secret trial. She would even be permitted counsel—a Nazi lawyer who, though he took no part in the proceedings, would make a short speech in her behalf. But even the lawyer assigned her would be hand-picked by the court itself. And the court would be not in the least concerned with any mitigating circumstances. It would seek to establish one thing, and one thing only: that Peggy O'Liam was, or had been, dangerous to the Nazi cause—to a state whose goal was world conquest.

Once that broad line of reasoning had been established, the girl was doomed. The death sentence would be coldly inflicted. And then—within twenty-four hours—she would be shot!

The cold fingers of nausea gripped him, and he knew that if he tried to speak to O'Shane, his voice could not be trusted. But there was nothing left to be said. He was scarcely conscious of the fact that O'Shane was speaking.

The older man had turned from the window. His face was grave, his habitual bluster gone.

"I feel a personal sense of responsibility for what has happened," Admiral O'Shane said wearily. "If that girl were a member of Naval Intelligence, trained for dangerous work, she would know—and understand—that having been caught, she must face whatever lies in store for her. But she's just a youngster, a civilian. She's done her best for her country—at my request. If she dies, then I sent her to her death."

That, Norton realized, was true. Yet strangely, he felt no bitterness toward the other man. Rather—deeply as he loved the girl—he cursed the circumstances that had swung her life into the orbit of his own. Now, when the surging memory of her youth, her loveliness, her eager zest for life rose up before him, he felt a fear for her that left him weak, wretched.

"At the hands of the German People's Court she can expect no mercy, no possible chance," Admiral O'Shane repeated. "I don't know whether the plan I have will offer much more."

Norton shoved up out of the chair. Hope blazed high in his eyes.

"Plan, sir?"

"Sit down, please," Admiral O'Shane said. "I don't want to raise your hopes. I particularly don't wish to do that. Chances for success are infinitesimal. You may well fail. If you do, your own life will be lost. And there can be no further attempt."

Norton wanted to shout that a single chance, however small, would be enough; that he cared nothing about his own life. With difficulty he remained silent.

O'Shane pushed a button on his desk. An aide entered.

"Send in Captain Wiegand," he directed.

A young man in the uniform of a naval captain entered the

room. His round rosy-cheeked face, blond hair, and blue eyes made him seem unbelievably young for his rank. He was commander of the United States submarine X36. When Norton had shaken hands with Wiegand, O'Shane explained:

"Wiegand sails secretly tonight, on a very dangerous mission. Confidentially, his goal will be the region of Chesapeake and Delaware Bays, now occupied by strong units of the German navy. His mission will be to harass and inflict as much damage on the enemy's ships as possible.

"Thank God, the capture of the Canal found most of our submarines in the Atlantic. Without the Navy, we can't hope to cut the enemy's line of communications across the Atlantic Ocean. We can only try.

"The point of this as it affects you, Norton, is that in the natural course of duty, Captain Wiegand's mission will bring him into the Atlantic off Assateague Island, where the enemy has a concentration camp. That camp consists of a number of tents just now. Barracks are under construction by American prisoners sentenced to hard labor. They aren't ready yet. At the southern tip of the tent camp are two tents set somewhat apart from the others, which house prisoners condemned to die.

"On Wednesday night Captain Martin Fleming of Naval Intelligence will be an occupant of one of those tents. Miss O'Liam will be in the other. Your specific assignment, Norton, will be to effect, if possible, the rescue of Captain Fleming. He possesses information badly needed by the Department. I need not point out to you that if, without endangering your mission, you can also effect the rescue of any other Americans who may be in the 'condemned' tents, the government will be pleased. Is that clear?"

"It is—and thank you, sir!"

"I'm not sure that you should thank me," O'Shane said seriously. "It's a nasty job. The entire concentration camp is enclosed by a barbed-wire fence, which we believe is electrically charged. If the sentries discover you, you will be shot, most certainly. Nor, should things go badly, can we risk the loss of one of our submarines at this time. Wiegand's orders are to leave the scene immediately should there be a slipup. If necessary, it will be his duty to shove off without you—all of you. I want you to understand that."

"I quite understand, sir."

"Further," continued O'Shane, "even if you succeed in returning to the submarine, you will be far from safe. Wiegand's mission borders on suicide—and you'll necessarily remain with him until he gets back to port. Good luck to both of you!"

While awaiting the plane that was to fly them to the Atlantic Coast, Norton and the blond submarine commander had lunch with Jock Rodgers.

"I'll be missing you, fellow," Rodgers said. "They're sending me up to the Pennsylvania front. They expect a second battle of Gettysburg up there in a few days. The Germans are trying to push our forces back across the Alleghenies. They've got forty divisions on our soil now, and they've taken a bite of our coastline from as far north as Chester, Pennsylvania, on the Delaware River, to Virginia Beach, below Norfolk. They're as far inland as Frederick.

"That's a pretty good bite. But it doesn't chew as easily as they expected. Despite their breakthroughs, they're having one hell of a time consolidating their positions. Apparently we Americans aren't quite as soft as they had us figured. They admit in their own communiqués that they are meeting stubborn resistance. Hell, we're just fumbling now. Wait until we get mad.

"The army's civilian spotter system is paying big dividends. Some farmer kid spots one of their tank divisions bivouacked for the night, and sneaks through their lines to the nearest telephone. Our air headquarters relays the word on to GHQ, and we slip around them with armored scout cars and cut them off. Last night we pocketed half a division and more than a hundred tanks near Unionville, Maryland.

"Our separate air wing is beginning to work, too. Instead of parceling out our squadrons all over the country when some politician lets out a yell, we're bunching them for defense where they're needed, and consolidating them with ground forces where the big pushes take place.

"They've been hammering away with their bombers at our industrial centers: Pittsburgh, Philadelphia, Bridgeport, Springfield, Massachusetts—even as far inland as Erie, Buffalo, and Detroit. What we lack in planes we've more than made up for in anti-aircraft defenses at those spots. Not a one of them has been successfully raided yet, though they did set a hell of a fire at Scranton with incendiary bombs.

"If our inland factories can turn out planes faster than they can bring theirs over and we can stalemate them for a while, we're all right. I'd feel better, though, if we had our Navy around the Horn and the Japs and Russians out of our hair."

"What's happening in the Northwest?" Norton asked.

"They're pushing down the coast, east of the coast ranges. Our line is at Eugene, Oregon, now. The Japs and Russians have taken Portland and Salem, but their line of supply has been nearly severed half a dozen times. It seems that every farmer who can throw a stone is sneaking down out of the mountains and letting fly.

"They're superior in concentration of equipment and in manpower, but they're getting the same kind of headaches from our people that they got in Finland. Funny thing, one of their chief reasons for holding us Americans in contempt has been that we're such a mixture of races. The Russians aren't finding that so funny at the moment. Up in the State of Washington there's a settlement of farmers who came to this country from Finland years ago. They've been aching for a shot at Mr. Stalin's boys anyway, and from letters they got from their relatives in Finland during the Russo-Finnish War, they know just how to go about it. They've been making 'Molotov cocktails.' And you know as well as I do what they do to a tank!

"The Reds have tried chasing farmers into the woods, and have found it suicide. Every tree begins shooting bullets at them. If they expect to push across the Cascade Mountains up there, they're going to have to learn Indian fighting."

On the plane bearing him and Captain Wiegand to the coast, Norton read an afternoon paper. Its news stories made no effort to minimize the seriousness of America's position. Its Air Force riddled, its bases gone, its Navy somewhere in the South Pacific and its armies locked in battle both on the East and West Coasts and along the troublesome Rio Grande, America was fighting a struggle for her very existence.

But the morale of the country had never been better. In 1940 the American people had talked somewhat vaguely of national defense, which had been a political football, a matter of appropriating money— and more money. And it had not been enough.

Now the American people talked of "our emergency." An

emergency called not merely for appropriations but for hard work and the laying aside of all thoughts of partisanship, in the common good. For sacrifice—by all, impartially.

There was a great and heartening difference. The political leaders of the country worked in smooth harmony. The workers offered their services "for the duration," not on the basis of a forty-hour week but on the basis of their physical abilities to meet longer and longer hours. Industrialists, many of whom had risen from a factory lathe to mighty executive berths, returned to their plants to man a lathe.

America did not follow the disastrous course that had been taken by quarrelsome, indifferent France. Before actual invasion, the country had awakened to the hard fact that only utmost sacrifice by all would save it. It became a point of individual pride, not duty, to make those sacrifices.

A great country built by sweat and hardship and sacrifice was returning to the precepts of its pioneers; was abandoning the good things of the present for the better things of the future—and being proud of the right, jealously guarded for centuries, to make its sacrifices voluntarily!

With a newfound faith both in itself and its leaders, America promised to be invincible. That there were dark days ahead was calmly accepted. A common danger had bludgeoned panic, defeatism, and differences of all kinds out of a now firmly united people.

After dusk, the plane bearing Norton and Wiegand landed at Manteo Municipal Airport in North Carolina. The woods to the west of the airport had been cleared and the field's runway strips extended.

The coastal airport lay at the junction of Albemarle and Pamlico Sounds, on Roanoke Island, north of stormy Cape Hatteras and not far south of Kitty Hawk, where years earlier the Wright brothers had demonstrated that man could fly—had thereby added another dimension to war.

A motor launch took them out into the winding channel to where the X36, her superstructure and barrel-shaped conning tower painted gray, rode at anchor, scarcely visible in the early darkness.

As they boarded her, Norton was puzzled. Every American submarine he had ever seen had been painted black. And the X36 bore no identification number.

He preceded Wiegand down the iron ladder from the conning tower to the control room. Five minutes later, traveling on the surface, they stood out to sea.

If Norton was puzzled by the submarine, he was no less puzzled by the boat's youthful commander. Wiegand, quiet almost to the point of shyness, spoke little. His name, combined with his blond features, fairly shrieked his German ancestry. Yet he was in charge of an American submarine.

He was, in addition, an extraordinarily capable commander. He issued his orders quietly, succinctly. And a crew that obviously adored him obeyed with well-trained swiftness. Morale and efficiency in the close quarters and bad air of a submarine could not always be held at a high level. They were surprisingly high aboard the X36.

When, with quiet politeness, Captain Wiegand invited Norton to share his cramped cabin with him, Norton, eager to learn more of his host, quickly accepted.

In a room crowded with gadgets, gauges, pipes, and valves they ate good food at a well-set table. Joachim Wiegand, warming gradually to a sense of trust in his guest, began to talk.

He was American-born, of German parents who had brought him, as a baby, to Milwaukee.

"My uncle," he said, "was in the German navy during the First World War. He was one of the surviving members of the crew of the German submarine U-156 that raided American waters during that war. It was the U-156 that planted the mine that blew up and sank America's armored cruiser San Diego off Fire Island.

"Now," said Wiegand, with a faint smile, "the tables are reversed. It is American submarines that will raid the shipping of the Germans."

Deftly Captain Wiegand probed Norton's unspoken thoughts.

"You are surprised, perhaps, that I—the son of German parents—should command an American submarine."

"Frankly, yes."

"If this war," said Wiegand softly, "does nothing more than banish the troublemaking, overworked word 'tolerance' from our language, then it'll be worth all the suffering that's ahead of us. We're just learning now that tolerance, if it is to exist at all, is something that must be taken casually, for granted, not something to make a speech about.

"So I'll make a speech about it," Wiegand grinned. "Let me tell you a story: During the First World War, I was a boy of seven in Milwaukee. My German name didn't help me. A name like mine was 'pro-German.' One day my schoolmates beat me up and tore my clothes and threw mud on me. An older boy drove them off. He picked me up. I was crying.

" 'What are you sniveling about?' he asked.

" 'They beat me up.'

" 'I know that. Why did they do it?'

" 'Because I am a German.'

" 'Damn it, you talk like some of my people. I'm a Jew. Now, you listen to me. Have you done anything to make them beat you up? Have you cheated them, or hurt them, or done anything to them you would not want them to do to you?'

" 'No. They beat me up because I am a German.'

" 'Shut up. That's no reason. You want to know why they beat you up? I'll tell you. Because they are a bunch of stupid, excitable fools. Germans, Jews, Swedes, Italians. What the hell's the difference? We're human beings—and Americans—in this country. They know that. They know it deep down inside. But you've got to remind them. You've got to treat them decent and forget they treated you rotten. And they'll be ashamed. It's up to you, not them. Do you understand?' "

Wiegand smiled. "That's how I met Jake Goldstein. We've been together ever since. He's my chief gunner—and one of the best marksmen in the Navy. He'd lay down his life for me. And I'd cheerfully cut your throat if you put a hand on Jake. You're surprised that, with my name, I should command this submarine. My name's no more of a handicap to me than Jake Goldstein's has been to him. We both play the game squarely, and we have no complaints.

"When war first broke out in Europe, a Gestapo agent came to me. He told me that my uncle in Germany was in a concentration camp and that if I expected him to get out, I would become a 'must' Nazi and give him information about our Navy. It wasn't pleasant to juggle the life of my mother's brother in my hands. I went to my superior officers and told them. They asked me to take a month's leave while they investigated. I did. They arrested the Gestapo agent. My uncle died in the concentration camp.

"I was raised in rank and given command of this submarine. I'm proud that my government should have as much confidence in me as I have in my government. And I'll take a special pleasure in helping you cheat the Assateague concentration camp of two of its victims."

Within the next few weeks, the team of Wiegand and Goldstein was to write American naval history. At dawn of the next day, Norton went into the control room just as Wiegand sighted a large steamship through the periscope. So confident was Germany of her mastery of the Atlantic that she was bringing men and weapons across without convoy. Captain Wiegand was to shake that easy confidence. He ordered the X36 to battle surface.

"Come along," he said quietly to Norton. "Watch Jake box her in."

On the submarine's decks, Jake Goldstein's gun crew went to work. Their first shot slashed across the ship's bow. As she changed course to make a run for it, they dropped a second shell neatly across her stern.

Still she sought to elude the American submarine. As a third shell ripped a hole in her side six feet above waterline, she hove to. Her crew took to the lifeboats while her captain rowed alongside the X36, bringing her papers.

She was the 15,286-ton *Berlin* of the German merchant fleet. She carried aboard her tank, field guns, a store of aviation gasoline, and some troops.

Wiegand sent a crew of his men to board the *Berlin* and examine her cargo. They hung time bombs on her and, as they returned to the X36, she exploded with a mighty roar, heeled over on her side, and went down.

In that first day of sea raiding, Wiegand and his men sank six Nazi ships, among them the speedy 1,811-ton armored destroyer *Karl Galster*, which had been sent out late in the afternoon in an attempt to hunt down and destroy the X36.

Recklessly, Wiegand braved almost certain destruction to bring his submarine within fatal range of the *Galster*'s five 5-inch guns, to blast a gaping hole in her with a torpedo that gutted her engine room.

On the second day, Wiegand further slashed at the Nazi sea communications by sinking five more ships, among them the *Neue Deutschland,* formerly the 26,943-ton *Britannic* of the British merchant marine.

That night, lying out in the Atlantic, they listened to radio news broadcasts from Chicago. A furious German Admiralty characterized the attacks upon German ships bringing reserve equipment and troops to the United States as "piratical barbarism" and "flagrant and inhuman violation of the rules of international warfare." The Admiralty promised that a continuance of "such tactics" would bring "annihilating retaliation."

Jake Goldstein, smoking a cigarette in the conning tower with Wiegand and Norton, grinned. "Cripes!" he said. "They can dish it out, but they can't take it."

Indignant because the lone American raider was painted the color of German submarines and wore no identifying number, the German Admiralty had placed a price on the head of its crew members. The equivalent of five thousand dollars per man was offered for information that would result in the capture of the unidentified submarine; twenty-five thousand dollars was offered, to be split among the crew members of any German vessel able to establish that they had sunk her.

"Hell," Goldstein said. "I ought to turn myself in. I've never been worth that kind of folding money before."

"Wait!" Norton said.

The 11 P.M. news announcer said: "The official German radio at Salisbury, Maryland, tonight announced that fifty American prisoners were convicted in the People's Court there today of crimes against the Greater United German Reich. Most of the offenders were farmers within the German-occupied territory who had been charged with destroying their crops or refusing to obey orders issued by German officers. Most have been sentenced to ten years at hard labor.

"The U.S. State Department has been unable, however, to obtain information concerning the sentences inflicted upon two American citizens found guilty this afternoon by the People's Court of what the German radio characterized as 'rank treason.' The penalty for treason is death.

"The two convicted persons were Miss Margaret O'Liam of Clinton, Illinois, and Captain Martin Fleming, a member of Naval Intelligence. Despite pleas for . . ."

Wiegand rose to switch off the radio.

"So they advanced their trials one day," he said softly. He sent a glance filled with sympathy at Norton. "Cheer up, my friend. It merely means that we'll have to get there tonight."

"But can we make it?"

"I think so. With luck—and we'll need luck, running on the surface without lights—we should be there by three in the morning."

"If the Captain please, sir," Goldstein said to Wiegand, "I'd like to go ashore with Mister Norton when we reach Assateague. He'll need help, sir, and . . ."

"And you'd like to get ashore and stretch your legs," said Wiegand.

"Yes, sir."

"We'll see."

Only once during their run were they in danger. That was when the sharp prow of a Nazi battleship had knifed out of the darkness ahead of them and almost rammed their craft. Traveling under blue battle lights, the warship had not seen them as it plowed past so close that they could distinguish her lines. It was the new 15,000-ton pocket battleship *Admiral Raeder*.

"We'll meet her again," Wiegand predicted.

At two forty-five that morning they were off the sandy strip that was Assateague Island. In the distance, through night glasses, they could pick out the outline of the tents of Assateague concentration camp.

On the deck of the submarine, Jake laid out the equipment he had assembled for their visit to the island: bolt and wire cutters, with insulated handles; a hatchet, a blue-lensed flashlight, revolvers, hunting knives, four black oilskins, a coil of rope, two trench shovels.

He inflated a gas-filled rubber life raft, and they got aboard. Lieutenant Wiegand stooped down to shake hands with them.

"Good luck," he said. His face was grave. "You understand that should you be captured, or should I be forced to leave here, the enemy isn't to know how you got on this island."

Jake, dressed in civilian clothes, nodded. "This won't take long," he promised.

They rowed quietly to shore. They pulled the rubber raft up onto the shore and partially covered it with a camouflage of sand, against possible detection by some wandering sentry.

Norton, his eyes straining through the gloom of a moonless

night, could see the wire fence a hundred yards ahead of them and, beyond, the tents. There was a row of many tents huddled together, and then two tents at one end by themselves. Norton blessed the methodical Teutonic nature that carefully placed condemned prisoners in their own separate locations.

As they crept forward, Jake's fingers suddenly squeezed his arm. Instinctively Norton dropped flat on his belly behind a clump of beach grass.

About a hundred feet to his left, some distance beyond the wire fence, silently strode a German sentry, a rifle across his shoulder. They huddled together, holding their breath. The sentry moved on— and down the line of tents. They crept forward to the fence. Jake studied it carefully.

"Probably charged," he said, and reached for the wire cutters.

"Wait a minute," Norton whispered. "These Germans are clever about such things. If we cut our way through, we may set off an alarm. Let's dig."

They found a section of the fence behind a mound that shielded them from the camp inside. They took turns, one watching, one digging silently, in the soft sand. Norton finished the hole.

"O.K., Jake. All clear?"

"Clear," said Jake. As Norton huddled down to wriggle beneath the fence, the other man whispered: "There'll probably be a guard or two at the tents. I'll take them. You get the girl and Captain Fleming out."

Norton saw his companion unsheathe a hunting knife. He nodded grimly. They crawled through the hole, took a careful look down the line of tents where the sentry had vanished. Noiselessly they sped across the soft sands toward the two tents, approaching from the side. Crouched there, Norton looked around the back of the tents and saw no one.

Jake, peering around the front of the tents, raised a warning hand of caution. Then the hand—his left—swept down in a signal that said, "Ready!"

Jake sprang. Norton plunged after him like a back following interference. He saw that there was one guard. And he saw Jake's left arm encircle the man to catch him as his right rose and fell against the guard's ribs. With a sound resembling nothing more than a mild sigh, the man collapsed. Jake was lowering him to the ground as Norton plunged into the near tent.

"Peggy!" he whispered.

"What the hell is this?" a man's voice asked.

He saw the outline of the man sitting up on a cot.

"Captain Fleming? I'm Norton, Naval Intelligence. This is a break. Where's Miss O'Liam?"

"Next tent. Am I glad to see you!"

He was throwing aside bedclothes as Norton ducked outside, hurrying into the other tent. Accustomed to the gloom, his eyes saw the girl sitting up in bed in terror. He half saw, half sensed her mouth opening to scream and slapped an open palm across it. His other arm circled her shoulders tightly, protectively.

"Peggy! Peggy, it's Doug. We're getting you out of here."

He felt her shiver a little, felt the tautness leave, felt a tear course down warmly against his hand. He took his hand away.

"Oh, my darling," she said, "I thought I'd never see you again!"

The others were waiting outside.

"I think that damned guard's due soon," Jake growled softly.

Captain Fleming was fingering one of the knives they had brought along. "If it's that black-shirted devil who used a whip on me this afternoon, I'd like right well to meet up with him."

Both Peggy O'Liam and Captain Fleming were dressed in black uniforms on the back of which had been sewn white circles of luminous cloth—a target, by day or night, for a guard's rifle.

They slipped into the dark oilskins that had been brought along and set out toward the electrically charged fence. They found the hole and wriggled through it one by one.

They looked about, saw no one. Norton lifted Peggy O'Liam into his arms, squeezing her with a mingled sense of triumph and exhilaration that made him want to shout. They set off at a trot toward the water.

Jake's sharp eyes found the partly buried rubber raft without difficulty. As they pulled it to the water's edge, Jake said, "Won't hold us all. I'll swim."

They got the raft into the water and headed out from shore. Norton, cradling the girl in his arms, shone the dim blue rays of the flashlight into her face for a fraction of a second. He saw a face pale and wan, hollow-eyed and haggard. He held her tight in blinding fury and asked:

"Oh, my darling, what have they done to you?"

"I'll be all right," she said, "—now. It was ghastly, Doug.

"You have no chance in their People's Court. Baron von Holtz was one of the five judges. I don't ever want to remember it again. And I need sleep so badly. I'm very tired."

"Of course," he said softly. "It's all over now."

"All over," she repeated. "It's all—"

The deafening wail of a siren drowned out her words. He felt her jerk in terror, and he felt fear run an icy finger up the back of his own neck.

"Easy, Peggy," he said. "We're almost there. We're safe!"

He looked around. Lights were springing on about the concentration camp. He heard a babble of voices, of shouting, as the siren died down. Then it was wailing again, a blood-chilling, vindictive shriek of derision. Men with lanterns were racing up and down. High on an observation tower, a searchlight swung its shaft up and down the sandy beach, then oceanward. It lacked the candlepower to reach them.

Norton leaned away from the girl, bent down toward Jake, who swam along behind the raft, holding on and pushing it.

"How much farther is it, Jake?"

"We're there now."

"Do you mean . . . ?"

Jake raised his hands, palms upward, in an expressive gesture, then grabbed the raft again with one hand, pointed to the left with his other. Norton followed the pointed finger with his eyes. It took him a minute to locate what Jake had seen against the horizon. A large ship— a destroyer, perhaps, or a cruiser, running a patrol across the path where Captain Wiegand would have waited for them. And now Wiegand and the X36 were gone!

Norton felt his last hope leave him. He felt licked, impotent and coldly furious. The siren rose and fell mockingly. By this time men were running along the beach. When the siren fell, he could hear the sound of rowlocks squeaking. They were dragging a boat out. It would not take them long now.

Peggy O'Liam sensed his thoughts. "Something's gone wrong, darling?"

"Yes."

"I'd rather drown than go back."

"We're not licked yet, Peggy."

But as he crushed her to him, he knew that they were. And as her arms tightened about him, he knew that she knew it, too.

He could hear the slap of oars somewhere behind them, and he thought bitterly:

To get this far—and lose!

CHAPTER 10

THE BATTLE OF CHESAPEAKE BAY

And then, when all hope was gone, he heard a rushing noise ahead. He saw the water turn white, saw a curtain of water rise and fall back from a submarine conning tower twenty feet away. A gray conning tower —the color of a German U-boat.

But it was the American X36 doing a quick "battle surface." He shook the sobbing girl in his arms and shouted, "We've made it, Peggy! We've made it!"

Captain Wiegand was up on the bridge while the submarine's deck was still awash. Members of the crew scrambled to the deck and pulled the rubber raft alongside. Norton, Captain Fleming, and Peggy were taken aboard. Norton leaned back down to give Jake a hand. Jake, treading water, shook his head.

"Get her below first," he said—and whispered to Norton, "I've swam out o' my pants."

While Peggy was being helped down into the control room, a sailor unlimbered a machine gun on the bridge. Another broke out a searchlight that swept the waters shoreward. Jake Goldstein, in shirt-tails, reached the bridge in time to man the machine gun as the searchlight picked out the two boats that were now pursuing them.

With deadly accuracy, contemptuous of the fire being turned on him by the approaching boats, the big gunner poured machine-gun bullets into them. One boat, riddled, began to sink; the other bobbed on the waters, unmanned.

As the Americans climbed down the iron ladder into the control room, Jake grinned. "Who said those Heinies are tough?" he inquired.

Captain Wiegand gave Peggy O'Liam his own tiny but snug cabin, moving his rig to a bunk in the torpedo room. Most of that day, they cruised underwater off the Virginia Capes. Shoreward, through glasses, they could see zigzagging Nazi destroyers and low-flying reconnaissance planes.

"Tonight," Captain Wiegand told Norton, "we are going to mine the entrance to Chesapeake Bay, just north of Hampton Roads." He spoke casually, yet Norton knew the task could be ticklish. Norfolk had become a Nazi naval base, the bay a great German-controlled lake.

They approached the mouth of it about dusk. Across the mouth were lined up a score or more of tiny craft. These were "drifters"; their job, to service a submarine net, hung from a boom, that extended almost all the way across. Beyond the net lay a thickly sown minefield. Drifters, anchored, formed a great rectangle about it and guarded its outer edges with searchlights. Inside the rectangle Nazi patrol boats maintained armed watch, while others kept the water between the net and the minefield under constant observation.

Altogether, any American submarine attempting to enter the bay would be virtually committing suicide. Yet Captain Wiegand said quietly, "I think we can get inside. We're painted gray. We carry no identification number, but it's possible they'll figure that we must be German—that no American craft would dare show herself here. It's worth trying. Whether we can get out again or not . . ." He shrugged. "We'll have to try that, too."

For the Nazi warships, a twisting, mine-free channel was maintained along the Cape Charles shore. Lying offshore in the dusk, the Americans watched a number of Nazi destroyers and cruisers come in from patrol and enter the channel.

Suddenly their own lookout cried, "Sail ho, sir! She's a battle-wagon!"

"Where away?"

"Dead astern, sir."

Behind them, plowing in from open sea, came a Nazi light cruiser, the *Karlsruhe*. They dived, sat quietly on the bottom, motors off, and listened to the whirring sound of her screws as she passed over them. Then they surfaced and fell in line behind her.

They followed her through the narrow channel between shore and the submarine net, then slowed down as they approached the edge of the minefield. She had reached that spot in the channel where two Nazi cruisers guarded it. As she came up to pass between the two, her blinker flashed recognition signals to them. Norton heard Wiegand read the signals off to a member of his crew, who wrote them down.

A fine drizzle had set in, and those on the bridge of the X36 were clothed in dark oilskins. Following in the wake of the *Karlsruhe,* Captain Wiegand flashed the stolen recognition signals. The men aboard the cruisers shouted greetings, acknowledged the signals, and did not bother to sweep this submarine's decks with a searchlight.

"We've made it!" Norton gasped.

Captain Wiegand consulted his watch. "We have fifteen minutes," he said. "Then the attack begins."

They located the new and mighty ships of Germany's First Battle Division riding at anchor. Wiegand lined up his submarine so that her torpedo tubes were trained directly amidships on the 40,000-ton *Adolf Hitler,* pride of the Nazi navy.

Exactly fifteen minutes later, shore sirens screamed and searchlights sent up their shafts of light through a low-hanging murky overcast. From above it, American bombers dropped screaming down in a surprise attack. Brilliant flares lighted up that section of the bay, and for the first time Norton saw America's bombsights, the finest in the world, begin to take their toll.

Breaking through the overcast, the bombers dropped their H. E. eggs and thermite incendiaries. Hits were scored on the aircraft carrier *Admiral Hipper,* which was set ablaze, and upon the cruiser *Leipzig.* Norton watched incredulously as one bomber, sideslipping its way down to 500 feet, dropped a bomb squarely down the funnel of the battleship *Scharnhorst.* She blew up with a terrific concussion that gutted her insides.

But the attack was being made against frightful odds. Nazi

anti-aircraft batteries were bringing down American planes, and from nearby Langley Field, Nazi squadrons were taking angrily to the air. Norton heard Captain Wiegand quietly order: "Torpedo, fire!"

Bursts of compressed air from the X36 sent a salvo of "fish" at the *Adolf Hitler.* They struck her amidships with a frightful roar. Norton saw a series of geysers, colored red and yellow and green, fly into the air, followed by pieces of deckwork, masts, and funnel. A billow of dark smoke puffed upward, and the great battleship went down.

The Germans thought this latest attack had been from the air and continued to rake the sky with their searchlights. Captain Wiegand brought his submarine about. He sent two torpedoes into the battle-ship *Tirpitz.* As the upheavals of water and wreckage subsided, Norton could see her list badly.

And then a searchlight from the *Gneisenau* swept the waters and found them. As it did so, Norton noticed with a thrill that the X36 was defiantly flying the Stars and Stripes. Wiegand ordered two more torpedoes fired. They exploded squarely against the damaged *Tirpitz.*

A dozen searchlights picked out the American submarine, but before guns could be trained on her, she went into a crash dive. A moment later Norton heard the thud of "ash cans"—depth charges. The X36 rocked and shivered. Once the lights within her flickered and dimmed. Even broad-shouldered Jake Goldstein went white at that moment. Captain Wiegand, utterly impassive, was issuing orders.

Their last possible chance was a ruse. The X36, lying quietly now on the bottom with motors off, released a lot of oil and some wreckage.

"We can only hope," Wiegand said, "that they'll see that and decide they've destroyed us. We'll know in a minute."

Another depth charge shook their craft. Then another. And then there were no more.

"We've fooled 'em!" Jake exulted.

"Yes," said Wiegand, smiling. "And all we need do now is find a way to get out of here."

All that night of September 5, 1945, the X36 lay on the bottom, listening to the throbbing screws of enemy destroyers. Mean-while Norton kept chatting with Peggy, trying to divert her mind from the horrors she had been through and the present tension. She seemed physically rested—but when she spoke at all, it was in a voice that was dull and listless. He realized that the past week had left her literally bereft of the capacity for emotion.

Once, in a tone that indicated merely that she wished to keep the conversation alive, she asked:

"Do you think Captain Wiegand will get us out of here?"

"I don't know how he expects to," he told her frankly. "But if any man can wangle it, he's the man."

Peggy smiled. "And if he can't," she said, "it will have been worth it. This night must have dealt Nazi pride a blow. And it will hearten our people." She hesitated. "Doug, if things go wrong, I hope you'll be able to come and be with me for—well, for the last moment. It will make it quite easy."

"I'll be with you," he promised.

A period of quiet came at dawn.

They heard and felt the X36's pumps go on. They saw the needle of the depth gauge begin to move counterclockwise from 250 feet toward 200. They were rising to the surface.

Norton went out into the control room. Even when the periscope had broken water, Captain Wiegand found it difficult to ascertain that fact except by instrument readings.

He was puzzled for a moment, then jubilant. "Luck seems to be with us," he said. "On an average, Chesapeake Bay has only one day of dense fog during September. And this seems to be that day."

It was. When they had crawled up to the bridge, they found themselves in a pea-soup fog.

As they lay there on the surface, the huge silhouette of a Nazi armored ship bore down on them. Captain Wiegand issued a quick order, and the X36 gave a series of sharp indignant blasts of her siren. The Nazi ship politely changed course!

They proceeded through the fog down the narrow winding channel blasting boldly and continually with their siren. And as they headed toward open sea, the crew, working frantically, shoved off the mines they carried on launching tracks near the stern.

Only once did they submerge, when they passed between the two Nazi cruisers guarding the channel. And now that channel, behind them, was no longer clear. They had anchored mines in it. They were safely in open sea when they heard the distant boom of an explosion. Later they were to learn that the Nazi cruiser *Friedrich Eckoldt* had struck one of their mines, which had rolled her bottom side up.

As Peggy had predicted, the daring attack upon the ships of the Nazi navy, the penetration of its seemingly impenetrable defenses, proved a bitter blow to German pride. The Nazi radio station at

Norfolk screamed its indignation at this "cowardly assault without warning" and promised "black reprisals." As for American pride, the crew of the X36, still cruising "somewhere at sea," became national heroes.

Meanwhile Wiegand and his crew continued to harass German shipping in the Atlantic. Though he had only six torpedoes left, he raided shipping lanes. He halted Nazi stragglers from convoys with shots across their bows. Then his crew boarded and sank them, using time bombs.

In reprisal, the Nazis burned the White House to the ground, threatening to destroy every government building in the nation's former capital.

In attempted reprisal, too, a Nazi squadron sailed out of Chesapeake Bay to seek out and destroy the American Atlantic Squadron, which, upon the capture of the Panama Canal, had been forced to hide out in the waters south of Cape Hatteras and await the arrival of Admiral Sterrett's fleet.

On the morning of September 10, 1945, the German squadron, consisting of eleven battleships, fifteen cruisers, fifty-five destroyers, four aircraft carriers, and train, found the Atlantic Squadron of nine battleships, twelve cruisers, forty destroyers, and five aircraft carriers, seventy miles off the Georgia coast.

In a raging sea battle that lasted all day, the Germans had the advantages of numerical superiority and greater speed. Against these the Atlantic Squadron pitted superior gunnery and fire power—plus decided superiority in the air. For it had picked its own scene of battle, and shore-based planes flew out from Charleston, Jacksonville, Miami, Key West, Atlanta, Pensacola, and New Orleans to help.

By nightfall the United States had lost three battleships, the *Arkansas, New York,* and *Massachusetts*; but the Nazi squadron, six of its mighty battleships sunk, set up a destroyer smoke screen and, turning about, limped back to base at Norfolk.

This victory, on the heels of the battle of Chesapeake Bay, put new heart into the American people. Within a week Nazi Germany's entire force of first-line battleships had been reduced from twenty-two to thirteen. Those thirteen, however, were enough to give her more than two to one against the six first-line American battleships left in the Atlantic. And for the time being, it would be hazardous to make any all-out attempt to sever Nazi sea lines of communications.

While Adolf Hitler's navy had suffered a tremendous setback, his military machine on land and in the air was rolling steadily westward and northward. Retreating American forces were blasting highways and railroads. The government commandeered great numbers of commercial trucks and private automobiles to move the machinery of coastal industrial plants inland. What could not be removed was demolished.

Aboard the X36, Norton and Peggy and Captain Wiegand had listened to radio reports of the naval battle.

"If only Uncle Burt could get the fleet up here now," Peggy said, "we might cut them off from Europe and get the better of them."

"I'm not sure," Captain Wiegand said, "that even cutting them off would turn the trick. I have an idea that Hitler is counting heavily upon one of two things. Either he hopes—in the thirty days or so before Admiral Sterrett can get the fleet up here—to swallow so much of our industrial triangle in the East that our own lifelines will be cut and we'll surrender. Or he hopes to roll his armies so deeply into our coal and farm and cattle regions that, even if his armies are cut off from Europe by sea, they'll be self-sustaining."

Norton nodded. "That's possible. And he can always bring reinforcements over by air. If his armies do get enough of a foothold to sustain themselves indefinitely, this is going to be the bloodiest and most prolonged war in the history of man. If Hitler thinks he can win without completely annihilating a hundred and forty million people, then he's mad. There'll be Americans fighting his troops for the last strip of sand in our western deserts. We're made that way. He'd have to lick every last one of us."

"Just the same," insisted Peggy, "I'd feel better about it all if only the fleet were here."

Even as the girl spoke, mild-mannered, pipe-smoking Admiral Burton Sterrett, commander in chief of the United States fleet, was draining his own cup of bitterness. While a whole country prayed for his safe and speedy journey around the Horn, he was spending sleepless nights aboard his flagship *Virginia*.

After leaving Pearl Harbor on August 9, he had made rendezvous in the Pacific with the California- and Balboa-based battleships *Maine, Missouri, New Jersey, Ohio, Utah, Montana, Wyoming,* and *Iowa*.

All the way down the Pacific Coast of South America he had

been harassed by lurking Japanese and Russian submarines. And it was his train—his oil tankers—that they struck at. To make the long journey, his fleet needed roughly 20,000 tons of oil a day. In his train he carried more than a million tons.

He was on the bridge one night when suddenly, from far back in the train, there came the muffled boom of an explosion. Great sheets of yellow flame leaped skyward. He took his pipe out of his mouth and swore softly. That flame represented a single tanker—and the 10,000 tons of oil that would fuel three battleships.

After that, five of the submarines were sunk by his aerial patrol before they got another of his tankers. And then, one night, another explosion, another leaping flame—another 10,000 tons of precious oil.

Night after night he paced his armored conning tower, worried and mildly profane. He tried new destroyer formations, increased aerial patrols. He drove his men hard and himself harder. But still the attacks persisted. Despite all his efforts, a third tanker went up in flames.

By the time he was off the coast of Chile, it seemed certain that he must part with a number of units of his fleet. He could leave them in some Chilean port—where they would be interned for the duration of the war. Or he could face the ugly possibility that he might have to leave them in a hostile Brazilian port. Or he could risk seeing them turn into derelicts as his supply of oil gave out.

He decided he'd figure out just how this nut should be cracked after he'd got his fleet through the Strait of Magellan.

Going through the Strait, "South of Fifty," was in itself enough of a nut to crack. It was September, there—spring in that region. His fleet entered the Pacific end of the Strait, and soon they were in a blinding rain accompanied by a lashing pampero, a sixty-mile gale of cold air sweeping down from the Andes. He led his mighty ships into the blinding mist and gale-lashed water, between the narrow channel's rocky shoulders. The men exposed on deck shivered in the icy wind, for they had come only recently from Hawaii. The giant 40,000-ton *Virginia* steamed along majestically. The unleashed gale, driving down at times almost vertically on her decks, gave the helmsman much concern as she yawed from time to time in the swift current.

The Old Man cursed his luck. He had been through the Strait before, but never in weather as filthy as this. It was difficult enough by day, and the short hours of spring made it necessary to steam also at night. He slowed the speed of his ships to ten knots and kept his fingers crossed.

All day and all night the wind whipped out of the north and west, mostly at their tails. The choppy seas, hurtling against the bows, threw spray on turrets and bridges over seventy feet in the air. In all ships every man was on watch, gazing into every cave and indentation that might harbor a submarine.

It was no time for anything further to go wrong. Yet something did.

The *Virginia* was nearing the Atlantic end of the Strait when the Old Man himself saw a group of bombing planes nosing into the stiff gale and heading directly toward him. He knew, without being told, where they came from—a base on the once-British Falkland Islands. And he did not have to see the black crosses on their wings to know whose they were.

He thought of his tankers, straggling along far behind him. And he thought of his pilots—the brave lads on his fifteen aircraft carriers who had been flying night and day patrols for endless hours without a whimper. And he thought, How in hell can we get a single plane off a flight deck smashed by spray into a sixty-mile following wind?

He knew of no answer to that question. As a sheet of spray hissed up at him, he shook a quivering, impotent fist at those oncoming bombers. And then he swore to himself and issued orders—issued them with his customary terseness, seeming calmness, and speed.

And down below, men shook their heads and said, "They've got us trapped. They'll bomb every tanker we've got. And the Old Man's up there calm as a kitten in a shoebox. Do you suppose anything ever will ruffle his fur?"

CHAPTER 11

DER FÜHRER DELIVERS AN ULTIMATUM

What the Old Man overlooked in that desperate moment—and he was ashamed of it for weeks afterward—was that every man in his crews and every pilot aboard his aircraft carriers was as stark fighting mad as he was.

They had gone through nearly twenty-four sleepless, foodless hours of the dirtiest weather any part of the world had to offer. They had developed hair-trigger nerves and an explosive anger that needed a target.

Those Nazi light bombers supplied that target. A low ceiling kept them within range of both anti-aircraft and machine-gun fire. But, even so, Admiral Sterrett's gun crews, marksmen though they were, would have all the worst of it. In those choppy waters, slippery decks would smear their chances. Nor could the great warships and their train, plowing through the narrow channel, hope to maneuver to duck the bombs that were coming. The odds were all with the German planes—unless the fleet could get fighting ships aloft.

It promised to be a suicidal effort. But the pilots aboard the aircraft carriers were in a mood to risk anything.

One by one the carriers edged close on shore, dropped sea anchors, let themselves drift back into the wind. And, one by one, flight officers told their pilots: "Ride the deck—all the way. Take off at half to three-quarter gun, not full throttle. Keep your tail down."

And a few of them added: "And may God be with you."

Into the teeth of the gale they trundled down flight decks that lurched and quivered crazily. Not all of them got safely into the air. One pilot yanked back on his stick to clear the mountainous wall of spray, and it caught him head on and pulled him into the water. Another stalled and spun to his death. The third died when the careening deck caught his left wing and crumpled it like paper.

Still another pilot had his undercarriage smashed flat as he was about to reach the crash net forward, but he got into the air anyhow.

Once in the air, they put their anger to work. Catapults aboard the battleships flung more fighting aircraft into the fray. A lucky hit by a Nazi bomber shot away the number one mast of the *Colorado* and knocked out the first stage of her fire-control apparatus. Swarms of incendiaries set three tankers ablaze before the anti-aircraft batteries knocked down their first Nazi plane.

But after that, the Germans found their hands full. Catapult and carrier planes slammed down on them like hornets. With utter abandon, an American pilot from the *Wasp* roared down out of the overcast, found himself out of formation and, single-handed, tackled half a dozen swift Nazi bombers. He shot down two before he realized that the remaining four had him bracketed.

To confuse the enemy pilots, he snapped his ship over on its back, shoved the stick forward, and rocketed up into the overcast. Before the swastika-marked bombers had time to scatter, he came plummeting back like a hawk to shoot down one more. Again and again he repeated the maneuver, and each time there was one fewer bomber in the air.

Not a single Nazi plane returned to its base. Cut off from retreat, they were hammered out of the sky by coldly furious and determined Navy flyers. Admiral Sterrett got his fleet—minus the three tankers—safely into the Atlantic. The storm abated, and he sent up his planes with short, clear orders:

"Fly to the Nazi-controlled Falkland Islands and blow up everything that offers resistance! But spare the oil tanks!"

Those orders were carried out to the letter. The fleet sailed into Port Stanley hours later, and under its big guns, no resistance was offered. The Old Man himself tore down the swastika and hoisted the Stars and Stripes. He ordered members of the skeleton Nazi government tossed into the brigs of his own ships, and filled his tankers with oil and his pipe with tobacco. He left one destroyer, one cruiser, and an airplane carrier to guard this newly captured American base and, puffing his pipe contentedly, steamed homeward up the Atlantic.

In the United States, however, the invading armies of Hitler, Stalin, and Hirohito were riding the tide of success.

Along the Pacific Coast, the Red and Japanese armies, heedless of terrific casualties, pushed southward, their left flank against the Cascades. Numerical superiority in men and equipment won them bloodily contested victories.

In orderly retreat, the American forces on the Pacific Coast demolished the fortified commercial port at Coos Bay, Oregon, the Navy yard and air base at Mare Island. A system of orderly civilian evacuation was perfected as West Coast residents moved inland before the advancing hordes.

San Diego withstood an attack by Mexican troops of the Revolutionary Army, but fell weeks later as Red and Japanese forces blasted their way southward through deserted San Francisco and Los Angeles. Nazi-led Mexican troops kept up a wavering series of attacks that necessitated keeping hundreds of thousands of American soldiers along the Rio Grande. El Paso fell in a breakthrough that pushed as far north as Rincon, New Mexico, before a determined American counterattack crushed the Mexican lines and rolled them back to Chihuahua.

In the East, meanwhile, Hitler's troops were pounding away with machinelike precision. They ignored territory south of Norfolk and smashed inland on a line from Baltimore toward Cleveland.

The great inland plane factories of the United States were working day and night in an effort to build up the country's riddled Air Force. The air arm had moved its GHQ from Columbus to Kansas City. New airplane factories, strategically located in thick woods, were constructed with incredible speed. Midwestern wooded hills became concealing hangars for new long-range bombing planes.

Still maintaining an almost continuous mastery of the air, Hitler's armies pushed relentlessly onward. Portland, Maine, was bombed into submission, and Nazi transport planes landed divisions of parachute troops who took over small New England towns. Receiving equipment by water and fighting inland, they began steady advances down the Hudson River valley and the New England coast.

Boston fell after a devastating attack by land and air. Beleaguered Providence, New London, and New Haven were forced to capitulate. Pressing north, south, and west in a triangular entrapment movement, the soldiers of Nazi Germany crushed stubborn opposition as their mechanized columns roared into the heart of industrial America and threatened to penetrate the meat and grain lands north of the Ohio and west of the Mississippi.

Twice they occupied Harrisburg, Pennsylvania. Twice they were thrown back out of the city by furious American counterattacks. A third time they captured it—and that time they held it.

A week or two after Admiral Sterrett had rounded the Horn, Peggy O'Liam and Lieutenant Doug Norton disembarked at Charleston, South Carolina, from the X36. They had been at sea with Captain Wiegand for nearly a month, and had watched him sink twenty-seven Nazi ships.

He shook hands with them, bidding them good-bye. He intended to put out to sea within the week. "The hunting won't be so good this time," he prophesied quietly. "They're on their guard now."

Peggy and Norton wished him luck before boarding a plane to Springfield. Two weeks later they learned, with shock, that Captain Wiegand and his entire crew had been lost 300 miles off Cape Hatteras when the X36 had been sunk by three Nazi destroyers.

They enjoyed little time together. At Springfield, Norton was assigned to rejoin Jock Rodgers on the eastern front near Pittsburgh. Peggy returned to her home at Clinton.

While in Springfield, Norton learned that the United States War and Navy Departments considered the situation exceedingly grave. The Nazi thrusts westward seemed irresistible.

America's new separate air arm was giving an excellent account of itself, but it had been formed too late. Often it hesitated to bomb military objectives because Intelligence reported that captured American civilians by the hundreds were being forced to guard repaired bridges and power stations and would lose their lives if these sites were bombed.

On September 30, 1945, Admiral Sterrett brought his fleet into Almirante Bay, where he rendezvoused with what was left of the Atlantic Squadron. The bay, on the Isthmus, only 150 miles west of the Nazi-held Panama Canal, was an almost completely landlocked harbor that had often been used by the United States fleet during its Caribbean maneuvers. It was one of the world's finest natural naval bases.

Following the occupation of the Panama Canal by the Nazis, the Panamanian government, friendly to the United States, had been overthrown. Upon the arrival of the United States fleet, officials of the Nazi puppet government flew to Almirante Bay. They advised the Old Man that in accordance with the rules of international warfare it would be necessary for them to intern every one of his ships for the duration of the war.

The Old Man grinned. "That's a nice bluff," he said, "but I'm holding aces. First, you haven't the force to back up your plan. Second, from Almirante Bay here, right across the whole Isthmus to the Gulf of Dulce on the Pacific side at the edge of Costa Rica, the land—five million acres of it—happens to belong neither to your government nor to the government of Costa Rica. It's legally American-owned property. You don't believe it? Then go examine your own government archives. Trace the Chiriqui Strip since the days of the Republic of New Granada. You'll find I'm right about it. Now get out of here!"

And before the Old Man sailed out of Almirante Bay, he hoisted another American flag.

In an effort to gain absolute superiority in both oceans, the Japanese had begun sending their navy through the Panama Canal from the Pacific to join forces with the badly riddled Nazi navy in the Atlantic.

Against this dread but expected eventuality the United States government had been on its guard. The air force had resisted every temptation to send a secret reserve of planes of all types into land combat where for weeks they had been desperately needed.

Now it hurtled its aerial reserves down in a smashing full-dress attack upon the Canal. Throughout one entire day American and Nazi planes fought vicious unending dogfights over Panama. American and Nazi pilots alike crashed in flames or floated to earth in parachutes to land in impenetrable jungles.

America won that battle—the greatest aerial battle of the war. And then the remnants of her reserve air fleet went to work on what had been their own Canal. They rained down explosives upon it—and upon the Japanese ships caught moving through it. They demolished locks and dams and left a third of the Japanese navy trapped securely in the Canal, with another third locked out in the Pacific.

The third that did get through to the Atlantic found itself confronted with Admiral Sterrett's fleet, which closed in on these intruding Japanese warships and hammered them to flinders. The Nazi navy, steaming south to reinforce the Japanese, turned and fled toward Europe. America had regained control of the Atlantic Ocean.

Yet it was not enough. In her few weeks of control of the Atlantic, Germany had put on the seas the greatest merchant marine fleet in the history of the world. By means of that fleet, and despite the heavy toll taken of it by Captain Wiegand and some of his fellows in the submarine service, the Greater United German Reich had managed to pile up immense stores of tanks, of guns, of ammunition, of war supplies of all sorts, in the occupied land on America's East Coast. Even though her lines of communication with Europe by water had been cut, she was prepared to fight a long-drawn-out war.

She could still transport additional combat troops to the United States by air. And America's air force was finding it difficult to intercept those enemy transport planes and bring them down at sea.

On land, Germany was piling up success after success. America, her industrial triangle either evacuated or largely in ruins, had been pushed back west of the Alleghenies. She was fighting now in desperation, to slap off the bombers that droned nightly over Cleveland and Dayton, Ohio; over Rochester and Buffalo, New York; over Indianapolis and Chicago and Detroit. Once a Nazi bomber had flown as far inland as Springfield, where it had dropped a 1,000-pound explosive bomb upon America's provisional capital.

With winter, the great Russian assemblies of tanks that had been landed in Alaska began to roar down through Canada toward the Pacific Northwest. That required the shifting of more American troops and equipment to that sector, and a weakening of badly needed defenses on America's eastern front.

Rumors persisted, too, that Germany was perfecting a new "secret weapon" of devastating power. A wretchedly tired, doggedly fighting nation merely shrugged off these boasts from the "New Fatherland" station at Norfolk.

As weeks passed, the secret weapon failed to materialize, although in the series of bombing raids that finally resulted in the

abandonment of Rochester, a gas-filled concussion bomb of horri-
fying power was used by Nazi airmen for the first time. American
soldiers an eighth of a mile from the spot where it exploded had
collapsed and fallen dead. Autopsies disclosed that death had come
solely through internal hemorrhages.

A dud found in the streets of Rochester was shipped for
analysis to the laboratories of America's Chemical Warfare Service in
Denver, Colorado. In Denver, too, America's finest physicists, chem-
ists, and inventors were quietly at work on problems of their own.

At the outbreak of war with the United States, Adolf Hitler had
promised he would have "an American Christmas dinner" in the
capital of the United States. He made good that boast. On December 24, 1945, in his huge personal seaplane, *Grenzmark III*, escorted by
a fleet of black Luftwaffe bombers, he flew the Atlantic in company
with von Ribbentrop and Goring, landing at Nazi-occupied Baltimore.

The Master of All Europe had set foot on American soil for the
first time. And the slight, intense-eyed, and still somehow comic man
who saw world dominion almost within his grasp was whisked to the
former capital of the last remaining great democracy on earth.

He had dinner the following day at the Mayflower Hotel in
Washington. The dinner had been preceded by a tour of inspection of
points of interest. His personal photographer, Heinrich Hoffman, took
pictures of the Führer as he posed in a trench coat, owlishly solemn, on
the steps of the now swastika-topped Capitol, at the base of the
Washington Monument, before the brooding statue of Abraham Lincoln, and on the snow-clad lawn of Mount Vernon.

Those photographs, released to American newspapers in the
Middle West, had a depressing effect that coined the phrase "Black
Christmas." However, that depression of a proud people was followed
not by terror but by a seething fury.

On Christmas night Hitler sat up late alone in his suite in the
Mayflower. He had found Washington more beautiful than he had
imagined. Some of the buildings had a classic simplicity that suited
him. But others made him shudder. He termed them "monstrosities."
And now he sat up sketching new structures of his own design to
replace those "eyesores" in the city that was to remain the seat of
government in his "New World Reich."

New Year's Day found him in New York City. Conscripted

American labor had long since cleaned its streets of rubble and glass and corpses. German Pioneer troops had thrown a pontoon bridge across the Hudson near the demolished George Washington Bridge, and Adolf Hitler's party rode triumphantly down Riverside Drive.

They stopped, so that the Führer could be photographed at Grant's Tomb, then sped on. He was in fine spirits, eager to see the skyscrapers. He visited the RCA Building in Rockefeller Center, the Chrysler Building, the enclosed observation tower on the 102nd floor of the Empire State Building, the buildings in Lower Manhattan's financial district.

The Statute of Liberty he referred to scornfully as "the gift of a vanished France to a vanishing America." And before returning to Germany, he promised: "This symbol of a decadent concept shall be soon replaced by a suitably virile monument to German youth, instrument of totalitarianism."

The spring of 1946 found America at the point of exhaustion. Every eastern coastal state from Maine to Florida had been wrested from her. Her oil lines were nearly severed, her interior supplies dwindling; her people (in a land of onetime surpluses) hungry. Her makeshift industrial centers in mid-continent were straggling behind the production of Hitler's European factories, her Great Lakes shipping reeling under savage blows, her soldiers fighting a bitter war that verged on stalemate.

Only the unquenchable morale of a people fiercely hugging their last bit of freedom kept America from going to her knees.

It was at that precarious juncture that Adolf Hitler came over by plane for the second time. He brought with him Dr. Hermann Strass, a distinguished German physicist—and a proposal that he had broached a month before. Hitler proposed a one-day truce during which certain "essential facts of the utmost importance" to both the government of the United States and that of the Greater United German Reich would be made clear.

Out of that proposal grew the historic Cincinnati Conference, held in the "neutral city" between the lines of the American and German armies.

To the Netherland Plaza Hotel in Cincinnati came representatives of the American government: the President of the United States, his Commissioner of National Defense, his Secretaries of Air, War, and the Navy, and their highest officers. Accompanying them at this meeting were men whose attendance Hitler had requested—a

number of America's leading physicists. Some of them were from
Columbia University, from Westinghouse, from Johns Hopkins Uni-
versity, from the California Institute of Technology, and from the
Department of Terrestrial Magnetism of Washington's Carnegie
Institution.

Awaiting them in the ballroom of the hotel were Hitler and his
retinue: his personal interpreter; his air, land, and naval commanders;
and Dr. Strass. As the American officials entered, the Germans rose and
saluted stiffly. Their salutes were returned and the leaders of both
governments gathered about a round table over which were hung
microphones.

The President of the United States spoke, and the interpreter
translated his words:

"It is but fair to tell you, gentlemen, that whatever you have to
say to us goes by radio into American homes. Yesterday our people were
dying a few miles from here in defense of their country. Since what goes
on in this room must affect their lives, it is only fair to them that their
government takes them fully into its confidence."

Hitler spoke—and the interpreter said:

"Herr Hitler agrees that, in this case, it will be wise for the
people to hear the news he brings. He wishes, first, to compliment the
American people upon their splendid fight. He expected collapse long
before this. He did not anticipate such stubborn resistance. He—"

The President nodded wearily. "We thank Herr Hitler for his
compliments," he interrupted, "but wish to know what brings us here."

The answer was:

"The humanitarian desire to save lives. I beg your permission
to read from notes prepared by Dr. Strass of the Reich Physical-
Technical Institute and approved by Herr Hitler:

" 'In the year 1935 one of your American physicists discovered
a new substance, a rare form of uranium today known as U-235. In 1939
two German scientists discovered that uranium, heaviest of the ninety-
odd known fundamental elements, could in this form be atomically
split. Your own scientists will tell you that when an atom is split the
amount of energy released is tremendous. In other words, by the year
1939 the physicists of the Reich, of Denmark, and of America were
frantically at work attempting to free and harness atomic energy—to
unlock the secrets of an energy that is even greater than solar energy, the
energy of suns.

" 'All of us knew the overwhelming implications. The man who unlocked atomic energy would revolutionize the world's existence. His discovery would be of far greater importance than the discovery of electricity, of fuel oils, of radio. For he would give his country a new source of heat and power. Its farmers would no longer need to depend upon sunlight or fertile soil. Fluorescent light could be cheaply piped into houses. Filling stations and oil-storage reservoirs would vanish, for between the halves of a walnut shell could be stored sufficient atomic energy to fly a plane across the Atlantic Ocean.

" 'All that, gentlemen, as your own scientists who have been racing us toward the goal of atomic energy can verify, was no more than a vision in 1939. Your physicists and ours stood on the threshold of a stupendous discovery. That threshold, it seemed then, might not be crossed in one hundred years. Our scientists had already released atomic energy, but only on a microscopic scale.

" 'The man—of your nation or ours—who first could produce great quantities of pure U-235 and could efficiently release its gigantic power, would give his country the secret of world mastery.

" 'I do not need to point out why. I simply tell you what, I repeat, your own eminent physicists in this room will confirm: that one pound of pure U-235 has the energy equivalent of three million pounds of gasoline; that it has five million times the power output of coal; and that—and this is why we are here today—it has the explosive power of thirty million pounds of TNT!

" 'And, gentlemen, we have now discovered the key to atomic energy. I beg you to remember its power—a destructive power beyond present-day comprehension. The power to blow entire cities off the face of the earth.

" 'Production of pure U-235 in the Greater United German Reich already is under way. Within one month, that devastating power can be unleashed against your cities, your people.

" 'Further resistance becomes utterly foolhardy. You cannot conceivably win this war. Herr Hitler proposes that you end it now, saving the needless destruction, during the next month, of the lives of your soldiers and ours. For but one month of grace is left you. After that we shall be ready. After that—literal and total annihilation.

" 'We are eager to have you examine our claims. That can be done now. Dr. Strass will convince your scientists that, within a month, the terrifying destructiveness of U-235 can and will be unleashed. He is—' "

The President of the United States interrupted: "You will tell Herr Hitler that his request that our physicists attend this meeting forewarned us somewhat. We fully understand the stupendous force—for good or for evil—of U-235. Tell him that, please."

The interpreter spoke to Hitler, who listened, then spoke.

"Herr Hitler asks if he is to understand that we are already on common ground. He wishes to know this: He wishes to know whether you concede that, in a war waged by one country in possession of large quantities of pure U-235 against another country having none, nothing but doom can come to the nation that does not possess U-235."

"We concede that," said the President of the United States, nodding.

Hitler spoke. The interpreter said:

"He wishes to know, then, whether the United States desires foolishly to continue a bloody war for another useless month, or whether you—as President of your country—prefer to end a stupid, losing struggle that, by your own admission, can end only in miserable defeat for your people.

"In short—Herr Hitler wishes to know whether you are prepared, now, in this room, to spare the people of the United States by signing an armistice, the terms of which Herr Hitler has already drawn up for your inspection!"

CHAPTER 12

CONCLUSION: THE TREATY OF CINCINNATI

There was a hushed moment of utter silence in that room. And in millions of homes throughout beleaguered America, men and women, white of face, sat speechless before their radios.

U-235! Atomic energy!

When the invasion of America had begun, Germany had boasted of having ready a mysterious death ray. The American people had not been alarmed, for they had been assured by their most authoritative scientists that so-called death rays were utterly impracticable.

But now, having listened to Adolf Hitler's solemn announcement and ultimatum, delivered by him personally in the presence of those self-same scientists and of one of his own, and having listened to their President's acquiescent brief responses, they were convinced that what Hitler said was true—that within thirty days, this irresistible new

189

force would be loosed by the enemy upon their defenders and upon themselves.

Now, fighting uncomplainingly for months against odds that had never disheartened them, Americans knew the foretaste of defeat.

In her home on West Main Street in Clinton, Illinois, Peggy O'Liam sat before a radio. Beside her sat Doug Norton. Apprehension lay like a cold heavy thing within them as they waited for the President to speak.

"You will tell Herr Hitler," he said to the interpreter, "that a dictated peace will be signed. First, however, I must insist upon a few brief words that, for the future of humanity, need be recorded here this afternoon."

Hitler listened to the translation, nodded indulgence. The President of the United States resumed:

"As you gentlemen have suggested, the development of atomic energy will mean a revolutionary change in the life of every human being now on earth. It can be an overwhelming force for good—or for evil.

"Accustomed to freedom in this democracy, we have attempted at all times to translate scientific or mechanical progress into terms of a better life for the great masses of our people. That has been our concept of progress. We have attempted to give our people more radios, more automobiles, more conveniences than any other people on earth have enjoyed. I think you will concede that we have had some success. And I, for my part, will concede that we have often stumbled or been clumsy. But we have not lost sight of our concept of progress.

"We are a so-called capitalistic nation. I find nothing wrong in a fair profit, honestly arrived at; I believe the great mass of our people respect the theory of honest wages for honest work—and treasure the right to their individual liberties. And some of our greatest corporations have been patrons of pure science. They have built great laboratories, put scientists into them, and given those scientists a free hand.

"It was so, here in America, with U-235. We saw its potentialities as a weapon of war, but even more clearly as an unlimited source of heat, of light, of power for peaceful production and transportation—all this at an almost incredibly low cost.

"We saw a new world in which the most densely populated country would have ample room for all its citizens to live in well and cheaply; a world in which this new wealth of energy would be shared by the people of every land and race and creed.

"International boundaries, money as we know it today, and poverty would vanish from the earth. So would war itself; for the economic causes of wars would no longer exist. That, gentlemen—that Utopia, if you like—was what we envisioned: a free world of free peoples living in peace and prosperity, facing a future of unlimited richness.

"In consequence, our scientists—both in colleges and universities and in the laboratories of great American corporations—were given a free hand to investigate the enormous potentialities of U-235.

"The moment your allies' first troops put foot on our soil, one of our first moves was to pick up and transport into the interior of our country the atom-smashing machines with which our physicists worked.

"From East Pittsburgh, Pennsylvania, we moved a sixty-five-foot steel atom smasher; from the Pacific Coast we moved a great cyclotron with which we had been splitting atoms. In Colorado, the best equipment that this country could build was supplied to its most ingenious and resourceful scientists.

"We were, as you have said, engaged in a life-or-death race with your country. Our goal, I must repeat, was the creation of a new, rich, peaceful world for all. To reach that goal, we needed to unlock atomic energy before you could; to produce tons of pure uranium-235 before you could do so; and then to master the world through the threat of its irresistible destructive force—a force we hoped would never have to be put to use.

"And now, gentlemen, you announce that you have solved the riddle of U-235. That within one month you will have begun large-scale production. I do not ask proof. I concede here and now that you have learned the secret of producing a weapon that must inevitably overwhelm and subdue any nation on earth. I concede that.

"And I tell you—all of you—that you are too late!

"You say you will be prepared to destroy us in one month. You are a month too late. Unless you can destroy us now, at once, this very afternoon, you are lost. For this country has been producing tons of pure U-235 for the past three weeks.

"And, as we sit here talking, bombers equipped with specially-installed fuel tanks, are flying high out of sight and sound, heading for every great city in Germany. The destruction they are prepared to unleash will be literally heard half-way around the world.

"I said that a dictated peace would be signed in this room this afternoon. Unless you wish Germany to become a charnel house, it will be. The choice is yours.

"Here, gentlemen, are our terms!"

In millions of American homes, families heard the paper that bore the "Articles of Peace of the Cincinnati Conference" slap down on the table. In millions of homes in Germany, frantic listeners heard a translation of the President's speech, and heard the babble of consternation among the members of the Nazi High Command. That consternation was duplicated in the Kremlin and in Tokyo.

And, 50,000 feet over the Atlantic, great United States stratospheric bombers cruised lazily toward Germany while awaiting instructions.

In the conference room Adolf Hitler, white of face and biting his lips against hysterical rage, conferred in a trembling voice with Dr. Strass. He listened to his military advisers—listened without hearing.

And then he said simply: "May I see the terms?"

He read the articles of peace in a prepared German text. They set forth much of what the President of the United States had said: that the desire of the American nation was for true peace and prosperity for all the world; that to preserve that peace for future generations it was necessary that the world's supply of uranium should fall only into the hands of those who would use it not for destruction but for construction. Temporarily, American engineers would limit the amount of uranium obtained by any and every other country, while American physicists would keep watch of the uses made of it.

"We have no wish," the President said, "to assume for long the task of policing the world. When the world is restored and made free, a Council of Nations shall take over the task we inaugurate now."

The President smiled wryly.

"You will notice, Herr Hitler, that while great damage has been done our country, we ask no indemnities, no reparations; we inflict no punishment upon the German people. That, if you please, is our contribution to world peace in the future. We do not intend to sow here, this afternoon, the seeds of some future war.

"We demand, first, that our bombers be allowed to land—unmolested—at airfields of the Greater Reich and fuel up with the gasoline without which they will be unable to return to America. If they *cannot* land, they have orders to drop the bombs they are carrying—and to detonate their bombs on the ground should they meet with any resistance whatsoever. Second, we demand that your troops now in America help us rebuild our country before they return home."

There was a buzz among the German delegation as the President's words were translated.

"There is one other condition—which will ensure your contribution. You are never to return to Germany."

When the interpreter had finished, Adolf Hitler jumped, quivering, to his feet. "Never!" he cried. "Never shall I submit!"

The President of the United States rose slowly. He nodded to the German marshals and to Dr. Strass. "Gentlemen, you have fifteen minutes in which to persuade your Chancellor."

At the end of that time Hitler remained obdurate. The President, his own face white, said, "I am sorry. You are making an immeasurable mistake. There is nothing—"

At this point one of Hitler's marshals spoke: "May we have five minutes more, please?"

The request was granted. The Germans were left alone. And, within three minutes after the President and his aides had left the room, a gunshot sounded in it. Five minutes after that, over all the world's radios came the solemn announcement:

"Adolf Hitler, Chancellor of the Greater United German Reich, is dead. At four-fifteen this afternoon the body of the man who conquered all Europe was found lying on the floor of the ballroom of the Netherland Plaza Hotel in Cincinnati. A pistol, from which a single bullet had been fired, was found beside him. According to his field marshals, who were present at the time, he committed suicide. There will be no public investigation, the American State Department said."

Two days later, on May 15, 1946, the American destroyer *Hammann* sailed from Baltimore with Hitler's body on board. Rumors that he had been slain by one of his own marshals persisted and gained general acceptance. But, by agreement, the circumstances of his death were locked for fifty years in the secret files of the American and German governments.

The capitulations of the Japanese and Russian governments followed within twenty-four hours of his death. Articles of surrender were quickly signed when authenticated reports from Russia made it known that an American bomber, dropping just one 500-pound bomb of the new explosive on the deserted Russian steppes, had blasted a hole in the earth several hundred feet deep and fifteen miles in diameter.

In the little town of Clinton, Illinois, on a night that had the soft breath of spring, Peggy O'Liam and Lieutenant Doug Norton set out from Peggy's home. They were to be married on the morrow. Admiral Sterrett was to arrive in the morning. Admiral O'Shane had promised to be there. Jock Rodgers was in town already. All day long a steady stream of Peggy's friends and fellow townsmen had been flowing to and from the porch of her home, where she had greeted them joyfully and made Doug acquainted with them.

Now, as the two walked arm in arm down West Main Street, he said solemnly, "I'm not sure you'll make a good Navy man's wife."

"Why won't I?"

"Your lingo's wrong. You mustn't tell people, 'Oh, I'm so glad to see you!' You must say, 'It's good to have you aboard.' "

She squeezed his arm, said even more solemnly, "I'll try to be a good wife, Lieutenant."

Their walk was a series of halts to accept still more felicitations. They met one of her old schoolteachers, and an old man, deaf in one ear, who loudly called her Maggie. His name was Matt Howard. "In the East," she explained after they had managed to get away from him, "I suppose he'd be a superintendent of maintenance. Here he's the courthouse janitor. . . . Oh, Doug"—she turned to him suddenly—"I'm tired of seeing people. Let's go for a drive."

He saw the restlessness in her face, sensed the tension of her nerves. He nodded.

They drove out Route 10. Coming back, as they passed rolling fields and hushed woods, he saw her lips trembling and he stopped and said softly:

"What is it, darling?"

"I'm afraid, Doug," she said. "Last night I had a horrible dream. I don't even remember it, but I woke up shaking with terror. So much has been crowded into these past months. I'm so glad it's all over—only—"

She looked up at him, pleading for understanding.

"—only, darling, there's something insidious about it. Like a drug. This town seems so small, so quiet, so deadly unexciting. This afternoon I thought: If I could only hear a gun go off! If something would only happen—something dangerous! I couldn't stand the quiet, the peace. I'm confused, dear, I'm mixed up. Does any of this make sense to you?"

He took her in his arms. "I know. You hate what you've been through. You're glad it is over. And you miss it." He grinned. "Wait until you have a child—or two, or three. They're sure to be troublesome little brats. They'll give you all the excitement you need. To say nothing of trying to feed them on Navy pay. We both have a lot to forget, my dear. We had to learn war. But we did. We'll learn peace, too."

His arms tightened around her, and the pressure of his lips against hers, as her fingers stroked his hair, was gentle.

They stopped at the courthouse square to see the statue of Lincoln in the moonlight. "This was Lincoln country, you know," she reminded him. As they looked up at the likeness of the tall, gaunt, gentle man who also had known the ordeal of war, a light went out in the courthouse across the way.

"Old Matt has finished for the night," said Peggy.

They saw him hobbling toward them. He squinted at them and said, very loudly, "Just finished clearin' my spittoons, Maggie. How are you, Lieutenant? Nice statue of Old Abe, ain't it? He was a wise man. Right here on this lawn he said, 'You can fool all of the people some of the time and . . .' Well, you know how it goes.

"One I like best, though, is the one that went: 'With malice towards none; with charity for all; with firmness in the right, as God gives us to see the right, let us strive on to finish the work we are in; to bind up the nation's wounds; to care for him who shall have borne the battle, and for his widow and his orphans—to do all which may achieve and cherish a just and lastin' peace among ourselves and with all nations.' "

Old Matt worried his left ear with a gnarled finger. "Them words seem kinda fittin' now, I guess. G'night, Maggie. Night, Lieutenant."

"Good night, Matt."

They watched the old fellow hobble off, and they looked again upon the statue's face in the moonlight.

" 'Peace,' " Peggy repeated, " 'with all nations . . . Lasting peace among ourselves'! It will be worth what has happened to have that, Doug."

He nodded. And when he kissed red-headed Peggy good night, on the front porch of her home, her lips were no longer atremble; they were the lips of the girl he had met that first day at Waikiki.

He had told himself then that it would be nice to kiss this girl. Now he told himself that he had only half succeeded in imagining how nice it could really be.

AFTERWORD: THE FINAL IRONY

No doubt the requirements of magazine serialization almost demanded that the final chapter of *Lightning in the Night* be reassuringly upbeat. Its "happy ending" idealizes American values and the secure, serene rewards of a hard-won peace. But nevertheless, the conclusion of Fred Allhoff's fictional scenario is not quite as rosy as he would lead his more casual readers to believe. Exactly what kind of a world has he left for Lieutenant and Mrs. Douglas Norton to live in?

This fictional World War ends not with a decisive conquest, but with a conference-table stalemate. Despite the enforced "peace" at Cincinnati, Greater Germany has lost virtually nothing but Hitler's leadership. She still retains her American colonies—and, according to Allhoff, her own atom bomb research is only a month behind ours! In the tranquil spring air of Clinton, Illinois, there already hangs, implicit and unspoken, the threat of a pre-emptive nuclear strike from long-range Nazi bombers. And can other countries be trusted *not* to misuse the uranium that the U.S. has pledged to share with "all the world" and which American physicists are supposed to supervise?

If this last detail seems eerily familiar, it's partly because *Lightning in the Night*'s final balance of power is not far different from that which existed in the years following the real-life World War II. Allhoff seems to have foreseen the actual aftermath of decisive armed conflict with Germany—namely, a Cold War between two highly armed nuclear powers!

And the international picture becomes increasingly dark the further we project Allhoff's fictional scenario into his putative future. The entire Nazi High Command is left intact, with no international tribunal to judge their past or future actions. Once armed with the Bomb, they can easily ape America's tactics and swiftly move to force the capitulation of Russia, perhaps dividing her territory with Japan. Imperial Japan, of course, remains a major power in the Pacific. Together with Germany, she can effectively isolate America from trade with any Asian, African, or European country, promoting an effective energy crisis.

Simply substituting Germany for the U.S.S.R. in recent history, it's not hard to imagine a "Jamaican Missile Crisis," a "peace-keeping" operation in New Guinea or the Philippines similar to our actual conflict in Vietnam, and a massive outpouring of foreign aid to preserve the tacit cooperation of right-wing Latin American nations. All of these "facts" grow logically from *Lightning in the Night's* last chapter, but even if Allhoff had drafted an extended epilogue, it would most likely have been cut before publication. After all, *Liberty's* main concern was with the United States' *immediate* future, and any editor would have blue-penciled Allhoff's lamentably accurate long-range prophecies simply because they seemed too far-fetched.